Her skin was soft under his touch, very soft...

The urge to slide his hands over more delicate areas increased and he couldn't help running his thumb along the inside of her arm.

Awareness grew in her gaze and she bit her lip as she nodded.

He leaned toward her, focused on her plump lip caught under her teeth.

"What else do you like?"

She opened her mouth to answer, but he didn't plan to let her get a word out. Maybe later. He bent his head to capture her lips.

And seventy-five pounds of fur jumped up on his side.

"The hell?"

Lyn gasped. "Atlas!"

"Af." Mindful of the dog's injury, Cruz gave Atlas a gentle shove.

The dog dropped back to all fours, his tongue lolling. Looking from him to Lyn and back again, Atlas lay back down on his belly.

Jealous. Damn dog was jealous.

EXTREME
HONOR

EXTREME HONOR

PIPER J. DRAKE

FOREVER

NEW YORK BOSTON

Copyright © 2016 by Piper J. Drake
Excerpt from *Ultimate Courage* copyright © 2016 by Piper J. Drake
All rights reserved. In accordance with the U.S. Copyright Act of 1976, the scanning, uploading, and electronic sharing of any part of this book without the permission of the publisher constitute unlawful piracy and theft of the author's intellectual property. If you would like to use material from the book (other than for review purposes), prior written permission must be obtained by contacting the publisher at permissions@hbgusa.com. Thank you for your support of the author's rights.

Forever
Hachette Book Group
1290 Avenue of the Americas
New York, NY 10104

HachetteBookGroup.com

Printed in the United States of America

First Edition: January 2016
10 9 8 7 6 5 4 3 2 1

OPM

Forever is an imprint of Grand Central Publishing.
The Forever name and logo are trademarks of Hachette Book Group, Inc.

The Hachette Speakers Bureau provides a wide range of authors for speaking events. To find out more, go to www.hachettespeakersbureau.com or call (866) 376-6591.

The publisher is not responsible for websites (or their content) that are not owned by the publisher.

ATTENTION CORPORATIONS AND ORGANIZATIONS:

Most Hachette Book Group books are available at quantity discounts with bulk purchase for educational, business, or sales promotional use. For information, please call or write:

Special Markets Department, Hachette Book Group
1290 Avenue of the Americas, New York, NY 10104
Telephone: 1-800-222-6747 Fax: 1-800-477-5925

To Matthew.
For believing in me. For your support,
patience, and caring, thank you.
大好き*—Daisuki*

ACKNOWLEDGMENTS

To Courtney Miller-Callihan: Thank you for your confidence in me and your never-ending patience.

To Lauren and Dana: Thank you for working with me to polish this story and make it even better.

EXTREME HONOR

CHAPTER ONE

David Cruz studied the woman standing in the front waiting area with equal parts irritation and interest. The room had an open design to accommodate dozens of owners and their dogs comfortably—enough space to prevent tussles the humans might not be able to break up without a trainer's help. Of course, the area was empty of other people and dogs at the moment and this little bit of trouble filled the room just fine on her own. Her neat dress suit had to have been tailored to a fit so exact, it might as well have been a military dress uniform. And she wore it as if she was ready for inspection, her posture perfect with her shoulders straight, her chin up, and her hands easy at her sides. If her thumbs lined up with the side seams on her skirt, he'd have wondered if a cadet had gotten lost from the nearby military academy.

The severe gray fabric didn't leach color from her face, though; instead the contrast set off her peaches and cream complexion. Made him think of a dish of ice cream on a hot day. And even standing still, she radiated energy. Charisma. Like she could burst into motion at a moment's notice and heaven help the man who got in her way. He had an urge to step right up and see if she could run him over.

Not likely, but it'd be fun to let her give it a try.

"Look, Miss..."

"Jones. Evelyn Jones." Her sharp tone cut across his attempt to address the current issue with any semblance of calm. "Any and all documentation you might need is right there in the folder I handed you. If you'll verify it instead of wasting both of our time trying to send me away, I'll be able to get to what I've been sent here to do instead of standing around engaging in a pissing contest."

Well, she'd come in ready for a fight.

Head held high and standing as tall as she could, her hackles would've been raised if she'd been a dog. The mental image was entertaining, to be honest, especially since her blond hair was pulled back in a no-nonsense ponytail combined with the stylish poofed-up effect. No idea why women did that but hell, she looked good.

And he did take a minute to appreciate her as she was: compact, curvy, and hot enough to catch the attention of every male on two legs walking the property. But her impact on the four-legged variety remained to be seen.

He could do without her glaring attempt at intimidation, though, and he wondered whether he shouldn't send her sweet ass right on back out the door. If she crossed her arms over her admittedly impressive chest or otherwise altered her body language to increase her aggressive stance, he would. If her attitude was enough to scratch his temper, the dog she was here to see would rip her to shreds.

"Your credentials aren't in question, Miss Jones." He raised his hand to forestall another interruption. He'd had plenty of experience with her kind of sprint-out-the-gate, establish–credibility-immediately personality. It didn't intimidate him one bit but he also wouldn't be rushed. "As I was about to say, you could wait here and be run over by the incoming class of two-year-olds or you can come on in to the office area and have a cup of coffee while I make a few calls."

She blinked and her cheeks flushed. "I...of course. A cup of coffee would be appreciated."

Somehow, he doubted that considering the sour tone of her voice. It took some effort not to grin at her discomfort. "Glad you decided to come along. The two-year-olds aren't a bad batch but their handlers are in some serious need of training. Go figure."

The corner of her very kissable mouth quirked. "Isn't it always the human side of the pair in need of the real training?"

Now, they had some common ground after all. At least when it came to civilians.

But if he wanted to be fair—and hell, who did?—Military dog handlers needed heavy training at the beginning, too. Especially if they wanted to reach the level of excellence required of a special forces working team.

He led her past the receiving desk and down a short hallway to a smaller area with chairs arranged for easy conversation. They had one of those little one-cup coffee makers and she seemed fine fixing up her own mug. He preferred his coffee brewed in a real pot and none

of those handy automated gadgets managed a strong
enough brew.

The whole host-and-good-manners thing dispensed,
he headed for his office. "If you'll just wait here..."

"It would save time if you showed me Atlas. I could
introduce myself to him while you're making your call."

He halted; his temper simmered back up to the surface. "With all due respect, Miss Jones, you're not
meeting Atlas until I've straightened out exactly what is
going on here."

"It's fairly straightforward. I've been brought in at the
request of the Pentagon to work with the dog you refuse
to introduce me to." At the edge of his peripheral vision,
her movement caught his attention. A slight raise of the
chin. "It would save you time if you would take my suggestion before I make a call of my own."

He studied her for the few seconds it took for his irritation to cool enough for polite conversation again. All
bravado and possibly some real bite behind her threat.
It depended on exactly who at the Pentagon had con-
tracted her.

"You could save us even more time and leave now."
He turned to face her, calling her bluff. Lesser men
backed down immediately under his glare. Took her a
full five seconds to drop her eyes. "As far as the United
States Air Force is concerned, Atlas was placed under
the care of Hope's Crossing Kennels with me as his official trainer. Currently, I'm willing to go through due
diligence and consider a joint effort if your consulting credentials are confirmed. But if you truly did your
homework on Atlas and this facility, you would know
you either work with us or you are escorted off the prop-

erty. This is not a general kennel where consultants are allowed to stroll in and work independently."

After all, Hope's Crossing Kennels wasn't just a training facility for domestic pets. And the trainers who lived here weren't civilians.

He strode into his office and resisted the urge to slam the door behind him. Bad enough she'd goaded him into a pissing contest. Instead, he managed a creditable quiet close without shooting her a dirty look as he did so. He stepped around his desk, fired up his computer. Logging in always took longer than he'd like. Then again, there wasn't a computer system fast enough to keep up with the advancing demands of security and surveillance needs and the equipment he had installed throughout the interior—and exterior—of the kennels gave him constant streaming feed whenever he needed eyes on a particular part of the property.

At the moment, Miss Jones remained seated and sipping her coffee. Good. Even better if her very attractive behind stayed put. It'd be a damn shame if she took her bluff further and did something stupid, like wander off.

Gaze trained on the video feed, he reached for his Bluetooth earpiece and made sure his smartphone was connected. "Call Beckhorn."

A few rings. "Beckhorn here."

Beckhorn always recognized Cruz's number so it wasn't a surprise when the man answered right away. Cruz was glad his longtime friend had been free enough to take a call at all.

"Please tell me you didn't send her." Not likely, since Beckhorn was at Lackland Air Force Base down in

Texas. But hell, influence didn't always have to do with geographic location.

A pause. "Unless I forgot I sent you a stripper for your birthday, I got no idea what you are talking about here. And I'm sure as hell I don't know when your birthday is off the top of my head."

Shouldn't. But he did. Visuals of Miss Jones doing a sensual striptease superimposed the real woman still sitting on the edge of a chair just outside his office. A lot of potential there, but he'd best file the fun thoughts for some later time tonight.

"A Miss Evelyn Jones arrived today with a very official statement of work to provide consultation for Atlas." And didn't that just chafe his butt. He was the best military dog trainer on the East Coast. He didn't need a...dog whisperer.

"Huh." Beckhorn had a few other choice utterances. Man hadn't lost his touch with the creative expletives. But then, men like him and Cruz tended to not lose the survival skills they'd accumulated over multiple deployments. "Send me scans of the documentation. I'll need to track it down but I'm gonna say up front I'm not surprised."

"There's a reason you flew me down there to meet Atlas." Cruz probably didn't need to remind Beckhorn but it could always be said for the benefit of the lady who'd left her seat and was now standing with her ear pressed against the door. Maybe he'd raise his voice a notch or two for her benefit. "The dog comes first. I won't waste time playing nice with any handpicked consultants if it compromises the dog's progress. If she's a help, she stays. If she's a pain in the ass, she's out."

Especially when some of the work he needed to do with Atlas went beyond the dog's recovery and more into what had happened to his handler. He didn't need some consultant tangling things up.

"Agreed. No worries from this angle." Beckhorn sighed. "Let me follow the audit trail and figure out what officer brought her in. Atlas is a high profile dog. Between the news spot and the articles published about him, the military is going to spare no expense to do right by him. But it also means others are going to want to make doubly sure Atlas has the best care out there. I'm surprised you don't have half a dozen consultants from various military offices and a few choice senators pounding at your door."

"This isn't about news coverage." Cruz tried to keep the growl out of his voice. "It's about giving Atlas what he needs to recover from where he's been."

And what he's lost.

Some people might not give a dog credit for emotions, but Cruz had seen dogs exhibit unfailing loyalty and self-less courage in the face of danger for the sake of their handlers. They experienced emotions. They loved. Deeply.

Atlas had seen awful things. Hell, so had they all. But Atlas had lost his handler—his partner—a man the dog had given his everything to. The dog deserved some sort of peace for the rest of his days if Cruz could help him. And Atlas's handler deserved to have the truth behind his death exposed, if anyone could find it.

"Based on your twenty-four-hour report, Atlas hasn't improved much." Beckhorn cleared his throat. "Not ex-pecting you to work miracles, but one of those would help your case in working with the dog solo."

"I'm not going to rush the dog." Cruz stood up and began to pace, irritated. Oh, not with Beckhorn, but with higher ups always convinced throwing more resources at a problem would lead to faster results. "He'll come around in his own time. I'm letting him get to know me and the facilities here. Not as structured as a military base, not as chaotic as a normal home."

"What are you going to do with the consultant?" Beckhorn tended to choke on the last word, but then, he had a thing about private contractors. Miss Jones might be different, but then again, she might not.

"I'll give it some thought." And he wasn't committing to anything. High-ranking sponsors from DC or no, if Atlas didn't like her, Miss Jones was out the door.

And it was about time to address the way she was lurking on the other side of his.

* * *

The door opened so fast under Lyn's hands, she pitched forward before she could catch her balance. She came up against a hard, very well-muscled chest.

Smooth, poised, graceful even. All things she wished she'd managed but definitely was not.

He wrapped big hands around her upper arms and set her back on her own feet. Cheeks burning, she forced herself to look up into his face. His brows were drawn close over his steel-blue eyes in the most intimidating scowl she'd ever encountered. No sense in fumbling for excuses. "I figured giving in to my curiosity about whatever you were doing was better than succumbing to the urge to go meet Atlas."

A noncommittal grunt was his only reply.

Good. Because she was fresh out of ideas for how to recover the professional manner she'd strapped on this morning as armor. She fussed with her suit, straightening the fabric and brushing away imaginary dust, as if setting her clothes to rights would bring back her confidence.

"For what it's worth, the doors around here are surprisingly soundproof." It would be the closest she'd admit to having pressed right up against the door trying to hear something, anything to give her a clue as to whether this man would cooperate today or if she'd have to escalate back up to her sponsor, the man who'd signed her contract, her employer. Thinking of the man in those terms made her grit her teeth.

And she wanted to talk to him like she needed a hole in the head.

David Cruz quirked his very sexy mouth in a half-smile. "Good to know. Maybe I'll cancel the order on the white noise generators for the offices."

Lyn blinked. "Overkill for a kennel, isn't it?"

His dark eyes fixed her in a somber stare. "We've all learned here to be prepared for every conceivable situation. It's kept the people, and some of the older dogs, alive when others didn't make it. We like to keep up the practice."

Oh man. Mental note to do some more research on Hope's Crossing Kennels. All her employer had given her was a newspaper article on Atlas, the hero dog returned from overseas, and the address for the kennel he'd been transferred to. She'd walked in ready to deal with the usual blustering egos. Strong personalities were a given with trainers working with dominant dogs all the time. But taking in the man that was David Cruz, really looking at him…

Lean and wiry, Cruz didn't seem to have an ounce of extra flesh on him. Everything about him was sharp, from the way he responded to every sound around them to the way his musculature showed through his snug tee. Cut wasn't the word for it. She thought she'd seen some fitness guys on the Internet call it shredded? Oh yes. His bronze skin and dark hair, combined with his brooding expression, stole her mental filter, leaving her with no sensible words from the start.

She was messing up this entire project and what she really wanted was to do the only thing she was good at: helping dogs. She'd turned down two private training contracts to clear her schedule for this. Her services were in high demand. And damn it, she could help Atlas.

But she'd made a mistake trying to bulldoze her way through Cruz. She shouldn't have tried to get around him or walk over him. Her employer would've sneered at her and cited a serious tactical error. But she wasn't military and she didn't have to maneuver her way to steady footing again the way others might. She could give a little, compromise, adjust to the situation and change her approach. And she could open her mind and learn before trying to shower everyone with her expertise.

"Has the status with Atlas changed?" She kept her tone soft, trying not to make it sound antagonizing.

Cruz's brows drew together and if it was possible, his expression darkened further. "How do you mean?"

She treaded carefully. "Newspaper article said he was pining away for his handler who died overseas."

A long pause. "He's eating."

Her heart skipped and then sank. It was a good sign if Atlas was eating. Bad news was they might not need her after all.

"To be fair," Cruz continued, "he's only eating on command. He won't eat if someone's not watching to make sure he does."

Lyn struggled to keep a politely positive expression. No gloating. No anything that might shut Cruz down again. "I appreciate your honesty."

"Yeah well, I try not to lie unless absolutely necessary."

But he hadn't had to share the whole truth either. Was he giving her a chance?

Whatever she said next might mean the difference between seeing Atlas and seeing her way out the front door. Her employer wouldn't be happy and she wouldn't be either.

Atlas's story had struck a chord with her. He'd gone to hell and back on the commands of someone he trusted, with unwavering faith he was doing the right thing. And that person was suddenly gone. Her father had always guided her to do the right thing. When he died, her world had been filled with a lot of people telling her what to do and every one of them had their own selfish motives in mind. It'd stopped being about the right thing and warped into presenting the right illusion.

Be real. Every dog recognizes a fake. And good men can see through it too.

"I'd really like to help." Honest. Simple. All the other reasons paled in comparison to this.

Cruz pressed his lips together in a hard line. She thought for a moment he'd say no. Fighting the urge to let loose an avalanche of reasons why she could and reiterate every point on her résumé supporting her expertise, she forced herself to stay put and wait. Five years rehabilitating abused animals in New York City and four years working as a private trainer to some of the most difficult human personalities on the West Coast had taught her patience.

"You've worked with dogs suffering from PTSD before." He made the statement a question.

"Yes." Quite a few in fact, but with a man like Cruz, she was getting the sense that less was more, at least when it came to credentials. He could and would check out her résumé later. He'd see her years of work, her awards and appearances at training conferences, in the paperwork.

No more bragging at this point and no more blustering. "Let's go."

She didn't have a chance to thank him, only hurried to keep up as he took long strides down another hallway and through a solid built door. They came out in the hallway to a set of kennels built directly against the main building.

Every one of the dogs came to alertness.

Cruz came to a stop at one. "We're not going to do the usual introduction and sniffing. I'm going to open up the kennel and bring Atlas out. I'm going to hand him off to you and I want you to do exactly as I did for him. Then you're going to give him back to me."

Lyn nodded. This was new to her. It didn't matter because she was up to handling anything this man might ask her to do. What mattered was Atlas.

Cruz gave a quiet command and opened up the kennel. A moment later he was leading a beautiful, muscled dog out into the corridor. The dog stood squarely on all fours and had the elegant lines characteristic of the Belgian Malinois breed. His proud head was chiseled and in good proportion to his body. There wasn't an ounce of extra flesh on him and in fact, he looked slightly gaunt.

Still, even among the working dogs she'd met, she wasn't sure she'd ever encountered a dog with this air of...fitness.

But there was something missing. Atlas was aware and responsive, but he didn't have the indefinable energy the other dogs around her were projecting. He wasn't engaged, vibrating with eagerness. Intelligence was unmistakable in his expression but there was no air of inquisitiveness. As if he didn't care.

Another murmured command and then the man bent down. Picking up Atlas, he wrapped his arms around the dog's chest and hindquarters in a secure hold. He then lifted what had to be around 70 to 75 pounds of solid dog and turned to her.

Lyn swallowed hard.

She held out her arms, watchful for Atlas's reaction. He remained calm in Cruz's arms and didn't even look at her. As the trainer stepped forward, she copied his hold on the dog, ignoring the accidental brush of Cruz's arms against her breasts. Once Atlas was securely in her hold, Cruz stepped away.

Atlas's fur was surprisingly silken and soft under her

hands. She resisted the urge to bury her face in his shoulder. God, he was a magnificent animal. Gorgeous, and so very sad. Her heart ached...and so did her arms.

How long was he going to have her hold Atlas? She leaned back slightly to try to take more of the weight in her back and legs as her arms strained.

She would not drop this dog.

"Okay." Cruz stepped forward and took Atlas from her.

As the dog left her arms, Atlas turned his head and touched her cheek with a cool nose and sniffed. Once.

"Huh," Cruz grunted. He stepped back and set Atlas on his feet. Then he returned the dog to his kennel with quiet praise.

Lyn waited, trembling a little. She should probably add some weights to her daily fitness routine. If Cruz had noticed how hard it had been for her, he might not...

"We start tomorrow."

"Excuse me, what?" She'd heard him. Only, it wasn't what she'd expected.

"That's the first sign of personal response I've seen out of him." There was a wry note in his words. "I'll take help where I can get it. You're staying at a nearby hotel?"

"Yes." Excitement zinged through her.

"Good. Give me the address and leave the attitude you came here with back at the hotel room." Cruz scowled at her. "This, right here, the you I see right now with the dogs is the person I want to see at oh-five-hundred tomorrow morning."

She wasn't going to argue, not when she basically agreed with him. It was going to be such a relief not to have to walk around with attitude for armor. Any soldier her sponsor had ever introduced her to had been a world-class asshole. The attitude had protected her, given her a way to stand up and not be treated as a doormat... and it was exhausting. But it seemed as if David Cruz was a different kind of military man and for the first time, she looked forward to working side by side with one.

But she was not going to say "yes, sir."

"You got it."

A grin spread across his face, lighting up his whole expression and doing evil things to her libido. "Well, you might be one of the better things that's happened all day after all."

Wow.

CHAPTER TWO

Seriously? You've been here for days and it's a woman who gets your attention?" Cruz stood in Atlas's kennel, leaning against the doorframe.

The dog in question lay in the far corner, probably enjoying the cool cement beneath his belly. Not that he didn't have the option of a cushy bed over in the other corner.

Right now, Atlas wouldn't even look at Cruz and the dog seriously appeared to have no shits to give on the current topic of conversation. He'd been that way since Cruz had returned from seeing the very pretty Miss Jones out to her car and hadn't moved in the several hours while Cruz was out working the other dogs under his care.

'Course, Atlas rarely moved, based on Cruz's experience both in having observed the dog back at Lackland Air Force Base and in the days here at Hope's Crossing. The dog might as well be a statue unless given a direct command. Then he'd obey, but it was like giving a robot orders.

When Cruz had seen Atlas respond to Jones, there'd been a spark. A ghost of the young dog Cruz had trained years ago.

And he would latch on to any incentive to get the dog to respond.

"Well, we'll see how you do with Miss Jones tomorrow morning." Not even a perked ear. Then again, Atlas didn't know the pretty stranger's name yet and it occurred to Cruz that he wasn't on a first-name basis either.

Been too long surrounded by just men and dogs.

Oh, he'd dated on and off since he'd arrived in Pennsylvania. A couple evenings here and there in Philly. He'd had a few hot women but nothing had lasted more than a few sweaty nights, and he had no plans to change the trend.

"I bet the club scene isn't your style either." Cruz preferred to spend some time every day hanging out in Atlas's kennel, talking. Gave the dog a chance to get to know him again, become used to his presence as a companion and not just as a temporary handler or his once-upon-a-time trainer.

But the indefinable moment when a dog chooses a new master? Hadn't happened yet. Not with Cruz or Rojas or Forte, the three best dog trainers on the East Coast. It'd been Calhoun that Atlas bonded to and now his handler was dead.

And contrary to bills of sale or certificates of ownership, it was always the dog's choice as to who his next master was going to be.

"We'll see what Miss Jones prefers to be called on a

first-name basis." He wouldn't admit out loud, even to Atlas, how curious he was about the things she liked to be called. Not as if Atlas was going to go around telling anyone stories.

His smartphone vibrated in his back pocket. Cruz reached for it and gave the picture password lock screen a tap and a swipe in the right places to get past the security. A little more effort than the usual pin or swipe to unlock apps that came standard with a smartphone, but maintaining higher security was a habit he didn't intend to let go.

An alert flashed across the screen.

"Hold the fort, Atlas. I'll be back."

In moments, Cruz strode into his office cursing. His computer was still running and it took less than a few seconds to authenticate and gain access past the screen saver protection.

A few seconds too many.

Whatever virtual intruder had tripped his network security was long gone. Best he could hope for was to follow any tracks left behind to trace whoever it was back to their source. 'Course, the person had only been nosing around the edges of the security system. They hadn't stumbled into it the way a random Internet intrusion would occur. No, whoever it was had known this system was here and had been testing to see just how sensitive the security measures were.

He glowered at his screen as he attempted to trace them back to their IP, only they'd gone through several servers. And by the time he did locate the originating IP, he cursed even more. Random computer terminal in a cyber café in Japan. Not likely.

Weird.

He didn't like weird. Nor did he believe in coincidences, so he locked down his computer again and pushed away from his desk, rising and heading for the door. Something like this didn't happen randomly, considering the other new things here at the kennels. There was Atlas's arrival and the circumstances around it, Miss Jones arriving to insist on working with Atlas, then this.

Atlas's handler had died for a reason, one Cruz was still looking for. Apparently there were other people looking for it, too.

"You headed out?" Forte passed him in the hallway. The owner of Hope's Crossing Kennels must've been breaking for lunch after a morning of teaching basic obedience classes.

"Yeah. We've had a security issue. No physical incursion, just a minor blip on the network. Secured now but I want to follow a hunch." Cruz didn't linger.

Forte called after him, "Let us know if you need us."

"Will do."

He and Forte had served together overseas. They'd gone out with less information in the past. Likely Forte would want answers later but it was good to be with people who wouldn't hold him up with questions when he was on the move.

Cruz crossed the front parking lot and headed for the private drive where his car was parked alongside the other trainers' vehicles. On his way, he glanced at the front drive and what could be seen of the trees lining the perimeter of the extensive property. His security wasn't just computer system based. He'd designed it all, from the access to any of the buildings to the kennels to the perimeter of the grounds they were built on. It'd been designed to maintain privacy in a civilian area but easily upgradeable if there was need, and they'd never had multiple nibbles until today.

There was only one new person, unexpected and unannounced, who'd shown up recently and she'd been there this very morning.

He entered the address to her hotel on his smartphone and set the GPS to direct him there.

Her attitude had been one thing, but her threat about calling her backers in the Pentagon? Maybe she was more than a simple civilian dog trainer. And maybe her interest in Atlas had grown from more than just the news coverage about his situation.

A man developed hyperawareness to survive overseas and there was a fuzzy line between hyperawareness and paranoia. Miss Jones arriving the way she had and hinting at high-ranking backing hadn't just gotten under his skin. Something was off.

Time to seek her out and ask a few pointed questions about her reasons for wanting to work with Atlas. And if any of her answers came across the slightest bit shady, she was out. Hell, he was tempted to keep her out of it based on his doubts here and now.

In his experience, any doubt whatsoever could mean the difference between success and failure, coming home alive and...not. Atlas's handler hadn't come home. And the circumstances around it were enough to make Cruz proceed with extreme caution.

He'd suffered a momentary weakness in telling her she could work with him on Atlas. Seeing her face soften when she'd gotten near the dogs—the way all her walls came down the minute Atlas was in her arms—had made Cruz think she really had come to help the dog.

But if the incursion on their network had been her, she must've gone straight back to her hotel and jumped online to start hacking into their system.

And she was good, too, if she could make it look like she'd done it from the other side of the world.

Well, he recognized her for what she was and he would be damned if he was going to wait until tomorrow morning to call her on it.

* * *

Lyn wiped sweat from her brow as she exited the elevator. She'd spent more time on the elliptical than normal, trying to outrun her thoughts on Atlas and her impressions of David Cruz. There was a lot to process from what she'd seen today. It didn't seem as if there'd be enough time to do the follow-up research she had planned before calling it a night. Through it all, she was sure she was missing something important about him. It was the kind of important that could eat away at a person and cause insomnia. The only cure she had for it was to burn off the anxiety eating her up and clear her head to track down the useful bits of information. Thus the visit to the hotel gym.

Bleh. So now her legs were about as useful as limp noodles and she wasn't sure she was even walking a straight line down the hallway back to her hotel room. But her mind was clearer and she already had some search strings in mind once she got in front of her laptop.

Everything about David Cruz shouted military. Not

uncommon for kennels providing trained working dogs to military and law enforcement. But most of the trainers she'd met hadn't had the edge Cruz had.

His level of tension as he walked into a room had been enough to make her nervous, an awareness of everything around him. She'd seen men like him on military bases, fresh back from deployment, but not a trainer working at a kennel out in the middle of suburbia.

But he wasn't a raging jackass either. And she'd come to associate the attitude with the kind of soldier. It was probably unfair, but it was exactly why she'd left home as soon as she'd gotten accepted to college and never gone back for more than a brief visit. The men her stepfather introduced her to had all set her teeth on edge with their overbearing demeanors and the way they patronized her.

David Cruz hadn't done any of that. If anything, she owed him an apology for the way she'd greeted him.

She barely glanced up as a man turned the corner at the far end of the hallway and walked toward her, then passed by without a word. Pausing at her door, it took two tries to slide her room key but finally she got the green light and turned the handle. As she walked inside, a loud thump made her look up from her phone.

Panic shot through her as a man dressed all in black straightened, her laptop bag in his hand. For a moment her mind froze.

What? Who?

She started to shout, but a hand covered her mouth as a hard body crowded her from behind, forcing her farther into the room and making her drop her phone.

She stumbled forward and another hand grabbed her left arm, twisting it behind her back.

Oh God. Her thoughts scrambled and scattered. This wasn't really happening.

The man already in the room walked toward her, his lips stretching into a leering grin. The rest of his face was hidden by a ski mask. He looked her over from head to toe and then his gaze settled somewhere south of her face.

"It's really too bad you came back." His voice sent chills down her spine and she struggled.

No. No, no, no, no!

Her captor only tightened his grip until pain shot through her shoulder. What should she do? What could she do?

The other man leaned close and the stench of cigars choked her. "I'm not gonna lie though, Miss Jones. I'm kinda glad you did."

She stared at him, shrank away as he ran a tongue over his top lip. It was all going in slow motion and she gagged in disgust.

"We weren't supposed to let her see us." The words rumbled in the chest behind her head.

"And she won't see our faces." The other man reached out and fondled her breast, pinching her nipple. Twisting. Pain and revulsion shot through her. She couldn't get away. "But we can show her a couple other things before we leave. Seems a shame to let the bed go to..."

Stop!

Lyn kicked out, hard, her foot catching the front of his shin.

"Ow! You bitch!"

Desperate, she bucked against her captor. The back of her head contacted with a hard jaw and she heard teeth snap together. A grunt of pain.

The pain in her shoulder seared through her and she didn't care. She needed to get away. Now.

A door crashed open and the weight of her captor slammed into her as they both fell to the floor.

"Hey!" the other man shouted.

An angry roar was all she could make of the newcomer. There were sounds of punches thrown as she struggled to see, trapped as she was. Then feet running past her.

The weight lifted off her as the man above her scrambled to his feet. She rolled to her back and drove her feet upward, catching him in the gut.

"Oof!"

"Fuck. Let's go." Both men ran out the door.

She sobbed.

A hand touched her shoulder and she flinched away. *No!*

"Hey, hey! It's okay. You're safe now. I won't hurt you." The statements were repeated over and over again. Slowly, the voice seeped through her panicked thoughts. She knew the voice.

David Cruz was crouching down in front of her.

She couldn't catch her breath and the sobbing wouldn't stop. She swallowed hard and tried to take a deep breath. Then another.

"That's it. Nice and easy. Take your time." Cruz crooned to her, his words soft and patient. "I'm not going to leave you. You're safe."

Good. Safe was good.

"I'm going to call the police now, Miss Jones."

"D-don't. Please."

Cruz's brows drew together. "Why shouldn't I call the police?"

She shook her head. "No. I mean, yes. Call the police. Just…"

He didn't seem to get angry at all. He only waited, watching her. His gaze trained on her face, not touching her. Not doing…things.

"D-don't call me 'Miss Jones,' please." The last word came out in a whisper. She'd have nightmares, for a long time. And the way the other man had said her name was going to haunt her forever.

"What should I call you?" So gentle. Was this how he won the trust of his dogs? She wouldn't blame them for trusting him.

"Lyn." She shifted, trying to move her left arm, and winced as the sharp pain came back.

"Easy there, Lyn. Call me David. Can I touch your shoulder?"

The sobbing hadn't stopped yet and tremors took over her body as reaction set in. Logically, she could register what was happening to her. Take a step away from herself and compartmentalize to catalog the damage, hear what David was saying to her. But she wasn't up for intelligible speech yet. She only nodded in response to David's question.

His touch was feather-light and still, it took effort not to shrink away from him.

"It's okay. You've been through hell just now. I won't ask more questions until the police get here." His check was gentle but thorough, and strangely her shakes stead-

ied when he touched her but started up again as soon as
he sat back on his heels. "Nothing broken or dislocated,
but he had your arm wrenched behind you in a nasty
hold. I'm betting the paramedics will still want you to
have it in a sling for a few days."

She blinked up at him.

"I'm calling in 9-1-1. They'll dispatch both police
and ambulance. You should be looked over."

For the first time, she took a long look at her hotel
room behind him. Everything, all her belongings, had
been tossed across the room. She hadn't brought much
with her but she had packed for an extended stay. All of
her clothes, her notes, were strewn everywhere.

Fear rose up in any icy wave and clawed at her throat.

"Why were they here?" They had to have been looking for something.

David shook his head. "I was about to ask you the
same. This looks too thorough to be a random robbery."

The one man had said something...

"One of the men, the one holding me, said I wasn't
supposed to see them." And she wouldn't think about
what the other man had said. Not yet. She'd tell the
police when they got there and David could listen
then.

"That so? We're going to have to see what the police
think." Somehow she suspected David was leaving
things unsaid.

Biting her lip, she wondered whether they were going
to come back for her.

"They won't get to you again, Lyn." David responded
as if he'd heard her thoughts. "And you did great in here.
I only heard a minute or two, but you let them know you

weren't going to give in without a fight. You were very brave."

Then why did the word "stupid" come more immediately to mind?

An awkward silence settled between the two of them. It stretched out until she fished for something, anything, to say. "I might be late tomorrow morning."

A surprised bark of laughter yanked her gaze back to him. He smiled at her, warm and comforting. And she wanted to slip into the curve of his arms to ward off the chill.

She'd only met him this morning and already she was going to ask him for more than she should. But what else was she going to do?

"Will you stay with me?"

He reached out a hand slowly, giving her plenty of time to watch the approach, and then cupped her cheek. "I'll be right here, the entire time. If you need to go to the hospital, I'll go with you there, too. Okay?"

"Okay."

CHAPTER THREE

How is she?"

Cruz craned his neck to look out the window. "Physically? She's a trooper. Arm's in a sling for a few days but she insisted on starting with Atlas at oh-five-hundred this morning."

That despite his assurance to her that it was completely fine for her to have started later. She'd mentioned she might be late, damn it. She should have taken the time for herself.

"That so?" Beckhorn's voice held equal parts surprise and admiration. Cruz shared it. "How's Atlas doing?"

"He's acknowledging her existence." And didn't that chafe his ass just a little bit. "She's out walking the perimeter with him now."

Speaking of, the pair came into view finally, far out across the grounds. Atlas kept pace with Lyn's short stride, adjusting to her changes in speed and coming to heel when she paused to check out flowers or whatever.

Dog still maintained an air of disinterest, but he was out there with her and not laying on his belly in the kennel.

"So he's making progress." Beckhorn pressed for more.

"Baby steps, my friend." Cruz chuckled. "Don't go reporting him as recovered any time soon."

"This mean you don't want me to keep digging into who sent her?"

Cruz leaned back in his chair, considering. Her fear had been real the night before. Terror, really. "She was damned shaken up last night. Take a look at the debrief I sent you, off the record. Someone was looking for info she didn't know she had. Or maybe she didn't have it yet."

"She's a liability." His friend made a grim noise.

"I had her check out of the hotel and gave her a place to stay here where I can keep an eye on her." He didn't entirely trust her yet but he was sure she hadn't been faking anything the evening before. Her reactions had been genuine.

"You're going to keep her around?" Beckhorn whistled, low and long. "Is she that hot?"

"It's not about that and you know better." Of course, Lyn chose to bend over right about then, checking out a pretty wildflower or weed or something, and he got a faraway view of her shapely rear.

Okay, she was hot.

But he wouldn't keep a liability around just for that. He had Atlas in mind.

"Yeah, yeah," Beckhorn continued, oblivious of the view. "What's the plan now?"

"We both know there was something to the way Calhoun died." It was a big part of the reason Beckhorn had called Cruz so soon for Atlas. He'd needed someone he could trust to oversee the dog's recovery before something unfortunate occurred. "Accidental friendly fire, my ass."

"It's the 'accidental' part in question. We both know it wasn't friendly even if the round did come from one of ours." Beckhorn's tone went flat. "What we need to do is both prove it and find out why. Calhoun reached out to you just before he died and whatever drunk text he sent you pointed to Atlas."

"At the time, the message hadn't made any sense so I assumed it was a drunk text." Cruz swallowed hard on the guilt and self-recrimination there. Not sure what he could've done from across a damned ocean but he still felt he should've realized something was wrong and helped his friend stay alive.

"It still doesn't make any sense." A string of curses followed. "Look. No ripping ourselves up for what we would've, should've, could've. We do the right thing now."

"Yeah." Cruz nodded even if Beckhorn couldn't see.

Lyn resumed her stroll and Atlas took up position by her side. Dog might play like he wasn't interested in the woman but he was engaged and Cruz would take whatever help there was to be had.

Of course, he might have more in common with the dog than he'd prefer to admit.

Last night, she'd suffered a bad scare. Things could have been far worse if he hadn't shown up when he did. He'd been ready to rip her a new one when he'd come to her door, ajar only because her phone had landed in the entryway. It'd taken seconds to change gears from being angry with her to charging in to help her.

He'd have still gotten through, but it would've taken longer for him to realize what was going on and to break down the door. She'd been very lucky.

In those moments, he'd become someone else. The man he used to be. The stranger he'd locked down after he'd returned from deployment. When he'd heard her in danger, he'd gladly embraced the old rage and the cold calm to rush the door. Eliminate the threats.

"You still there, man?" Beckhorn brought him back.

A cold chill passed through Cruz as he realized he'd come to his feet. Maybe he hadn't completely put the other him to rest yet, but it'd take some time to ease back and he hadn't been all too relaxed as it was. It'd been why he'd come to spend time at Hope's Crossing. "Yeah. Here."

Now. Just a minute ago? Not so much. Seemed like Miss Evelyn Jones had a way of pushing all sorts of buttons with him without even trying to.

"You wanna share what you're thinking? I can almost hear the gears turning in your head."

Way across the field, Lyn had come to a halt. It was Atlas's posture that got Cruz moving. "I'm going to have to call you back."

* * *

Atlas noticed the stranger first. Lyn thought it might be one of the other trainers, but in seconds it was clear he wasn't. She'd met both through the course of the day and neither of them had the same build or stance. Dressed casual in dark jeans and button-up shirt, the stranger came through a thick grouping of trees out of nowhere. He caught sight of her and grinned. She recognized it. Oh God, she'd recognize that grin anywhere.

Fear rushed through her and she stumbled back a step, instinctively bringing her hands up to ward off the stranger without thinking.

A deep growl broke through her shock and Atlas surged forward, ripping the leash off her wrist before she could close her hand securely back around the leather.

"Atlas!" *Oh no, no.* She couldn't leave him, wouldn't. Last night, the intruders didn't seem to have any weapons on them, but this man might.

But he blanched white at the sight of the oncoming dog. He backpedaled a few steps and then turned and ran straight back through the copse of trees.

Atlas plunged through after him.

Lyn ran after them both.

"Are you crazy?" The bellow came from behind her but Lyn ignored David and kept going. His angry shout was gaining on her. "Stop! I got this."

Reckless, more afraid for Atlas than anything, Lyn sprinted through the trees and came out in another field. The stranger lay on his back, yelling in pain with Atlas over him. He'd only made it halfway to the fence.

"*Los! Los!*" David caught up and passed her by. "*Los!*"

Atlas didn't let up.

"I'm just lost! I came in here by accident!" The man was shouting.

David let loose a curse and turned to her. "Lyn, come here."

Her heart in her throat, she ran to his side. She should say something, tell Cruz who the man was.

The man's screaming became shriller and words scattered from her mind.

"Here, focus here." David's words cut across the awful sound. "You can do this. Go to Atlas, grab his collar, tell him '*Los.*'"

"What? I..."

He grabbed her good arm and gave her a light shake. "Quick. Before he gets through this guy's guard. Atlas can and will kill. You need to do this."

His gaze caught her, steel blue and hard. Not cold. Urgent.

She nodded.

He let her go then and she stumbled toward Atlas. She needed to get to him before he killed this man.

"Not on his left, go to his right."

Obeying David's instructions, she changed the direction of her approach.

Atlas was so fast, he was a blur. He had the man's forearm between his teeth and was shaking his head back and forth. As she hesitated, there was a sickening crack.

"*Los!*" The word fell out of her mouth as she lunged forward and grabbed for Atlas's collar. "*Los*, Atlas, *los!*"

Atlas released his hold and she dragged him back as the man crab-walked away from them on one good arm. David was on him in a split second.

"I'm going to sue! You're all crazy here! I'm going to sue!" The man babbled as David hauled him to his feet.

He was covered in blood and his arm hung at an awkward angle.

Lyn swallowed back bile and knelt down next to Atlas, keeping a firm hold on his collar. She couldn't stop shaking. "Good boy, Atlas. Good boy."

Atlas's attention was on the man and he whined with eagerness but stayed with her.

"Lyn." David sounded calm, completely ignoring the threats of the injured man. "Take Atlas back to the kennel and check him over."

"What about..."

"Police are en route. The silent alarm went off when he broke the perimeter. I'll wait here for them; you take Atlas back. Go around the trees so I have you two in my line of sight."

That, she could do. The farther away she could get from the man, the better. "Okay."

She fumbled for Atlas's leash with her bad arm, ignoring the ache in her shoulder. Didn't want to chance letting go of his collar until she had the leash in hand. When she stood, she had to tug twice for Atlas to come with her, but he did.

They made it a couple of yards before she noticed Atlas was walking funny. She turned to look him over, bending to run her hands over his chest and shoulder.

"Oh no." She'd thought the blood splashed across his chest belonged to the man. But as she ran her hands through his fur, her fingers found a gouge in his flesh.

Sirens approached in the distance and two men came running from the main building. David's partners.

"What happened?" Forte skidded to a stop next to her and Atlas gave a warning growl. Rojas continued on past, toward David and the intruder.

"Easy," she murmured to Atlas. Not good if he went for one of the trainers. Not good. They needed them. "He needs help. He dove through the trees over there and must've gotten torn up on his way through."

"Seriously?" Forte started to kneel but halted and straightened as he took in the dog's posture. "Okay, Lyn, he's not going to make this easy. I need to talk you through this."

"What do I need to do?" Too much time was passing and Atlas was hurt.

"Kneel down and get your arms around him. Don't lift him. Don't hurt yourself. Just hold him. Talk to him. Let him know it's okay for me to take him from you. If you don't, he's not going to let me touch him."

It wasn't what she'd been expecting. But she didn't waste time waiting for an explanation. She squatted in the grass next to Atlas, murmuring soothing nonsense phrases as she did. His growl quieted but he didn't take his gaze off Forte. Copying what David had done the day before, she wrapped her arms around Atlas's chest and hindquarters. Her shoulder ached but she ignored it. Instead, she kept talking to Atlas, coaxing him to calm and listen to her.

When his posture relaxed, Forte kneeled next to them both, nice and slow.

"It's okay. He's going to help." She kissed Atlas's head, whispered against his fur. "Good boy. Good boy."

It wasn't what the dog was used to hearing, but his ears turned back in her direction. He was listening.

Forte got his arms around Atlas, keeping up a steady soothing monologue of his own. The dog remained still with the handoff, heavy panting the only sign of his distress.

"Let's get him to the main building. We've got a triage room." Forte's words were grim. "Grab the phone out of my back pocket. Vet's on speed dial."

Embarrassed, Lyn fumbled at his backside as he strode across the field. "Which…?"

"Left cheek, my friend. We're friends now, right?"

A laugh slipped out before she had too much time to think. One more fumble and unintentional grope and she had the phone. It was easy to find the vet on speed dial. She was in the top five favorites on the front screen and labeled as "Vet."

Easiest thing to do in the last twenty-four hours.

* * *

Cruz strode through the doors of the triage room they kept on site. Atlas lay on the table and Doc Medicci was shaving away the fur around a nasty slice across his shoulder.

Forte stood by, helping with the now calm dog.

And there was Lyn.

He zeroed in on her. "Is any of that blood yours?"

"I'm sorry," she whispered, her gaze locked on Atlas. "He went right through the trees and must've tore himself up on a branch. It didn't even slow him down."

"It's not the first time we've seen something like this." He was concerned. Of course he was. But the intensity and prey drive these dogs had resulted in accidents like these in the past. In this case, Atlas had moved to protect Lyn.

Currently, Cruz was fairly overwhelmed with the need to take care of her himself.

"Relatively superficial this time." Medicci didn't even glance up from her work. "I'm not finding any other damage. I'm going to put on a dissolving suture. Keep it clean and restrict him to light exercise until it heals. If it gets red or irritated, call me."

In short order, Atlas was back on his feet.

"Go get cleaned up, Lyn. He's fine now and you're swaying on your feet." Forte's tone was gentle, not angry.

Cruz caught Forte's attention and his friend gave him a brief nod.

"Let's go." Cruz reached out for Lyn and herded her toward the door, careful not to touch her.

Did she realize she was shaking?

"The man. He was the same from yesterday." Lyn's voice trembled. She took a breath and the rest came out in a rush. Atlas padded over and leaned against her leg. "He had a ski mask on but I recognized his grin. The way he looked at me. It was the same guy, I swear."

Cruz clenched his teeth against the wave of anger as it washed through him. He sucked in cooler air as he struggled to rein in his temper. He hadn't recognized the man, possibly because the man's expressions through the ski mask the night before and the grimace of pain he wore today when Cruz had gotten a good look at him were vastly different. But he could understand why Lyn had recognized the grin. And he wanted to wipe the guy from the face of the earth for putting that kind of fear into her with just one expression.

"I'll update the police." Forte's cool helped anchor

him. "You go on and wash up or Sophie will have all our heads for not showing up to dinner."

His heartbeat pounded in his ears, but he focused on Lyn. "They'll handle it for now. Let me take care of you."

Not going to think about his words too much. It was what he meant, so he said it.

The cabin he'd put her in late last night wasn't far. Its proximity to the main building and kennels was the reason he'd given it to her in the first place.

When she fumbled at her pockets for the key, he reached up behind the lamp fixture high above the door and pulled out the spare. Once he had the door open, he kept an eye on Atlas. The dog didn't signal that he detected any humans.

In fact, Atlas had simply walked along with Lyn calm as you please, as if he hadn't broken training and gone after a man not so long ago.

They entered the cabin and he flipped on the light, then nudged her toward the kitchen.

Once he had her there, he turned on the brighter kitchen lighting and turned to her. "Let me get a look at your wrist."

She held both hands out to him, palms up.

"Don't strain your shoulder." He tucked her left arm back in its sling. As gently as he could, he touched the angry red abrasion around her right wrist.

"He didn't mean to do it."

"He had other things on his mind." Cruz agreed. She must've tried to hold Atlas when the dog had lunged after the intruder. Atlas had literally ripped the leash off her wrist. "Any sharp pain when I do this?"

He bent her hand at the wrist, carefully testing the range of motion.

She shook her head. "I don't think anything is broken. Only lost a couple of layers of skin is all."

"Well, let's make sure it heals up quickly." He put a hand on either side of her waist and hoisted her up—hiding a grin as she squeaked—and sat her on the kitchen counter. First of all, he liked her sound effects. Wondered what others she might have. Second, she didn't flinch at his touch. A good sign she was recovering from the previous night's scare even better than she might notice herself.

Atlas gave a short bark.

"*Af.*" Cruz watched as the dog's ears came forward, considering. Then he lay down on his belly, head up, watching.

Dog definitely had a thing for Miss Lyn Jones. And wow had Atlas woken up. The difference between yesterday and right now was night and day.

Cruz shook his head.

"I'm sorry." Lyn shifted on the counter.

"No. Not you." He turned and pulled a go bag from under the sink. A quick rummage inside and he pulled out one of his personal med kits.

"What is that? How do you know where things are?" Lyn craned her neck to see around him. "Is every cabin stocked like this?"

"No." Setting the kit on the counter beside her, he opened it up and pulled out a few supplies.

"Then how do you know where everything is?"

"This was my cabin."

She paused. "Oh, um."

He waved a hand toward the rest of the cabin. "It was more secure, so I put you here and I moved out to the guest cabin closer to the edge of the property."

"But you had to move all your stuff?" She sounded uncomfortable.

"Not really. I don't keep much aside from essentials." He realized he was starting to scowl, but it wasn't because she was making him angry. Why was it that the woman could be attacked twice in less than twenty-four hours, hurt both times, and worried about him having to move his stuff? "It really is okay. I prefer to be farther away from the main house anyway. Too many guests on the property once the basic obedience classes get started."

"Okay." She was chewing on her lower lip, still concerned.

Saying more would only make her think on it harder so he decided to drop the topic. Nice to know she did care about putting others out of their way. He'd have done it regardless, all things considered. But it made it better to not be taken for granted.

"We're going to clean your wrist and get the blood flowing a little. Then I'll get some antibiotic ointment on it."

She didn't comment. Her dubious frown made him smile though.

"Trust me, I know what I'm doing."

"You're not going to tell me it's not going to hurt, are you?" She narrowed her eyes.

He shrugged. "It's not gonna tickle exactly."

"Joyful." She held out her wrist to him.

It took less time to clean her wrist under cool running water in the sink than it had to patch up Atlas. Her skin was delicate, smooth and silken to touch. If her wrist was this soft, he couldn't help but wonder about other, more tender places.

Nope. *Keep on task*, he ordered himself. He patted the area dry and spread the antibiotic cream over the abrasion as gently as he could.

"For such big hands, you've got a really light touch." Her words were slurred a little. She must've been coming down off the adrenaline kick. Considering last night and today, she had to be exhausted.

"Yeah?" He wrapped sterile gauze around her slender wrist, mostly to remind her not to bump it into things.

"Your fingertips are calloused, a lil' rough."

That didn't sound like a compliment. "Sorry."

"No, I like it. It feels kinda good on my skin."

Her heart rate had picked up, fluttering at the pulse point under his touch.

"Yeah?" The urge to slide has hands over more delicate areas increased and he couldn't help running his thumb along the inside of her arm.

Awareness grew in her gaze and she bit her lip as she nodded.

He leaned toward her, focused on her plump lip caught under her teeth.

"What else do you like?"

She opened her mouth to answer but he didn't plan to let her get a word out. Maybe later. He bent his head to capture her lips.

And seventy-five pounds of fur jumped up on his side.

"The hell?"

Lyn gasped. "Atlas!"

"*Af.*" Mindful of the dog's injury, Cruz gave Atlas a gentle shove.

The dog dropped back to all fours, his tongue lolling. Looking from him to Lyn and back again, Atlas lay back down on his belly.

Jealous. Damn dog was jealous.

CHAPTER FOUR

Rest. Relax. For how long?" Lyn sat on the couch in the main area of the cabin, tapping her fingers on the windowsill. It wasn't as if she'd broken anything.

David had left only a few minutes ago. And to his credit, he'd mentioned something about lunch as he'd left.

It was already past mid-morning so unless he planned to starve her, lunch couldn't be too far off.

Patience had never been one of her virtues, though.

"At least he left you with me." She turned away from the windowsill and studied Atlas.

The dog lay stretched out on the floor with his head on his paws, as close to her perch on the couch as possible. He'd opened his eyes and lifted his big ears in her direction at her movement.

"You are my job, after all." She continued to consider him.

His attitude really had changed overnight. The look in

his eyes was still somewhat reserved in her opinion, but he was more obvious about listening to her. Not as aloof or disinterested as yesterday, or first thing in the morning, for that manner.

Good signs, all of them.

David was a good dog trainer. She had no doubts after having seen him greet the other dogs at the kennel. Every one of the dogs in the care of Hope's Crossing Kennels jumped to their feet at his approach, eager for a word from him or the chance to work. His body language was always relaxed, confident. He moved with the kind of easy readiness—potential for explosive action in every muscle—that commanded respect. The dogs were sensitive to it, acknowledged him as a dominant in the territory. With him, there was no question as to who was in charge.

"But you need more than clear leadership," she murmured to Atlas. He blinked and blew a huff of air out of his nose.

She held out her hand in a loose fist, the back of her hand toward him. He considered for a long minute before lifting his head and extending his nose. One sniff. Then he returned to resting on his paws again, looking away from her. Not interested in more than acknowledging her.

"It's good to have this time to get to know you." She always talked to dogs when they were relaxing. If she'd been working with him instead of enjoying quiet time— and there was a difference—she'd give him clear and concise commands instead of conversational commentary. Even eager-to-please dogs still needed to understand what it was a human wanted them to do and they didn't precisely speak human. They learned to recognize short commands combined with body language. Any human could speak a command, in any language, and it'd still take a dog a minute to really understand what the human wanted unless the human copied a known trainer exactly in words, tone, and gestures. Then the dog probably made an educated guess.

"You're smart enough to know what we all want from you," she murmured. "But obedience and working aren't what you want to do right now, are they? You've lost your heart."

She didn't blame him. Being heartbroken was something she could understand.

"I've never had my heart broken by a boyfriend, mind you." She leaned her head back against the couch's arm rest. Confiding in dogs was one of the most secure ways of getting something off her chest. And opening herself up to them gained their trust in return, every time. "I think human hearts break, too, when the people we live for disappoint us. Like our parents. I have trust issues."

Of course, if David was to walk in, he'd probably think he was interrupting a therapy session. Only she was the one on the couch talking about her emotional baggage while Atlas was the shrink listening.

There was a method to what she was doing, though. Atlas was getting used to the cadence and tone of her voice. Her scent surrounded him in this room. And every movement she made was being cataloged in a library in his mind associated to her. The introduction process was a long one, and the more time the dog had to interact with her, the more comfortable he'd be because he'd know what she was likely to do.

Her phone rang, the tone bringing her bolt upright in her seat. Atlas was on his feet beside her, his entire body tense and his ears forward at alert. A low growl rumbled from his chest.

"Sorry, Atlas. Easy." She took a deep breath, calming herself so the dog would take her cue and go back to resting.

Damn it. As much as she hated the distinctive ringtone—or rather, the caller it was assigned to—she figured she better answer it before the caller decided to blow up her phone again.

"Hello, Captain Jones." Neutral. She was going for a nice, civil exchange.

A pause. "I have repeatedly instructed you to call me 'Father.'" The voice on the other end was surly.

Make no mistake, his feelings weren't hurt. In her twenty-eight years of experience, he'd gone around in a perpetual state of dissatisfaction with the world. Well, at least twenty-five. Theoretically, the first few years of her life hadn't been formative in terms of actual memories. Her mother had married him when she'd been just a toddler.

Instead of arguing the point, she decided to go for pleasantries. "I hope you've been well. Is there a reason you're calling?"

"Don't try to sidetrack me, miss. Each time you insist on your lack of respect for familial ties, it becomes more of a habit. One of these days you're going to do it in front of admiralty and the reflection on me will be absolutely inappropriate. I will not have it." His words came low and fast, as they always did whether they were speaking face to face or over the phone. Given the choice, she preferred the distance. Then she could pretend the admonishments didn't give her cold chills anymore. The impact of his intense, quiet speeches was worse for her than all the screaming in the world.

"You're one promotion away from Rear Admiral." She commended herself for a cool, even delivery there. "Surely your service record outweighs the impact of a few words from me."

Besides, he hadn't ever let her call him "Daddy" or "Dad," and not "Papa," ever. Not what had come naturally to her as a child. It'd always been "Father" for as long as she could remember. Proper. Formal. And pronounced properly as soon as humanly possible.

"It's amazing you ever graduated from college." His words dripped with disgust. *Oh, what a surprise.* "Even basic classes and interaction with professors should have demonstrated that perception is a distinct advantage in every situation. Never underestimate it."

What will people think? echoed through her childhood. "Of course. I do remember those lessons from you."

"Then apply what you learned." A command, not a request. With him it was never a request.

She waited. He'd called her and she'd asked why. He could either continue to rant or actually get to the reason for this contact in the first place.

"I was informed you experienced an attack." Was that a note of discomfort? Surely not.

"There was an incident at my hotel last night. I gave a detailed report to the police." She waited to see where this was going.

There was an intake of breath. "Did you see your attackers well enough to identify them?"

A leering grin flashed across her mind's eye. Her heart kicked hard in her chest and she swallowed the sudden taste of bile. Atlas was on his feet in front of her, pulling her focus with a somber stare.

She was safe. Atlas had made sure of it.

Regaining her composure, she stood and tried to walk off the residual nerves as she answered, "Not last night."

Maybe her stepfather was concerned? Hard to tell with him, but there was always room for surprise in the day.

"No? It would have been useful if you could give a sketch artist something to work with."

Ah. Of course. How easy it was to find a shortcoming. "The man I saw was wearing a ski mask. The other attacker came from behind and I never saw him."

This was her stepfather's chance to express concern. Two attackers. Didn't he wonder how she'd come through in one piece?

"As your point of escalation on your current contract, I was notified about the encounter and your physical status but not given the details of the sequence of events." He paused. "I assume you were able to trigger an alarm of some sort to call for aid."

Actually, no. And if Cruz hadn't arrived when he had, she wouldn't have been able to. Something she was going to fix, and soon. Maybe one of those tiny, super loud air horns to carry in her purse. "Not quite, but help was close by and the police were called as soon as possible."

She was reluctant to mention Cruz saving her. It wasn't that she wasn't thankful. She was. But the idea of admitting to her stepfather that she'd needed rescuing stuck in her throat. She should have been more aware of her surroundings, should've been able to guard herself better. The nature of her job had her traveling alone most of the time and right now the idea of staying in a hotel gave her more than a moment's hesitation. Suddenly cold, she shuddered.

"You've changed to a hotel with better security?" It was more of a statement than a question. Another assumption.

He made those a lot. And basically considered you an imbecile if you hadn't done what he considered the most logical, best, or expedient thing to do.

This time, she was fairly certain he would be surprised but not disappointed. "Not a hotel. I've moved into guest accommodations directly on Hope's Crossing Kennels property."

Silence. Then, "Is staying on the premises a common practice when you are consulting?"

Oh no, judgment could stop right there. "With private clients, of course not. However, this is a professional kennel facility and it makes absolute sense to be as near Atlas as possible while I work with him. It maximizes my access to him and the increased exposure could potentially speed his recovery."

There, refute that *line of reasoning*.

"Indeed." Another pause. "And security is sufficient on the premises?"

Was he actually concerned for her safety? She checked her incredulity. She was getting petty and letting it go was still a work in progress. Recent years working on her own had helped her maturity in dealing with him but this contract and the sudden uptick in conversations dragged up too many old habits. It was time to think more constructively. "Security here is better than most hotels. Gated entrance, video surveillance, and dogs with various levels of advanced training." She paused. It seemed thorough to her so she considered what else might be useful information to provide before he needed to prompt her again. "One of them has been caught."

"How?" His voice turned sharp.

Puzzled, she answered, "He showed up here at the kennels while I was working with Atlas this morning. Atlas apprehended him."

And she was incredibly proud of Atlas. She paused in her slow pacing around the room and turned to give the dog a soft smile. He was still in front of the couch, sitting now.

"Ah." Her stepfather cleared his throat. "I wasn't aware. It's not likely you were targeted at random at the hotel, then. Do the police know why this man seems to have targeted you specifically?"

"That's a good point." It galled her to acknowledge it because any time he had one it was an assumption he was right about all things, in perpetuity. "The police took him into custody. I haven't heard anything more."

Silence.

"I guess you were only notified about last night's incident so far?" She was walking out on thin ice and at any minute it was going to crack under her feet.

She didn't want to think about the attack last night or the man showing up this morning. But there was a reason he'd come after her and there was another man still out there. It might be more trouble for Hope's Crossing Kennels and she didn't want to repay their generosity in letting her stay with the danger. Uneasy, she started to pace again. Maybe she should discuss this with David.

"I'm sure I'll be notified shortly. I'll also take steps to ensure there isn't a delay in this kind of update in the future." So matter of fact.

If he only said it was because he cared, it'd make all the difference. Instead, he made it sound like he was just making sure he could call in expedient damage control in case she managed to embarrass him. She used to think he was planning a political career the way he worried so much about appearances. But the two of them had never been on the same page, so neither understood the other's aspirations.

She'd given up trying to share a long time ago.

"You were the one who wanted to be involved in this particular military case." He had to bring it up. "There are quite a few eyes on the dog. He's been prominent in the news and other media outlets."

Of course. "I'm making good progress for having only recently met Atlas."

"Good. I expect personal status reports." Crisp. Maybe even cheerful? For him.

There was quite the range of moods from him today. She couldn't remember the last time she'd been on the phone with him for this long.

"Via e-mail?" she asked hopefully. *Please.* E-mail would be so much less awkward than phone calls.

"Secure e-mail correspondence with me, always. Use the encryption program I sent you." He sounded distracted now. Already done with her and on to the next thing.

Actually, she was relieved. It'd been a weird conversation. "No problem."

Still, she was surprised he was interested enough in Atlas and her work to request actual status reports. Of course, this was the first time her line of work had overlapped with anything remotely related to his, and as the main holder of her contract she supposed it did reflect directly on him.

"I'll send you some background on this kennel and the man working with you on the dog."

She blinked. "I'd planned to research both the kennel and the people I'm working with already."

"The research should have been done in advance, but you wouldn't have the resources to access much more than names and public record." He made it sound so dismissive.

Well, she wasn't a private investigator and as a civilian, she was limited to what a good Internet search could find for her. He had another point. She was never going to be someone to spite herself by turning down valuable information just because of where it came from.

"Background information would be helpful." There. As close to a thank-you as she was going to manage through gritted teeth.

"Remember. Your performance reflects on me and that dog is a military asset. Conduct yourself professionally." His admonishment sparked her temper again. "The man you're working with is former military. Don't let him run over you on this case. Men like him are still military even after they've left active duty. Arrogant sons of bitches. Do not let him take credit for our family's work."

Hello, pot, calling kettle black.

And there was no way her stepfather could know about the...almost moment between her and David. Something she hadn't had a chance to think about, but she should. Until she did, though, her stepfather needed to recognize this project included real souls. Not just assets listed on a report. "That dog's name is Atlas. And I am always professional. I'm very good at what I do."

Damn. Too much. She shouldn't have taken the bait. Shouldn't have gotten defensive about her abilities.

"We'll see." He ended the call.

Of course. He always had the last word. And damn, but it'd left her reaching for a comeback again. Too slow. Flustered. He'd won that round.

She tapped her foot, restless. Atlas hadn't budged from his spot over by the couch, but he was sitting up and watching her. Another good sign. Even if he wanted to maintain a little detachment, he was tuned in to what she was doing and what her moods were. Engaged. Very positive considering yesterday he'd been completely disinterested in life in general and people specifically.

No harm in continuing a bit of therapeutic venting in Atlas's direction. Dogs were excellent listeners. "I lived and breathed to please my stepfather when I was a kid. He was never home. The few times he came back, I wanted to show him everything I'd done while he was gone. How good I'd been. And somehow I got it into my head that if I could just do well enough in school, win enough awards, excel at sports, then he'd come home to stay. Every time he left again, it broke my heart." Her eyes grew hot and she blinked against dryness. The tears had long since burned away when it came to this set of memories. "When he finally sat me down and informed me how very little I mattered in the bigger picture of his career and his life with my mother, my heart was in pieces on the floor. I was extra baggage. Someone else's genetic contribution to the continuation of the human race. And out of honor, he'd see to it I had the basics to grow up and contribute to society. That was it."

She huffed out a soft laugh. Atlas gave her one of those doggy raised eyebrow looks.

"By the time I realized I had nothing to do with his decisions, I thought I hated him. Really. It took a long time to realize no matter how mad I was at him, how much I said I didn't care, I was waiting for the one time he'd say I'd proved him wrong or made him proud." She chewed on her lip. It'd been a bitter taste, admitting it to herself. "He's not a bad man. His priorities are different from...basically the rest of the warm-blooded, caring portion of this world."

Atlas settled back down on his belly, his head raised as he continued to listen to her.

She stepped toward him and crouched down to sit back on her heels within arm's reach of him. "We're all assets to him. We each go in one of two buckets: useful or useless. And to be honest, even if I built my career on my own and in spite of his doubts, I still want to prove to him I'm not useless."

She sighed. And Atlas sighed too.

"I want to say it's not a primary driver." Studying the beautiful contrast of black in the tan of Atlas's face, calm settled over her. "And it's not. I came here for you and your story. Just reading what happened, I wanted to get to know you. And now that I've met you, I want to see you happy again."

Because broken hearts could heal. It wasn't a whimsical child's refuge, it was her very real belief and she wanted it for Atlas.

CHAPTER FIVE

Cruz hesitated at the door to his cabin, now guest quarters. Atlas hadn't sounded any kind of alarm at his approach, but then the dog knew his step. If there was a window open somewhere, the dog might have caught his scent, too. Also familiar. It would've been confirmation: someone who belonged was on his way and not a stranger.

He shouldn't be disappointed Atlas hadn't given a warning bark on the approach of a known human.

But Atlas was waking up from the pining he'd been doing. Engaging with the world and people again. Maybe it was unfair to expect leaving him with Lyn Jones for an hour or two would trigger a full transformation in the dog, but Cruz had kinda hoped it'd be that easy—for Atlas's sake, and so they could make more progress in tracking down the mystery of his old friend's cryptic message.

Atlas's handler, Calhoun, had sent a random text to

Cruz in the middle of the night a while back. It hadn't made any sense. Cruz had assumed it'd been a drunk text, honestly. Then Calhoun died. As far as Cruz was concerned, the message and the tragedy were connected in a bad way, no matter what the official report said. Cruz needed Atlas to puzzle out Calhoun's message and his old friend deserved having his last request fulfilled.

One step at a time. He'd see how things had progressed with Lyn and Atlas first, then figure out his next actions. Considering how he'd left Lyn, there was a spark he needed to follow up on there, too.

Juggling the packages he carried into his left hand, he freed up the other to give a quick knock. Lyn's soft acknowledgment came from inside, not directly on the other side of the door but definitely in the main room. He let himself in.

"Brought some choices for lunch." Stepping inside, he noticed the guest cabin was mostly dark. The only light was streaming in from the windows. Plenty to see by, but a relief from the midday sun beating down outside.

"Smells good." Lyn had been...sitting? She rose from the middle of the floor and Atlas came to stand on all four feet as she did it.

Funny.

"I've got a couple of choices from our favorite sub shop. Cheesesteak or meatball parm. Which would you like?"

Her eyes widened.

Shit. Maybe she didn't like either option.

"Are you a vegetarian?" He probably should've asked before they'd made the lunch run but he'd been in a hurry to tuck her away someplace safe and get back to the police who'd responded to the call this morning.

She blinked and placed her hand on her belly. "No. I was just hoping you hadn't heard my stomach growl when the word 'cheesesteak' came out of your mouth. I'm starving."

Good. Otherwise, he would've been making a second run out for food because he sure as hell wasn't going to let her go hungry as a result of his lapse in thought. Generally, he tried to be considerate and shit. With this woman, though, he was constantly off his game.

Atlas stood in the middle of the living area watching him, expression and body language decidedly neutral.

Well, the pair of them had him off balance. Cruz might have a chance to regain it if they could avoid an encounter requiring police follow-up for more than twenty-four hours. All things considered, anyone would be a little unhinged.

He headed for the small kitchen table in the breakfast area. "Let's not keep you waiting anymore."

Pulling the foil-wrapped subs out of the bag, he placed the cheesesteak in front of her and took the meatball parmesan for himself. Plenty of napkins went in a pile in the middle of the table. Added bonus, he flipped open a carton containing French fries drowning in melted cheese.

Lyn pulled out a chair and glanced back at Atlas mid-motion. The dog's ears swiveled forward. Cruz bit back his first impulse comment and waited to see what she did.

She gave a slight shake of her head. "Atlas, *auf.*"

The dog hesitated and then lay down on his belly, head still up.

"*Blijf.*" She gave the dog a long look and then turned, seating herself.

Atlas watched her back and glanced at Cruz. Then the big dog set his head between his paws, turned away from the table as if he hadn't wanted any people food anyway.

Cruz approved. No way was he going to feed any dog in their care this kind of junk food. And yes, he saw the irony. But the dogs at Hope's Crossing Kennels were fed balanced meals based on their weight and level of activity. Cheesy, greasy, bombs of comfort food were not figured into their dietary plans.

She glanced up to meet Cruz's gaze. "I did some research into the command you taught me earlier. Most of my clients have their dogs trained to respond to English commands but Atlas and I have been figuring out how to work with the Dutch vocabulary he recognizes."

He'd planned to work with her and Atlas on that after lunch. On one hand, her initiative was on point and he approved. On the other, he was inexplicably irritated at the implied censure in her tone. As if he'd meant to keep her communication with Atlas limited or been testing her. She was probably fishing to see if he'd been doing just that but he wasn't going to take the bait and respond.

Whatever passive–aggressive crap she was anticipating, he didn't play those games. So he remained silent and kept his expression neutral, continuing to set out their lunch.

"I'm not going to lie; I'm really interested in trying this." Lyn quit staring at him and unwrapped the cheesesteak. "I've never had a real Philly cheesesteak anywhere near Philadelphia."

Cruz raised an eyebrow. "Your work doesn't bring you to Pennsylvania very often?"

She shook her head. "I'm mostly on the West Coast. Seattle, Portland, several cities in California."

She had the sandwich up and had turned her head to the side, trying to fit the entire end in her mouth. As long as they were being honest, Cruz really enjoyed watching her try. How much a lady could fit into her mouth was always an interesting question.

And he was definitely going to hell for that thought.

Then her eyes shuttered closed as she had her first bite and chewed. "Mmm."

His pants suddenly got a hell of a lot tighter. "Good?"

"Oh yeah." She chewed some more, savoring. "That is really good."

"Have some cheese fries." He pushed the carton over to her and got up to get them each a glass of water. She looked like she was about to inhale the cheesesteak and he wanted to be sure she had something to wash it all down before she choked.

He also needed time to get his stupid grin under control because watching her enjoy a simple sandwich was incredibly entertaining. In all sorts of ways.

"What kind of cheese is this?" Lyn asked. He glanced back to see her studying the end of a coated fry before popping it into her mouth.

Bad, bad pictures flashed through his head. *Jesus*.

"Cheez Whiz." Not his favorite, but then Rojas had been the one to actually go for the food. "It's one of the favorites on-site."

"One of?" she asked even as she took another bite.

Even eating messy, she was cute. Hot. Both.

He returned to the table with glasses of water and sat down again. "Everyone has their taste. I like my cheesesteaks better with real provolone."

"Hmm." Another bite and a very thoughtful look of concentration as she pondered. "It wouldn't go over the fries as easily."

He nodded. "True. I still like the fries better with Cheez Whiz."

She sighed, studying her now half a sandwich. "It's too bad this is so very *bad* for us."

"Doesn't hurt to enjoy once in a while." Life could be short. Painfully so. Living for the moment helped. This was fun, much improved from her indirect attitude earlier. "If you like it that much, we'll have to make sure to take you into Philly and have you order your own at one of the classic places for them."

She chewed some more, swallowed, and took a sip of water. "Aren't the best places Pat's and Geno's?"

He shrugged. "Probably the ones you hear about most often. There's Jim's on South Street too. A lot of places in Philly do a good cheesesteak. I like Tony Luke's on Oregon Ave."

The cheesesteak in her hands had more of her attention than his words did. No issue there. He liked a woman with her priorities straight.

There was a lot to like about Lyn Jones from what he'd seen over the last day, and he'd rather focus on the positive. The way she could enjoy a good sandwich every bit as much as a swanky meal in an expensive establishment was high up on his list of good things about her so far.

"You think Atlas would do well on a socialization

walk through the city?" She was back to the fries and looking at him with a clear, crystal green gaze. He decided not to tell her she had cheese on the corner of her mouth, or that he wanted to kiss it off.

"Maybe not today, but not out of the question later this week if he keeps improving." He glanced at the dog, who was steadfast in trying to ignore them. Normally he didn't eat in front of the dogs. No need to tease them with what they couldn't have. But it didn't hurt their training to have temptation around them sometimes. "I was thinking maybe I'd take you out to dinner and give him the night off."

She swallowed. Hard. "Dinner. Like a date?"

Ah. Maybe not. "That was the idea. Maybe I read things wrong but I thought we had a moment back there."

"Oh." Her fair cheeks flushed pink. "No. Yes. We did. I just…"

"It's okay if you'd prefer not." He schooled his expression to carefully neutral. She was important to helping Atlas and he didn't want her to feel uncomfortable working with him just because he'd asked her on a date. Dumb idea anyway.

She bit her lower lip but had the grace to look him directly in the eye. "You're a very nice man, David. And I can't thank you enough…"

He held up his hand. "No need to thank me."

He'd slam his own head into a wall before letting her accept a date with him as a thank-you for what any decent person should've done for her. Interested in her? Yes. But everything in him rebelled at the idea of pressuring her. He liked his women willing and he didn't exactly have a problem finding them. This just needed to quit being so damned uncomfortable.

"I'd like to keep things at the professional coworker level...and friends. Is that okay?"

How could he say no? He wasn't an absolute dick. And besides which, his priority was Atlas. The dog needed for them to work well together and David wasn't about to let his hormones screw anything up.

"We're good." He gave her what he hoped was a reassuring smile. "Totally professional and no hard feelings."

She let out the breath she'd been holding and gave him a small, unsure smile.

He pushed the fries closer to her and handed her a napkin. "Have another fry. You'll need the energy this afternoon working with our friend here."

* * *

"Agility?" Lyn studied the course. It wasn't the standard agility course she was used to seeing but rather a more rugged course. There were items specific to K9 training like the broad jump, catwalk, and brick wall jump. The Catch-A frame was completely new to her. The car door jump and window jump were actually painted in more realistic colors as opposed to the standard white. The equipment was familiar to her but not part of her usual clientele's goals.

David took the lead off Atlas. "He can do all of it. Easily. The question is whether he wants to."

She nodded. A dog learned exponentially faster with internal drive. Incentive could help too, but a trainer learned to align training with the natural drive of the dog for the best results. Which meant finding a situation in which the dog wanted to perform a particular action.

At the moment, Atlas was sitting next to David and not even looking at the agility course. Not interested.

"What're we using for incentive?" She'd used treats usually for clients, but the K9 and military trainers didn't always have the same practices.

David pulled a tennis ball from his pocket. Atlas watched the slow arch of the ball as it crossed the distance between them. Lyn was happy she caught it. It would've been insanely embarrassing if she'd dropped it considering how much time David had given her to catch it.

"He gets this after completing each exercise." David lifted his chin toward the ball in her hands. "Then we'll see if we can get him to do the whole course for the ball."

She raised her eyebrows. "That's assuming a very fast learning curve."

He shrugged. "This is all review for him. He used to run a course like this for the sheer joy of doing it. If we get him back into a mood to do it at all, I don't think it'll take long for him to demonstrate how easy this is for him."

She laughed. Atlas did seem to have his fair share of pride. "Okay."

"Walk to each obstacle and give the command. Let's take them one at a time and see how much he needs to obey."

"Obedience." She frowned. "We haven't confirmed he's consistently obedient yet."

Only a few commands this morning and during lunch. Every time, she'd seen the pause, the consideration, as Atlas had *decided* whether he wanted to obey.

"He's still got solid obedience." David spoke with utter confidence, almost irritating. "There's a delay but he doesn't ignore commands. He just doesn't care enough to execute immediately."

She frowned. The delay in behavior might not be a big deal in the civilian world. Some regular owners might not even think twice about the delay even if it became a habit. But...he could be testing her. "The delay isn't acceptable for military work."

David shook his head, no hint of whether he'd been leading her to saying so or not. Just responding. "Not at all. But then, at his age, he might not be redeployed at this point. It really depends on how well he comes through this."

So cold. Matter of fact. She kind of hated David a little bit for the way he casually talked about Atlas like that. As if it was all about practicality and not about an injured soul.

Her heart ached for Atlas. Part of her wanted to cut him slack, let him have the leeway in his training to ensure he'd be allowed to retire and enjoy life here. But Atlas was a working dog. He might not be happy no longer working. It had to be up to him. Find his balance again and working might be what he lived for.

"You do basic obedience with every dog here, right?" Seemed as if she'd seen the other trainers working with various dogs. Both Alex Rojas and Brandon Forte had been out with various dogs all morning.

"We make sure every working dog here trains for

thirty minutes in obedience every day. Then they spend time in their specialization." Still brisk and all business, David pointed toward the kennels. "Any puppies Rojas breeds are also taught basic obedience as a package deal with the buyers. We use the time in the basic obedience classes to confirm the new owners are a good fit for our dogs."

Good practice, assessing the owners to be sure they could handle the dogs they were purchasing. The trainers were less likely to lose track of a puppy somebody might decide to abandon. Too many people purchased a dog, invested in training, then dropped it in a shelter rather than admit to the breeder they'd decided they didn't want the dog anymore.

Perhaps she was reading too much into his tone. He was being practical but maybe he wasn't uncaring. She realized she was biased because of her dealings with her stepfather, looking for callousness in David. But David had been very generous with answering questions. Especially considering she'd turned him down earlier, he could've taken a completely different tack. She appreciated his willingness to really work with her.

"How many of your puppies go to private homes?" She'd thought they specialized in working dogs.

David studied Atlas. "Not every dog is suited for military or K9 work. We start assessing temperament right away and do our best to find good homes for the puppies not suited for working. They start training early and we watch them for the right combination of prey drive, aggression, intelligence... all of the traits necessary for them to be successful."

"And those same traits make them difficult home

pets." High aggression and intelligence made for destroyed homes when those same dogs became agitated in a high-density neighborhood or got bored while owners were away at work or even on short errands. It was amazing what level of destruction a single dog could do in the wrong environment.

David's grin drew an answering grin from her. It was ridiculous how much of a difference his expression made from his previous attitude and how happy she was for them to be on the same page when it came to training. She'd butted heads with other trainers in the past and the experience had been frustrating. She'd really thought he would be another one of those when she'd first met him. This—and seeing him with Atlas—was proving her wrong in the best of ways.

It'd been the right decision not to go out to dinner with him. This level of professionalism was something much better, even if he was also one of the most distractingly attractive men she'd ever worked with.

"Well, I might not have the same commands you'd use." She figured it would be best to clarify before she confused Atlas. "I did look up the basic Dutch commands but I need to do more studying."

David swept his arm out toward the course. "Let's give it a try and take those spots where we run into them. I can give you the correct command if Atlas is looking like he's up for the course."

Good point. First step: see if the dog was actually willing. This entire exercise could end quickly if he only walked up to the first obstacle and sat there.

"All right. Let's give this a try."

CHAPTER SIX

Please tell me you're not going to keep her here on a gorgeous Saturday while the rest of you all pretend it's just another day of the week."

Lyn looked up at the speaker, an extremely attractive Asian woman with way more energy than anyone ought to have at 0500 on a Saturday morning. Seriously, the woman literally exuded vitality.

"Sophie, we are holding no one hostage." From his position behind the breakfast counter in the communal kitchen, Brandon poured a new cup of coffee. He added cream and sugar then held it out to her.

He was going to give her caffeine? Seemed like a questionable choice.

Lyn wasn't a morning person by nature. Most of her clients preferred to meet at reasonable times in the morning, like nine or ten. However, Hope's Crossing Kennels had a much more active routine than the average home owner. The trainers were up and beginning morning chores by 0500, as they put it. The early morning was filled with feeding, then basic obedience for the working canines and the boarded guest dogs. Later in the morning, people would begin arriving for obedience and agility classes with Alex while Brandon and David took the working canines through specialized training. The afternoon went along the same lines, with various dogs getting individualized attention. Evening saw people arriving for more classes into the night.

The trainers of Hope's Crossing Kennels easily worked sixteen-hour days, with long breaks in the slow times of the afternoon to balance out their long hours.

Lyn's involvement was solely regarding Atlas but she sure as hell wasn't going to sleep in when David was up and getting started with the freaking dawn. What she hadn't anticipated was how ragged she'd feel once the weekend hit and they were all still getting started right on time.

One never appreciated sleeping in on the weekends until one couldn't. It'd been especially hard to climb out from under the comforters this morning. The guest bed was warm, cozy and comfortable. David's bed.

Lyn took another sip of her own coffee. No good could come of her brain being allowed to continue half-asleep at this moment.

"You all may continue with your routine," Sophie was saying, coffee mug in hand and a stolen piece of bacon in the other. "But your guest here might not know there are options for her. Like actually leaving kennel grounds and enjoying a day off."

"We take days off." Alex sat at the table across from

Lyn and gave her a grin. She lifted her mug in acknowledgment.

Sophie scowled in his general direction.

David slid a plate of eggs sunny side up and bacon in front of Lyn and her attention snapped to the wonderful smell of breakfast. She lifted her fork. "Thank you."

"No problem." David was already digging into his own plate of food.

He'd been incredibly considerate through the entire week. Breakfast was always like this at the kennel. They ate together, went through the day's schedule and any potential issues. Lyn was included as a contributing member. Maybe not one of the inner circle, but a part of a team. It was refreshing, interesting, as compared with the solo work she usually did in her training and consulting business.

"The least you could all do is introduce us properly." Sophie had a plate of breakfast by now and she seated herself.

Brandon sat next to her, absently passing a plate of iced breakfast rolls over to Lyn before offering it to Sophie, too. They smelled heavenly and Lyn immediately bit deep into golden, pillowy goodness. When blueberries burst across her tongue, complemented by the vanilla lemon icing, Lyn closed her eyes to focus every fiber of her being on enjoying the flavors.

Alex chuckled. "Pretty sure Lyn's going to be your friend forever if you keep bringing baked goods on your visits while she's here. And you know who Lyn is because as soon as you noticed we had a guest you followed Brandon around until he told you. Not sure any other introductions are needed."

Lyn finished chewing and swallowed, coming up for air before taking another bite of happiness. They all accepted the other woman with an easy air of long acquaintance. She was like a little sister, running around bugging her big brothers for attention. Brandon glanced at Sophie as she reached over him for salt and quickly stuffed his own breakfast roll in his mouth.

Well, mostly big brothers. There was something else going on there but it wasn't Lyn's thing to get into the middle of those situations.

"Lyn, it's a pleasure to officially meet you." Sophie extended her hand across the table. "I'm Sophie and I do the accounting for the kennels."

"She also keeps giving us all reason to keep up our cardio, otherwise her baking would make us fat." Despite his commentary, Alex helped himself to another sweet roll.

Lyn quickly wiped her hands on her napkin and reached out her right hand to accept the handshake. "You made these? They're incredible."

"It's a hobby." Sophie's slender hand caught hers in a firm grip.

Nice. Lyn hated limp handshakes.

Sophie gave her a friendly smile. The sort of open, genuine smile Lyn couldn't help but return. "I was going to do a little shopping in New Hope today. Why don't you join me?"

"Oh." Lyn glanced at David. "I don't want to miss any work with Atlas."

"Today's his rest day. No plans besides easy exercise time and relaxing with him." David didn't look up from his plate. "You can always spend time with him after you get back."

The week had been interesting, learning how to take Atlas through the various specialized training. They'd only covered agility and scent training this week, with one session on bite work. David had asked a friend from the local police force to come and wear the big protective suit when they'd done the bite work.

It'd been frightening and fascinating to see Atlas spring into action. She'd worked with K9s in the past but Atlas, as an Air Force military working dog, was on a different level. His aggression was higher if at all possible, and his speed was heart stopping. Plus, there'd been a distinct difference between biting to apprehend the way K9s did and biting to kill the way a military working dog needed to.

"Can we speak privately for a minute?" She put her fork and knife on her plate. "So we're on the same page about Atlas."

David didn't respond but pushed his chair back and rose.

In minutes, they were down the hall in his office. She still couldn't stop blushing when she looked at the door. Eavesdropping hadn't been the greatest moment of her life.

"Is this because of yesterday's bite work session?" She wasn't going to waste time circling the question.

David met her gaze directly. "What is this? And why do you think it is?"

"I was surprised by the directive to bite to kill." She'd been transparent about it because it seemed to be the way they worked best together. "I've appreciated the way we've been able to work together up to yesterday but it seemed like yesterday's session broke something."

Silence. Then David sighed and dragged a hand through his hair. The gesture only made her want to run her own fingers through.

"It was a reminder about how different civilian dog behavior is from what we need Atlas to be for military work." David didn't sound happy about admitting it. "And your anxiety can transfer to the dog. Atlas needs to be able to do those things without hesitation."

Atlas hadn't seemed to hesitate or consider at all the day before. In fact, Lyn had been elated because his response had been the best she'd seen all week. "There was no delay in Atlas obeying any command yesterday."

"No," David agreed. "Not a fraction of a second of hesitation. He was almost too eager to kill something threatening you."

Lyn blinked. Closed her mouth on what she'd been about to say.

"You were nervous. He responded to protect you with deadly force." David shoved his hands into his pockets. "It's excellent in terms of his engagement and the progress you're making with him. It was almost dangerous for my friend while you weren't used to controlling what Atlas could do."

True. The protective suit was more than sufficient in most cases but if a dog really wanted to kill the man inside, it could eventually happen.

"I figured a day off from the more intense training would be good for both of you." David brought her attention back to him by tapping a finger on the big calendar he had on his desk. "You can come back later today and spend some quiet time walking the grounds but let's give him some time to unwind and you some time to get more comfortable with his capabilities."

"Okay." She hesitated. "I thought you might…"

"You're doing great." He cut her off before she could voice the self-doubt. It was one of the only times he did interrupt her. "Seriously, we couldn't have made this much progress with Atlas without you."

"We're doing great," she countered, happiness filling her as he smiled at her assertion. "I couldn't do this without your expertise either."

"So go take a day and hang out with Sophie. New Hope's a nice town to walk around."

She gave him a bright smile and walked out of the office. The idea of a day out to clear her head and be around another woman was suddenly a fantastic change of pace.

Sophie was still in the kitchen with Brandon and Alex, chatting about the various dogs. When Lyn re-entered, Sophie stopped. "So. Conference complete. Are you allowed to come out to play or do you still have homework to do?"

"My schedule looks open for the day." Lyn snagged an extra piece of bacon from the plate on the breakfast counter. "But I'm looking for a more adult kind of fun day."

Brandon choked on his coffee.

Alex cracked up laughing.

David stopped in his tracks behind her.

Lyn kept her gaze on Sophie, refusing to look back to see David's expression.

Sophie's smile broadened into a crazy grin. "Oh, New Hope is the *perfect* place. Wear comfortable shoes."

* * *

"That tea set was amazing. Why didn't you buy it?" Lyn asked as they waited to be seated.

"No place to display it right now." Sophie sighed. "I love tea sets and I've got an everyday set at home to use, but a set like that one? It needs to be displayed and used. Too gorgeous to tuck away in a cabinet."

"That wasn't the first time you've gone to look at it, either." The shop owner had recognized Sophie.

Sophie grinned. "The goldfish set is my favorite, but I always stop in to see the new pieces she has on display. The designer has a catalog and comes out with new themed pieces every year. The new Phoenician bird design is incredible. Oh, and there's this older ladybug themed set of teapot, cups, and platter."

The way Sophie chattered on about tea sets and good afternoon tea services made Lyn's stomach growl.

Sophie laughed. "We'll have to go someplace for afternoon tea sometime, or maybe I'll put together one at the kennels and Boom can join us."

"Sounds good to me, especially if you're baking again." Lyn hoped she'd be around long enough, but then, her project with Atlas was open-ended based on his progress, so it was a possibility.

"Question for now is, what will you have here?"

"You haven't led me wrong yet today." Lyn settled into the seat and set her shopping bags at the side of the little table. "What do I absolutely have to try?"

Sophie had been a fantastic shopping companion for the morning, whisking Lyn off to New Hope to explore quaint shops up and down a historic main street. They'd browsed and chatted, exploring locally made clothing and art. With Sophie as a guide, Lyn had learned more history about the area than she'd ever thought possible.

"Hmm." Sophie pondered for less than half a second. "The boys have been feeding you mostly hot subs and pizza, I'm guessing. Maybe some Chinese takeout."

Lyn groaned. "Yes. Do any of them cook? Ever? I've had more General Tso's this week than I've had in the last two years combined."

She hadn't wanted to insist on fresh salads or grocery runs when she was only a guest.

"This one, then." Sophie reached across the table to point out a sandwich. "It's roast turkey and cornbread stuffing and cranberry, all on toasted white bread. So good."

It sounded delicious. "Perpetual Thanksgiving."

Sophie nodded. "Not a bad thing, as far as I'm concerned. But feel free to pick anything that looks good. With this restaurant, you can't go wrong with anything on the menu. Plus, it's a fun place."

It was obviously popular. Every table was taken and the servers bustled between seated customers. The atmosphere was warm and the servers were good-natured. Friendly in the way only people who enjoyed where they worked could be.

Their orders were taken by a cheerful girl who looked to be high school age, maybe first year of college.

"What's the story here?" Lyn had no doubt Sophie would know. The morning had been a fun, quirky litany of stories.

"Hah. This place has an incredibly young owner, who is also the chef." Sophie nodded toward the back. "Came up with the concept when he was...fourteen, maybe? It's the nation's first restaurant completely run by young people."

"Really?" Lyn raised her eyebrows. The menu was well put together with some complex flavors in those items. "That's young. Very young to be starting a business."

She wasn't familiar with labor laws for minors in this state but it seemed far-fetched.

Sophie nodded. "It's an inspiring story and they had the support of friends and family. Dinner is all fixed price style, European influence now. It's a definite romantic hot spot."

"And have you been here for a particularly good date or two?" Despite chatting about shopping preferences and art, they hadn't touched much on personal life. Lyn wasn't sure if it was off-limits but she figured it couldn't hurt to ask.

"Nah." Sophie sipped water. "I'm too busy with work to deal with the insanity of dating. Every few months I try to go out with a guy or two. There's a couple of awkward dates with inane conversation and I swear off men until I forget just how painful dating can be."

"Ah well, I can completely understand." Lyn played with her straw. "It gets worse when you travel all the time. Most guys don't want to wait a couple of weeks for a second date. So even if I find someone remotely interesting, he's moved on by the time I'm back in town. Or he's decided I wasn't interested because I keep telling him I'm out of town."

Sophie nodded in understanding. "Tough situation. But then again, you've been here about a week now. You usually in one place for this amount of time?"

Lyn shook her head. "Most times, a client consultation is just a few hours. Training sessions are the same. I try to schedule clients in the same area together to make a trip out cost-efficient. Depending on how the dog and the owner are doing, I might come out every week for a month then switch over to once a month for a while to make sure the training stuck."

Sophie gave her a knowing smile. "Stuck with the dog or the owner?"

Lyn laughed. "It's almost always the owner who needs training. Once the dog figures out what a command means and which command a particular human is trying to give them, they're generally good if there's consistent practice. It's more about figuring out the right routine for the whole household so the dog is behaving the way the owner wants. Not always as easy."

"Brandon says most of the time dogs aren't bad, they're just bored." Sophie glanced out the window as if the man would materialize.

Lyn didn't blame her. Her own thoughts had been drifting back to the kennels, too. Wondering what David was doing with her out of his hair and how Atlas was doing.

"Yeah. A bored dog gets destructive," Lyn confirmed.

"So your specialty is more dog psychology than actual training, isn't it?" Sophie's face lit up as their food arrived.

Lyn took a minute to try her sandwich. "Mmm. Good call."

"Mmm." No words from Sophie either.

After enjoying their first bites—because good food deserved proper attention—Lyn pulled her brain back to the last question. "It seems like psychology, but getting where a dog comes from and how he or she is thinking makes training exponentially more effective. Besides, dogs are some of the most honest creatures you can work with anywhere."

Sophie nodded, more knowledge in her eyes than Lyn had anticipated. Lyn shifted in her seat.

"The boys work with dogs for a lot of the same reasons, you know." Sophie's tone had become softer, more somber.

"Not sure I get what you mean." And Lyn wasn't sure she wanted to.

Sophie popped a French fry in her mouth. "Brandon grew up in this area. Did any of them mention it to you? He left for the military right out of high school and didn't come home to stay until he was ready to retire from active duty. He started Hope's Crossing Kennels as soon as he got back."

"Okay. Guessing you grew up with him?" Lyn leaned her chin on her hand, interested. The kennels looked fairly new, with all up-to-date equipment, so she'd guessed they'd been established recently.

"Yup. I was his next-door neighbor growing up. Once he bought the land for the kennels, I made sure his finances were all in line to keep him in the black." Sophie's expression grew distant and maybe a hint obstinate as she continued, "He wanted to make a place for himself because no place felt right when he got back. It's hard to find a comfort zone when they return from overseas. The contrast, the change from deliberately stepping into danger every single day to being surrounded by people running from place to place completely unaware of what could happen...there aren't words for it."

Lyn nodded. Her stepfather hadn't ever stayed for long. And it'd made her bitter. But this was the first time someone had given her this perspective.

"Alex and David arrived as soon as the main building and kennels were built. They all had experience as handlers. They put together their business model to provide basic and obedience training for the community and to train working dogs for military and police units." Sophie seemed to have forgotten the rest of her sandwich, working her way through the French fries instead. "It didn't take long. Brandon was a hometown hero and they're all gorgeous."

Lyn chuckled. "I hadn't noticed."

"The basic and obedience classes are packed with single women who've suddenly decided having the protection of a dog at home is a good idea." Disgust colored her words but Sophie waved it away. "They eventually settled into business and now people come from hours away to work with them. And their dogs are the best. They provide working dogs to police units all over the country and to the military, too."

"David's training techniques are incredibly effective." Lyn admired him for his work with any of the dogs on site, especially Atlas. It took a rare person to put pride aside to work in the situation they had. Lyn was lucky Atlas was responding to her and thankful David was coordinating with her in Atlas's best interest.

"To hear some of the ladies talk, David is incredibly effective in a lot of ways." Sophie studied her.

Lyn hoped her face was completely blank, fighting the heat rushing up to her cheeks. "I wouldn't know and I don't think it'd be appropriate if I did."

Sophie raised a single, perfectly groomed eyebrow in a high arch. "No?"

"It's not professional." Saying so had sounded perfectly logical when she'd had the conversation with David at the beginning of the week. Here, with Sophie, not so much. Lyn didn't want to be so short—not when Sophie had been so nice all morning—but Lyn wasn't sure how to turn this into an easier-going chat.

"Weak." Sophie shook her head. "I like you. And I'm straightforward with people I like. So I'm going to say this: this isn't a corporate environment. Plenty of people can work together plus engage in extracurricular activities."

Oh, and Lyn had been imagining them. Working with David every day was an exercise in self-control and mental focus. Every time he bent over to pick up a tennis ball, she was presented with the most grope-able ass she'd ever seen. And the other day he'd taken off his shirt in the afternoon for a few minutes to switch out to a clean one. The sight of all those wonderful muscles rippling underneath his skin had left her drooling, just a little. Luckily he hadn't noticed.

"We're both focused on Atlas as a priority." Might be the truth, but also another dodge.

"True. And he's important. I get it." Sophie nodded. "It's not easy under all the scrutiny either. Since Atlas was in the papers, people are coming out of the woodwork, aren't they?"

"There's a lot of oversight." As personable as Sophie

was, Lyn kept her stepfather's interest to herself. Not that she wanted to hide it. But it'd just complicate things and be a whole lot more history to share than she was ready to do in one sitting.

"Which means a lot of stress, maybe some anxiety." Sophie pinned her with a direct look. "And there is very obviously tension between you."

"Maybe." Okay, a lot. But Sophie had already laid it out there and Lyn wasn't ready to say it out loud. "Why do you have an opinion about it?"

Sophie had said she liked Lyn. And Lyn hadn't been this close to another woman in years. Sophie could be a real friend someday if things here worked out. Lyn didn't want to mess it up with a fight over David.

"David is one of my best friends. He's become a big brother to me. If you hurt him, I'd have to come after you." One French fry was popped into Sophie's mouth and another was waved in the air between them. "But if you might be good for him, it's my duty as a little sister to get involved and get things moving since the two of you are obviously being obtuse about it."

CHAPTER SEVEN

Cruz stood on the main street people-watching, basically.

Tourists were walking by and giving him a healthy amount of space on the sidewalk. Considering the sheer number of visitors on a Saturday afternoon, he was more than happy to be free of the crowds of people. Of course, part of the reason why he'd been given so much space was probably because he was in a shit mood and wasn't bothering to keep it from showing on his face. He wasn't going to check out his reflection in a storefront window to confirm.

He'd spent an entire morning up at McGuire, accessing SIPER Net to view the report on Calhoun's death, and he didn't have answers. Only more questions. He'd have preferred to bring the report back to his office where he could read and re-read and brainstorm, but those kinds of documents were secure and accessible only via SIPER Net. Which meant if he wanted to refresh his memory on the report, he had to drive up to McGuire and sign in to a secure location to gain access. No taking anything out with him.

All he wanted now was to sit down, have lunch, and brain dump the questions he had so he could compare them with his other notes at home later. Why he'd stopped in New Hope on the way home was a question he wouldn't answer to Forte or Rojas, but he'd be honest with himself.

Lyn and Sophie had come up to New Hope.

And knowing Sophie, there was no way the ladies had finished their shopping yet. Add the knowledge of how hungry Lyn got around lunchtime—she basically had an internal lunch bell inside her belly—and he was pretty sure they'd be seated in one of the trendy places along the streets eating their way through a menu.

What he didn't know was what he was going to say when he found them. Joining them would probably happen. He wasn't the type to give bullshit excuses for why he was around town either. He had promised Lyn they were good when she'd turned him down for a dinner date. And he'd been careful to keep things professional and easygoing through the week as they focused on Atlas's rehabilitation. But this was their first day away from each other. He'd wanted to check in on her and hadn't thought twice about stopping.

Now that he was here, though, he wasn't sure if she'd think it was creepy.

He'd consider himself creepy.

Maybe he should go home and pick up fast food on the way.

As he turned to head back to his car, he caught sight

of a man across the street. The guy was doing a good job blending in with the wall of tourists checking out the old railroad station. Only he'd been there for as long as Cruz had been standing around debating whether to continue finding Lyn and Sophie or leaving. No other visitor had been hanging out for as long. There was only so much time a person could spend staring at an old building. Photographers and artists were the only exceptions that came to mind.

This man had neither a fancy camera nor tripod. No art supplies either. He was dressed like a tourist but wasn't. Fit beneath the t-shirt and jeans; wearing work boots, not sneakers or loafers. Plus, the way the man stood kept the wall at his back and all approaches in easy view.

Definitely not the usual person out to enjoy the sights and shopping.

"David!" Sophie's voice erupted about a block down the street as she and Lyn emerged from a restaurant.

His person of interest didn't flinch. Despite remaining in his relaxed position leaning against the wall, the man's balance shifted easily to a more ready-for-action position. Interesting.

"Didn't you hear us?" Sophie arrived at his side and gave him a friendly punch in the arm.

"I heard *you*. Entire street did, too." Cruz tore his gaze from the other man to focus on Sophie and Lyn before Sophie made a bigger scene. "It's never good to reinforce bad behavior."

Sophie gasped in mock outrage and Lyn choked on a laugh.

"You two just finished lunch?" He'd might as well chat with them and make sure all was well.

"Oh, actually, I think I forgot something at the shop down the street." Sophie made a big show of fishing through her shopping bags. "I better go try to find it."

Obvious. So incredibly, painfully obvious.

Lyn leaned over to look in the bags, too. "I'll…"

"No, no." Sophie waved a hand. "Stay here and chat with David. I'll only be a minute."

Before Lyn could say anything else, Sophie was walking at a fast clip down the street expertly dodging other shoppers on the sidewalk.

Damn. He was pretty sure a grenade had just fallen into his foxhole. If he stayed, it was likely to be a mess. If he made a run for it, Sophie would shoot him down in his tracks.

Lyn cursed under her breath.

He studied her. "You don't have to wait with me if you don't want to."

What? He didn't see any reason to pretend politeness if either of them was uncomfortable.

She looked up at him with wide eyes, her lips parted in surprise. Her very kissable…Shit. He should go.

"I don't mind waiting with you." The words came out quick, with a weird note of panic.

Oh, even better. Creepy might not be a strong enough word for the reaction he was inciting in her.

He did not want to be the cause of it. "It really is okay. It's your day off. You should get to relax."

He took a step away, then suddenly stopped. Because her hand had shot out to snag his wrist.

"I really don't mind." Her grip on his wrist was firm, not hesitant.

Interesting. He turned his wrist in her hold until she

released him and he caught her hand in his instead. "No?"

Her fair skin turned a pale pink over her cheeks. He wondered if other parts of her flushed when she was embarrassed.

She left her hand in his, relaxed and warm. "Feels weird being out and about instead of working with you and Atlas."

"It's been an intense week." So was this...moment. Or whatever it was. He rubbed his thumb over the back of her hand, enjoying the softness of her skin. Hanging around was becoming a better and better idea.

She nodded. "He's coming along very well. And I've enjoyed the opportunity to learn from you."

Very well was an understatement. Atlas's transformation over the last several days was continuing. His responses to commands had become quicker, more enthusiastic. The dog was starting to actually pay attention to his surroundings and listen for commands. His desire to *work* was coming back. And that drive was key in a military working dog.

"There's a lot more to this concept of balance you've been talking about than I'd initially given credit to." Cruz had been skeptical at first. The whole dog-whisperer technique of head shrinking a dog had been tough to keep an open mind to at the beginning. Most of his training had to do with understanding the natural drivers of a dog and making sure training coincided with those instinctive impulses. "It's good to see him engaged."

Of course, Cruz had some reservations. The rehabilitation they were doing with Atlas was good now. But in the future, the question would be whether Atlas had become too attached to a single handler again. They'd have to cross that bridge when they came to it.

Lyn, though, had lit up thinking about Atlas. "Seeing him in action is exhilarating. I knew the military service dogs could do amazing things, but seeing it in person is a whole new level of wow."

She'd said "wow" several times through the week. And every time, Cruz had pondered how he could make her say it in bed. Completely inappropriate, but hell, as long as the thoughts stayed locked inside his brain they couldn't hurt. And they were definitely entertaining.

Cruz grinned. "Atlas is capable of more. Maybe we should take you out and rig you up for some of the more adventurous training exercises. A little rappelling, maybe even take you to one of the bases and arrange for a jump out of a helicopter."

Could be a lot of fun. Though it'd depend on how she faced the challenge. Atlas had done it plenty of times, but back then his handler had been practiced in the action first. If Lyn was nervous or afraid when she tried, Atlas would react to her anxiety.

"Really?" Lyn's eager expression and her genuine smile made Cruz rethink. She'd come through some crazy shit already. A little hop out of a helicopter wasn't likely to daunt her.

"We'd need to get you trained first." He wanted to take her out on those new experiences himself. Savored the idea. And if he imagined a few other naughty experiences, too, who could blame him? Adrenaline was a great aphrodisiac.

She probably looked fantastic in rappelling gear. All those nifty straps.

Probably unaware of his line of thought, Lyn shrugged. "Training is usually for the human half of the pair anyway. The canine just needs clear leadership."

He snorted. Once in a while—okay, more than sometimes—she sounded like a textbook waiting to be written. If it'd been anyone else, Cruz would've probably rolled his eyes. But from her, he'd kind of gotten to enjoy listening. It wasn't as if she was wrong.

Occasionally. But not always.

A movement at the edge of his peripheral vision drew his attention. "Why don't we talk about it more after you get back to the kennels? You and Sophie must have more shopping planned."

As much as he hated to cut this conversation short, there was something not right out here.

Lyn's smile faded a fraction. "Oh. Yeah."

On one hand, he hated to dim her happiness even a little bit. On the other, if she was somewhat disappointed to have him suggest she go do other things—especially after a week of working side by side with him from dawn to dusk—maybe she'd reconsider her decision to keep things just professional between them.

Something to file away for later. For now, he wanted to send her and Sophie safely on their way so he could satisfy curiosity.

"I'm glad I ran into you today, though." He made sure to catch her gaze and hold it until the blush came back into her cheeks. He might be pushing his luck but hopefully it didn't harm his chances to let her know he was still interested.

"I am too." She ran the tip of her tongue over her lower lip.

Instant hard-on. Even more because it'd been a self-conscious reaction on her part and not a purposeful invitation. Lyn didn't do coy as far as he could tell.

He watched her head on down the street and disappear into the same store Sophie had gone back into. He'd bet money Sophie had been in there watching them the whole time. Childhood friend of Forte's or not, she'd become a little sister to all of them. Complete with the nosy tendencies.

With both of them occupied, he started his own easy walk down the street toward his car.

His friend, the tourist who was not a tourist, finally left his perch by the wall and meandered off on his own. Only the man's path took him toward the stores.

Cruz let a group of passing tourists obscure his line of sight for a minute and cut down one of the small alleys. Two minutes later he was back on the main street a couple of blocks up from where he'd been with a clear view of the stores where Sophie and Lyn were shopping.

The other man's target might not be anyone Cruz knew. But he was too close to the ladies.

A minute later, Cruz was on another one of those little side streets coming up behind his not-a-tourist leaning against the wall pretending to wait for someone inside a store.

Cruz advanced at a leisurely pace so his footsteps wouldn't cue his target in and deliberately shoulder-bumped the guy as he passed.

"Oh, sorry." He turned to face the guy, looking him straight in the eye.

The man stood straight, balanced forward over his toes, definitely ready for action. "No worries, man."

Cruz studied him. "You sure about that?"

A pause. The man's eyes narrowed. "Just out for a little sightseeing."

"This small town is good for that." Cruz was absolutely sure the guy couldn't care less about small-town atmosphere and historic points of interest.

The man smiled, the kind that left a greasy sort of residue impressed in the mind. "Ex-military, right? You've got the look. What service?"

Yeah, the other man had the look, too, despite the unkempt facial hair and generally sloppy way he dressed. Far away, he'd appeared fine, but up close his t-shirt was stained and left partially untucked. His jeans were torn in places no fashion designer would've planned.

"Air Force." Cruz left it at that.

"Navy SEAL." The other man jabbed his own chest with a thumb.

Well, said a lot about a man when he felt the need to specify Special Forces. Cruz was willing to bet the other man wasn't active duty anymore. Wouldn't be hard to find out.

Either way, even a man who could reach the level of skill to be Special Forces could decline, lose his edge. Combat shaped soldiers in a variety of ways and as much as people wanted to think it was for the good, sometimes men got twisted. Or they already were and service had brought out the jagged edges in them. This man was not a shining example of a military hero by anyone's definition.

"What brings you to New Hope?" Cruz genuinely wondered.

"Ah, let's be real. I'm following your girl." The other man shrugged. "You'd already figured it out or you wouldn't have dropped by for this . . . discussion."

He'd guessed. Had been hoping not. Cruz was glad they weren't going to pretend coincidence. But then again, the guy being forthright was its own kind of message.

"Why?" Cruz was getting tired of the chitchat.

"She's working with a dog and that dog is carrying a whole lot of trouble along with it." The man spat on the sidewalk without ever taking his gaze off Cruz. "Anyone with a brain should stay far away from that shit."

Charming. Message received.

"What's it got to do with you?"

The man tilted his head. "Look, I'm just keeping an eye on things here, making sure no one gets too nosey. It's what guys like us do, right? Guys like you and me, we keep an eye out for trouble to ourselves and our own. Nothing wrong with that."

He paused.

"You understand, don't you? You'd have a brother's back, wouldn't you?"

Cruz considered. There was a whole lot of meaning in those questions. Overseas, deployed out in the middle of nowhere, a serviceman had to rely on his fellows to keep him safe. No man could survive in the middle of that chaos alone for an extended period of time without *someone* to watch his back.

Normally, it went unspoken. If someone had to ask the question, it was a threat.

From then on, the soldier had to wonder if the people around him really had his back. Or if they'd let him take a bullet and become just another casualty of war.

"Look, I'm just watching." The other man held up his hands. "I won't bother you, you don't get in my way. Agreed?"

"Look but don't touch." Cruz kept his tone pleasant. "Always happy to meet another serviceman."

The guy smiled again. "I owe you a drink sometime. You have a nice day."

Cruz turned on his heel and walked away.

Pulling out his phone, he texted Sophie.

Shopping trip is over. Need you two to head back to the kennels. STAT.

In less than a minute, Sophie responded.

???

Irritated, he typed faster.

There's something wrong here. I need you to go home now. I need to know you are both safe.

Sophie was strong-willed but she also knew when to listen.

Headed to the car.

That taken care of, Cruz circled around yet again. He wanted to know if his newfound friend had a partner in town. It shouldn't have been as easy as it was to sneak up on this guy. If he was a Navy SEAL, he wasn't the best of the best. Cruz had worked with a few teams in his time deployed and guys like this one made it into the Special Forces teams but they didn't last. If Cruz could figure out who this guy was—and he intended to—he was willing to bet the man had a dishonorable discharge. There were bad apples even in the most elite parts of the service. Sad reality. And obviously, the man had either thought Cruz wasn't worth the effort of even trying to mislead or he'd been sent to give Cruz the threat in addition to keeping an eye on Lyn.

Finding a good vantage point, Cruz pulled out his phone.

"Yeah."

"Beckhorn, you know if there are any parties particularly interested in Atlas's case?" Cruz asked the question quietly. The line could be tapped but he doubted it. At least not yet. This would let Beckhorn know that there were indeed interested parties.

"Can't imagine why," Beckhorn responded in an uninterested drawl.

"He's been in the papers and all." Cruz watched Sophie and Lyn emerge from another store, chattering as normal as you please. They headed straight for the parking lot and got in Sophie's car.

A small amount of tension unwound as they headed home toward safety.

"I get the occasional inquiry about him. Nothing outside the standard check-in." Beckhorn snorted. "Come to think of it, you owe me a progress report."

Perfect opening.

"I'll get it to you this afternoon." And Cruz would send along a couple of encrypted pictures of his new friend, too.

"I'll look forward to it."

"Yup." Cruz ended the call.

Now all he had to do was be prepared for Sophie and Lyn when they caught up with him later. They'd be expecting answers once he got back.

CHAPTER EIGHT

I'm glad I ran into you today.

Every time she remembered those words—and the look in David's steel blue eyes when he'd uttered them—Lyn's cheeks burned and other parts of her did things she didn't ever talk about to anyone.

Maybe she should feel uncomfortable. Or intimidated.

Nope. What she wanted to do was rewind back to the day she'd asked him for professional space and take back what she'd said. Or better yet, go back to the moment he'd almost kissed her and take things into her own hands.

Because every day she got to know David Cruz, she wanted him more.

If he'd been the least bit bitter or defensive or even indignant about her turning him down, she could dismiss her attraction to him and convince herself he was just another guy. Instead, he'd not only honored her request for professionalism but he'd gone on without any of the distance any normal person would create after the rejection. He'd made it easy for her to continue working with him. And she'd learned so much about him because of it.

And now she was pacing in the cabin again—his cabin—because he'd been concerned for her safety. For Sophie, too.

Sophie hadn't argued, only driven straight back to the kennels. When they'd returned and Sophie had explained to the guys, Brandon had insisted on seeing Sophie home—in a different car. All Sophie had told Lyn was that the men of Hope's Crossing Kennels didn't make requests like that unless there was a real issue.

Great. So now what? She'd have to wait until David returned to find out.

'Course, considering his military background and habits and…everything, he'd probably only tell her what he thought she needed to know. Which was next to nothing. As generous as her thoughts had been toward him a second ago, now she was thinking about him from this perspective and *everything* about David Cruz shouted military for all that he was honorably discharged.

Military equaled distance. Military meant you were never equals. Military meant you were forever shut out of a part of his life.

She'd spent her childhood watching her mom wait for her stepfather to come home. And when he was home, he wasn't. Not really.

Gah. Frustrating. So much of what she respected about David had roots in the deeply ingrained military honor he embodied. He wasn't just a man who used to wear a uniform. He was a man who made a uniform what it was. She couldn't help admiring the qualities. And she couldn't help being wary of what it'd mean to get involved with a man like that.

She'd hated it in a stepfather and sure as hell wasn't looking for it in a relationship of her own.

Her phone rang and she rushed to answer it without even checking the caller ID, hoping it was David. Impulse now. Logic later. "Hello?"

"Miss Evelyn Jones?" An unfamiliar voice was on the other end of the line.

Her heart dropped into the bottom of her belly. Why was she so disappointed? "Yes?"

"I'm Officer Hanley." The man cleared his voice. "I was responsible for taking your report from the night of the attack."

"Ah." She vaguely remembered the man. Sandy blue hair. Light-colored eyes. It'd been a difficult night, one she'd been actively trying not to dwell on. "Hello, Officer."

It wasn't her intention to sound flat. All the warmth got sucked out of her voice. Her mouth had gone dry. Maybe he needed to ask her a few more questions about the night at the hotel.

He went on when she didn't say more. "It's not normally our practice to call, and you seem to be with good friends, but in a situation like this I felt you would want to know…"

She waited as he trailed off. After a long, drawn-out second she grew impatient. "Yes?"

"The man who was taken into custody the next morning made bail today." The words came out in a rush, like ripping off a Band-Aid.

Stunned, Lyn almost dropped the phone. Cold fear twisted her gut and her heart rate kicked up until she heard it beating in her ears.

It's really too bad you came back.

She did a slow turn, frantically scanning the room. Alone. But the curtains were all open and the night was dark beyond the windowpanes. Any minute his face could appear, peering through the glass. The hunger in his eyes. She remembered...

"Miss Jones?" Officer Hanley sounded concerned, maybe regretful. He hadn't wanted to give the news to her.

"I'm here." She yanked her thoughts into place, tried to pitch her tone to calm and grateful. "Thank you for letting me know."

"Like I said, miss, it's not something we usually do but all things considered..." He cleared his throat again. Maybe it was a nervous habit. "Anyway, the guys at Hope's Crossing are good men. Stick close to them and you'll be fine. The man will see his day in court."

Of course. Officer Hanley couldn't refer to him directly as the man who'd attacked her. Innocent until proven guilty and all that. "I understand. Thank you again."

He blurted out a few more reassurances then ended the call.

Lyn clutched her phone to her chest. After a moment she shook her head, pocketed the phone, and rubbed her hands together. Nervous. Scared.

This entire trip had spun her world around. She traveled alone all the time! Now, she was jumpy in a cabin on private property with better security than any hotel had. She wanted to be mad at somebody. The men who'd attacked her—there'd been two, not just the one—and whoever had sent them. Thugs like that had to have some sort of boss to tell them what to look for.

Only she didn't know what she could possibly have. None of her clients gave her anything of value in print. They arranged for direct deposits to her bank accounts for her training and rehabilitation services. She never had access codes to their property or to any sorts of diagrams of their estates.

There was no reason for those men to have been looking through her things that night. And now, they were both out there. Loose. And angry with her.

Stars shot through her vision and she realized she'd been holding her breath. She let it out in a whoosh, then deliberately took air back in slowly. Hiding in the cabin like a mouse was a bad idea. They wouldn't need to come find her. She'd terrify the life out of herself.

She snagged a jacket and a small flashlight David had left for her before heading for the front door. Her hand on the doorknob, she froze. Maybe he'd known. That would explain why he'd sent her and Sophie back from New Hope earlier.

It didn't make sense, though. Telling her and Sophie would've precluded any hesitation. Not that they'd been slow to follow his request. There just wasn't any reason she could think of for him not to tell her. Unless he hadn't wanted to frighten her.

But he'd been so serious, with so much conviction in his statement about her safety. His expression alone had been enough to unsettle both her and Sophie. The actual reason couldn't be much more of a leap. Could it?

No way to know while she was still in the cabin. It might be dark outside but all the paths between the buildings were well-lit and the dog kennels and main house were in clear line of sight. Anyone on the paths would be seen by the people in the main house and most of the dogs on the property. She'd walk quickly and get from point A to point B. Calling one of the guys to come get her seemed like overkill.

As she stepped out into the night, the dark didn't close in on her. Solar lights lined the walkways and there were overhead lights at intervals along the paths, too. She headed directly to the main house but paused as she heard the low tones of David's voice over by the kennels.

Instantly calmer, she turned toward the sound and followed the covered walkway along the side of the main house. David was within shouting distance. The others probably were inside or similarly close by. Everything was a lot calmer. All she needed to do was not be alone.

"You can't be mad because we left you alone all day."

She stopped in her tracks. It hadn't been all day. Then she realized he was talking to Atlas.

Leaning against the dog's kennel with his broad back to her, David looked as relaxed as she'd ever seen him. Was there a single t-shirt he owned that didn't fit him like a second skin? If there was, she'd hide it or give it to Atlas to sleep on. Fitted clothing suited her just fine.

"Everyone needs a day off, including you." David carried on his conversation with Atlas. "Definitely her. She works hard as any person I've ever met, in or out of the service."

She couldn't help a smile. Funny, but the casual talk

probably got Atlas used to the sound and cadence of David's voice. After all, she did the same thing. Dogs were good listeners.

"Besides, she took you for a walk before she left. It's not like you didn't get time with her." He might've sounded jealous. Maybe.

Or wishful thinking on her part. Hard to tell.

"At least she likes you." Definitely some chagrin there. "I might've broke the camel's back today. Situation came up and no time for an explanation. She's the kind of lady who likes to be informed when things are happening. So I'm betting she is not too happy with me now."

Well, she hadn't been a while ago. Then there'd been a phone call and panic and she'd been reserving real anger until she found out if he knew what was going on and hadn't told her. But this, this didn't sound like the same thing.

David pushed off from the kennel and squatted, resting his elbows on his knees and balancing easily on the balls of his feet. "You and me, Atlas, we know what it is to be sent out into unsecured territory. Overseas, we went in ahead of anyone else. Drop zone, airfield, absolute middle of fucking nowhere. We went in to pull others out. And we're okay with it. It's what we signed up to do."

There was a pause. Lyn thought hard about what David was saying. Years ago, other military wives would talk to her mother about safe, well-established Air Force bases well within American territory. They'd made it sound like there was minimal risk. Of course it was awful when husbands had to deploy, but there'd never been a hint of the kind of danger David was talking about to Atlas. What he and Atlas had survived—it was something she'd known some select few had to do, far removed from anyone she knew or cared for. Only, it wasn't so far removed anymore.

"But she should be able to enjoy a safe afternoon shopping. That town is a freaking tourist attraction. It's the small, historic place to go around here to walk around and have a relaxing day." Anger was seeping into David's voice and an answering low growl issued from Atlas in response. The rapport between the two of them was getting stronger. "Instead, I see a man who shouldn't be there. Bad news. And my gut tells me she wouldn't have to worry about any of it if it weren't for us."

Why? Who? And what did they have to do with any of it?

Too many questions. She put her hand over her mouth to keep from blurting them out. If she walked up now, it'd stop him and she was *not* about to pretend she hadn't overheard.

David sighed. "She looked like she had a good time today. Hated to cut it short."

It took every ounce of will she had not to lean forward and listen harder. The breeze was blowing toward her, away from Atlas. But if she made any noise now or if the wind changed, Atlas would let David know she was near. And David was one of the best trainers she'd ever worked with. He'd be able to read Atlas clearer than printed text.

"Not sure how to proceed at this point, Old Man."

She scowled. Atlas wasn't old!

But then she took a breath and counted down slowly, letting the air back out silently. She'd heard her stepfather call his war buddies "Old Man" the few times she'd been around them. It was a thing, she supposed, and even the passing point of similarity to her stepfather knocked her feelings about Cruz back into a jumbled mess.

"If it were Calhoun or any other soldier, I'd brief her. Give her the details and let her decide. But she's not a soldier. And she shouldn't have to worry about these things." A pause. "She's a solid trainer. And she's done you a lot of good. She deserves better than being sucked into whatever shit storm we're about to go into next. Something is about to break, somewhere. I feel it in my gut and you've been on edge all day. We both know it's coming, whatever it is. And I want her clear before it does."

"Oh no. You are *not* sending me away." She slapped her hands over her mouth. Then wondered how the hell they'd moved while she'd been listening in the first place. Fantastic the way she didn't even pay attention to what she was doing when she heard epic statements of idiocy.

David and Atlas were both on their feet.

Since there was no sense lurking around the corner, she walked the rest of the way to them, trailing her hand against the chain-link of the kennel so Atlas could snuffle her fingertips.

"Listening long?" David didn't back away from Atlas's kennel and she decided she didn't have any issues with stepping into his personal space.

Being near Atlas was only a partial excuse.

"Well, I still have questions so maybe I didn't listen long enough." She lifted her gaze to his.

Steel blue eyes, the color of storm clouds. Wow, but she liked looking into them. At the moment, his brows were drawn over them, giving him a severe expression. She ought to be at least somewhat intimidated by it but maybe she was building up a tolerance. Besides, being here with him was so much better than a couple of alternatives.

He came to a decision while she was pondering those. It crossed his face and then he seemed resigned. "What do you want to know?"

She swallowed. "Everything. Whatever there is. Whatever is going on. Because I'm already all sorts of caught up in it and I think you worry about what it means."

His lips pressed together in a thin line.

She nodded. "Yeah. You do. And I do too."

"There's a certain safety to not knowing the details." He wasn't just standing there anymore. He was looming.

And it wasn't going to scare her. Not anything he'd do. Because there were two men out there who'd already taken her sense of safety and ripped it to shreds. "Only when you're sitting, waiting, hoping the bad things won't come to find you. You sent me back here today and I followed your lead because it was the right thing to do at the time. But I won't be staying here forever. I need to know what I'm facing when I step off this property."

He opened his mouth.

But she wasn't done yet. "The man who attacked me already set foot here, so even this place isn't perfect.

Now he's made bail and he's walking around free as you please. While you and Brandon and Alex are here with the dogs, there's a line of defense. Isn't that the way you put it? But no place all on its own is safe. The dogs are kenneled and you all have to sleep sometime."

"Never at the *same* time," David muttered.

She blinked, caught by surprise. The idea of the men each taking a turn in sleep and being awake was unsettling. Whether it was because they never let go of their military habits or because they were actively expecting trouble, it wasn't something normal people did. The realization settled over her that Hope's Crossing Kennels had never been a simple kennel.

This place had always been more, from the first day she'd walked into the office. It and the men who ran it were more than simple civilians with a shared love for dogs. They were men who'd survived hell and come to live with the rest of them again. And their survival skills had never been forgotten or even set aside, only concealed for the peace of mind of the community.

"He won't get to you. I'll be here for you." David's voice came to her—soft, serious, and sincere. A promise.

When she refocused on him, it was with a new awareness.

"You can't be everywhere." She looked down at Atlas standing pressed against the chain-link next to her. The big dog was as close as he could physically be with the fence between them. "No one can. We all live with the chance something will happen."

Her stepfather had explained his reasons for being away from home to her and her mother over and over again. He was away so she and her mother could sleep safe at night. Every time he'd said it, the words had come by rote, a quote or a mantra, rather than words said with sincerity. She'd always said the same to him in reply. There was always a chance something would happen while he was away.

Back when she'd started, it'd been with a whole lot of teenage angst. In her mind, she or her mother could get hit by a bus and her stepfather would've been too far away to do anything about it.

"Maybe you're right. The more information you have, the more prepared you can be." David leaned in closer, until his heat whispered along her skin. Not looming anymore. Definitely not looming. "Seems fair enough."

"I want the knowledge I need to protect myself." The way she'd gone out on her own to learn how to shoot a gun the minute she'd reached adulthood.

"What will you do armed with information? Go hunting?" His words whispered against her hair.

"No." She shivered.

"Good. Going hunting would be stupid. Will you run?"

She shook her head. "I'm not sure. Running sounds futile if someone with any kind of skills or obsession is after me. It depends on what is actually going on. But once I have the full picture I can make an informed decision. Something that makes sense."

"Okay." But he didn't wax eloquent with the things she needed to know. "Why did you come out here, Lyn?"

Frustration sparked and she clenched her jaw. Changing gears wasn't going to help her.

"I got the call from the police." Seemed like a long time ago. Being out here with David and Atlas always made time pass faster. But hold still, too. Like they were all in their own little bubble. "They said I should stay near friends."

Of course, these two were the closest she had to friends anywhere. Not just nearby. Sophie might become a friend if they kept in touch. But the side effect of traveling all the time tended to be a whole lot of acquaintances and virtually no close friends. Even the town she had on her driver's license as home wasn't anything more than a place to send junk mail.

"Are you worried he'll come after you again?" David's hand came up toward her face slowly, his index finger extending and exerting gentle pressure under her chin to get her to look up at him.

When she met his gaze, she was drawn in closer without ever moving. They were in the eye of a storm and the air directly around them had gone still.

"Yes." It took effort to get the affirmative out. Frustrated, she pushed forward with the conversation. "Doing nothing but waiting was going to drive me crazy. I was getting cabin fever."

His nod was almost imperceptible. Still, something settled inside her. He got it.

"Whatever is going on, you know more about it than I do." She licked her lips; her mouth had gone dry.

His gaze dipped, focusing on her mouth. "I might. I know something. I'm not sure it's related. But this next question is important."

Can I kiss you?

She was doubtful that was the question he was going to ask. But the moment was drawing out and she very much wanted for him to ask it. "Okay."

"Do you think I would hurt you?"

"No!" It popped out before she had time to think about it. Anger burned up from her chest and spread outward. She scowled. "Of course n—"

He kissed her.

CHAPTER NINE

His kiss wasn't light or gentle or teasing. His lips came down on hers with heat and firm pressure. His hand moved from her chin to cup the back of her head, urging her to tilt for him. She did, opening her mouth and giving him access, too. His tongue swept in, hot and searching. She answered in kind and they explored each other.

This was...*wow*. More than wow. Heat swept through her and she reveled in the sensation he sent coursing throughout her body with his kissing.

It was a long time before he let her up for air and when he did, she realized she was clutching the front of his shirt with both hands. Oh hey. How about that?

"You need to get over this."

What?

Shocked, she started to step back but David's hand was still on the back of her head and his other arm came around her waist. Tucked against him, she looked up to see him glaring at Atlas through the chain-link fence.

The big dog had reared up and put his front paws on the fence.

"You can deal," David said to Atlas. "Don't even tell me you gave Calhoun this kind of interference when he was with somebody."

Butterflies tickled her and she buried her face in David's chest as she giggled.

"What? That's seventy-five pounds of canine jumping up on me if it weren't for this fence." Despite his words, amusement colored his tone and his arm remained firmly around her waist.

"With the two of you, there isn't anything that can keep me worried." She smiled up at him, enjoying the fit of their bodies against each other.

David gave her a lopsided grin. "Good. I'd like to say we make a solid team but Atlas here is working for you but not with me, if you get what I mean."

"Ah well, he's a free agent for the time being." She didn't want to ruin the mood. But it'd be stupid to pretend Atlas wouldn't be returned to duty once they'd gotten him back to one hundred percent responsiveness. The big dog was too good to retire yet.

"True." David pressed a kiss to her temple.

"So." She could barely believe her own audacity but the last few days, the last few minutes in particular, were all about personal evolution, apparently. "Where were we before Atlas expressed his opinion?"

Because she'd like to get back to that. And explore. In detail.

Okay, maybe she wasn't as daring as she could be. Yet.

"Here." David caught her mouth for another hot, fantastically mind-blowing kiss. "But I think we should all head someplace more private."

"All?" Catching her breath was a challenge.

He tapped her nose. "Don't go thinking too hard because it's not anything too exotic."

Keeping one arm around her waist, he snagged Atlas's leash and gave Atlas the command to sit. There it was again: the half-second of consideration before Atlas made the decision to follow the command. David didn't comment, but he didn't have to. They both recognized it. He simply opened Atlas's kennel.

More rehabilitation required before Atlas would be ready for duty.

"Since you feel safest with both of us," David commented as he hooked Atlas's leash onto his collar, "then both of us will see you back to your cabin and stay there with you through the night."

He'd just invited himself to her cabin. For the night. Yep, she'd heard the key points there.

A thrill rushed through her. It might've been better if she'd invited him but she was definitely not opposed to the idea. Especially considering how nice it was to be tucked against his side as they all started walking back to her cabin. The lighted paths had less contrast and the dark beyond them wasn't as sinister. She didn't jump at every sound. It was a world of difference in company she trusted.

Her heart just about burst out of her chest once they got there, though. The idea of going back inside, where she couldn't see anyone coming..."You're definitely both going to be here. All night?"

It took everything she had to suppress the shiver when

her mind went into overdrive and images of a man's face peering into her windows flashed across her vision.

His arm tightened around her waist, grounding her and bringing her back to reality. "We'll keep watch."

"Just tonight?" And that was the issue, wasn't it? She'd forgotten momentarily about the danger out there. His kiss had blown it right out of her mind but it was still there.

He didn't push her inside the cabin, or even nudge her. She swallowed hard and walked in on her own. The attack hadn't happened here, after all. But at the hotel, she'd been shoved inside. And next, they'd hurt her. They'd been about to do worse.

A whine cut through her thoughts and Atlas shoved his head under her hand. His cool nose pressed against the inside of her arm as he wriggled his head, demanding her attention.

"We'll be here and we'll take each night as it comes." David was still outside. He'd stayed back and given her space with her fear.

She was grateful for it. Every door—every time she'd walked through one—she'd shoved this far back into the corner of her mind. Mostly, it'd worked. But not tonight. Too many thoughts were crowding her head and she wasn't able to compartmentalize the way she normally would. Maybe David had seen it all this week when she hadn't been completely aware.

Even knowing he was with her and wanting him there, she wasn't sure she wouldn't have panicked a little in that moment if he'd been right behind her. "I'm sorry."

He shook his head slowly. "No apologies. Not ever."

She opened her eyes wide against sudden, unexpected tears. "I'm kind of embarrassed. But I really appreciate...this."

He was being incredibly considerate, and thoughtful, and patient. She couldn't say the words without the emotions spilling over, and tears weren't sexy. She wanted to recover the excited moment earlier, not be stuck in this echoing fear now.

David only gave her his smile, the one that had never failed to tempt a return smile from her over the last week. "I can stay out here. Atlas can keep watch inside."

"No!" Her response was immediate and maybe a little horrified. "Please don't stay out there. Come inside."

The last ended on a whisper. Even if it was him, someone outside would freak her out even more.

"Okay." He stepped inside slowly and shut the door behind him.

Immediately, the imaginary vice around her lungs eased. She rubbed Atlas's head absently, taking comfort from his weight as he leaned against her leg. Her embarrassment was evolving rapidly into something else and her cheeks burned with shame.

"Hey." David's voice was quiet, coaxing. "You don't need to be embarrassed. And this is all about what will make you comfortable. You're safe with us and everyone here would go the extra mile to see to it that you feel that way. Nothing you say or do is wrong."

She laughed then, but even to her ears she sounded like she was on the verge of tears. Maybe this was what hysteria felt like. This unhinged, out-of-control feeling. Like she could lose it at any minute. "I'd really like to forget what made me come out in the first place and what made me lose my mind when I came back in here."

"Would you feel better staying someplace else?" Another completely rational, patient question.

He was a good guy.

She shook her head. "Honestly?"

"Honestly."

She lifted her gaze to his face, taking in the solid lines of his jaw and his serious countenance. His expressive eyes and those lips that'd completely scattered every rational thought from her mind not too long ago. "I'd like to go back to how I felt when you kissed me, because that's the best I've got in my short-term memory currently and it was way better than any kiss I remember ever."

Too much information. Definitely. And embarrassment was taking on whole new levels.

David's eyebrows rose during her comment and the bastard started to look *smug*. "There's a high bar set there. I'm going to need to try to outdo myself now."

She opened her mouth to yell at him. What she'd say, she wasn't sure, but she'd come up with something witty on the fly because he was going to be impossible to work with if she let—

He closed the distance between them and bent to capture her mouth. She hadn't dodged. Her mind had been too preoccupied with generating witty commentary. Which was a lost cause because his lips burned into hers until she gasped and he deepened the kiss until she was drowning. His tongue teased and coaxed her until she responded in kind.

"*Foei.*"

She was breathless and off balance, leaning into David and blinking to clear her vision. David had an arm around her and the other out, holding Atlas at arm's length. The big dog had tried to jump on David again but this time David had caught him and held him back, balanced on his hind legs.

"*Foei*," David repeated. "That'll be enough of that."

There was a long pause as man and dog stared each other down. Atlas finally settled back on all fours, then sat. Lyn had never been caught in the middle of a pissing match between men before, but somehow she imagined it'd be something like this. Probably.

"He'll be all right sleeping out here," she whispered. Maybe she was being disloyal to Atlas. All things considered, she'd make it up to him tomorrow with extra-long walks and a whole lot of belly scratches.

Tomorrow.

David nuzzled just behind her ear and caught her earlobe between his teeth in a gentle nibble. Then he brushed his lips over her ear. "Both of us can make do out here while you get some rest."

"What?" She jerked her head back, almost catching his chin as she did.

He kept hold of her and brushed her cheek with his thumb. "You've got a lot going on inside your head right now and you are the definition of vulnerable. I'd be a complete ass to take advantage of you."

Please. Take advantage.

"I want to re-establish your sense of safety first." He just had to sound incredibly reasonable. "And then, take you out on a real date."

"A date." She repeated the words slowly, rolling the idea over and over in her head. Now that he mentioned it, she'd hated saying no the first time he'd asked. Still, he was being incredibly stubborn at the moment and part of her didn't enjoy the way he was holding out. Mixed messages.

"I figure I should at least buy you dinner before I try taking advantage of you." He winked, and there was enough heat in his voice to make it clear he was interested.

Her resistance evaporated. "You are incorrigible."

He screwed up his face in mock dismay. "Sorry. Can you use a smaller word?"

"Impossible." She balled her hand into a fist and thumped him on the chest.

"That's only one syllable shorter."

"Bad!" She thumped him again. "You are a bad, bad man."

He laughed and snuck a kiss, which she gave him. And she nipped his lower lip for good measure. "I plan to be."

"Good." She was pouting and smiling at the same time and she didn't even know how he'd managed it.

He grinned. "See? Bad. Good. I can handle the easy vocabulary."

"Tease." She threw it out there as an accusation.

"I'll add it to the plans." He grinned. "Limited vocabulary. Excellent memory."

"Fine." She blew out a breath. "I guess we'll be calling it a night then."

A very frustrating, probably restless night. His kisses alone had her melty and tingly and wound up in all sorts of ways. God, how would it be when they did get all tangled up?

He nodded solemnly. "It would be a good idea."

"But not together." She might've sounded disappointed. And it served him right if he heard it and felt guilty.

He kissed her. Kissed her until she melted for him, all the rigid outrage gone as she pressed up against him trying to fit herself against the entire length of him. She wanted to touch everywhere. When he let her up for air, he gave her a smile that meant bad, bad things. "Not yet."

* * *

"David? Are you hungry?"

Define hungry, he thought, because first thing in the morning his appetite was focused on something much more satisfying than pancakes.

He didn't open his eyes. Instead he considered his surroundings, how close Lyn might be, and most important, whether he had his pants on. He shifted a leg, took note of the loose slide of something too soft to be denim across the top of his thigh.

Nope.

He did have a light blanket across his lower half. The thin fabric protected him from the chill in the cabin but it definitely wasn't enough to hide him from the light of day. While he was mostly certain Lyn found him attractive, she might not appreciate the part of him most awake first thing in the morning. At least not yet.

Lyn sighed. "Different question. Bacon? Yes or—?"

"Yes." There wasn't ever another answer. Ever. He opened his eyes and sat up. It'd been a long night and he hadn't gone to sleep until a few hours ago.

Lyn was already headed back to the kitchen area so he couldn't get a look at her expression yet. Her hips swayed as she walked, though, which could've been a torturous tease if he hadn't already spent a week or so appreciating her walk. So she wasn't throwing anything special into how she was getting around for his benefit. Biggest issue at the moment was her not giving him any clues as to whether she was upset with him for the way last night had played out.

He'd been trying to be a good guy. Do the right thing. His balls were blue enough to torture him without her being angry with him this morning.

"Did you sleep well?" Safe question. He hoped.

Her gaze shot up and pinned him to the couch. "Did you?"

Not quite mad, but definitely touchy. He'd have to proceed with caution.

"Well…" He drew out the response to give himself time to think. "I stayed on watch until Forte texted me a few hours ago to let me know we've got an eye on the grounds. Then I was up for a while longer, thinking of you."

God, he enjoyed the way pink spread across her cheeks. He planned to tease her more often. This was also a good sign. He'd take whatever he could get.

From the middle of the floor, Atlas snorted and rolled on his side.

No opinions from the peanut gallery, thanks.

Not that he had any delusions of the dog being a mind-reader, but there was no doubt Atlas was aware of the pheromones floating all over the place. Dog probably had a better idea of Lyn's mood than David did.

"If you were so…interested, maybe you shouldn't have insisted on sleeping out here last night." She turned to the stove and a second later, the sizzling of bacon filled the room with mouth-watering aroma.

He took the opportunity to snag his jeans from where they were hanging over the end of the couch. "Seemed like we were on the same page, but you did get some upsetting news yesterday. Wanted to give you time to ease into things."

Plus, he'd still been on edge after the run-in with the other ex-soldier earlier in the day. He didn't trust himself to keep things light and easy. Her first encounter with him should be at his best for her, not when his old issues were so close to the surface. She'd seemed to appreciate his reasoning last night.

Of course, she'd given him a look that could kill a man when she'd closed the bedroom door.

As she set a plate on the table, it landed with a loud *thunk*. He winced. Maybe she'd reconsidered overnight.

Enough.

He stood and got himself into his pants while she was still being stubborn giving him her back. Then he stepped over Atlas and came up behind her in the kitchen, putting a steadying hand around hers on the skillet to keep her from whacking him across the head with it. Other hand on her hip, he ground his own into her backside so there was no way she could ignore the raging hard-on he still had even zipped up inside his pants.

"Believe me, I wanted to join you in your room last night." He leaned his head close to the side of hers and nipped her ear. "But same reasoning applies this morning even if we both lost some sleep from frustration."

She didn't try to step away but her back was straight as a board and her shoulders squared.

"You're being very considerate. And I should appreciate it. I thought about it a lot last evening. I don't like the mixed messages and I don't like running hot only to be put into a forced cool down. You had me incredibly wound up last night and then you decided it was all about the chivalrous thing to do."

He swallowed hard. Okay. He backed up a fraction and gave her room. "I'm sorry."

After a moment, she sighed, turned off the heat on the stove and placed the skillet down safely. Then she turned into his arms. Rising up on her toes, she pressed a kiss against his jaw. "But you had good intentions. I'm hoping talking about this will prevent a repeat and that you'll make it up to me."

No sane man would ignore that hint.

He kissed her, enjoying the sweet honey taste of her mouth. He also gave thanks she'd changed her mind about keeping professional distance because even the minimal space between them due to the clothes they were wearing was too much. He sincerely hoped she'd be as interested in pursuing this thing between them after he clued her in to all the other shit going on around them.

And the thought effectively chilled him. A man didn't need cold showers when he had this much insanity to deal with inside his own head. His mood was grim by the time they'd finished breakfast and gathered up Atlas to head back to the main house.

"It's a vet visit for you, Atlas." David noticed Atlas had been much more amenable to commands this morning. Small battle won there. He expected to have a few more instances like last night's contest of wills before Atlas made the decision to listen a hundred percent of the time. It was a turning point between every dog and handler. The trick with Atlas was to get him to a point where he would accept a new handler at all.

Lyn held Atlas for Doctor Medicci while she checked on the healing scrape along his side. Atlas stood still under examination, amazingly responsive to Lyn's encouragements. David stood back and let the ladies work.

"He's healing well, not showing any signs of pain." Medicci murmured as she ran her hands along Atlas's back and legs. "You kept him on light exercise, right?"

"Easy training and daily walks. No running for any real distance," Lyn answered. She paused then added, "Mostly. He's an active dog."

"Mmm." Medicci sounded noncommittal but not angry. Atlas was looking good and they all knew it. "On principal, he should be kept to light exercise a while longer but as long as the area around the wound is free of redness or swelling, he should be fine. Sutures will dissolve on their own."

"Got it." David figured he'd keep the training review at the current pace. No need to rush Atlas, and Lyn was working wonders with the dog in general.

"While I'm here, I'll do his basic exam and take samples for the standard tests." Medicci took out her stethoscope and pressed it to either side of Atlas's chest.

Things looked to be fine until Medicci took out the big scanner and passed it over Atlas's back. She frowned, checked the device, then passed it over him again more slowly. "He's chipped, isn't he?"

"All military working dogs are." David pushed away from the wall and came to stand at Lyn's side. He ran his fingers through Atlas's coat along the dog's right shoulder, seeking the small bump under the skin he'd encountered grooming. "It's right here."

"Whatever that is, it's not a functioning microchip." Medicci shook her head. "I just used this before I got here on two other dogs. It's in working order. His chip must've malfunctioned or been damaged."

It wasn't likely, as small as the chips tended to be, but anything was possible.

"I'll remove it now and we'll re-chip him to be safe." Medicci reached for her sterile implements.

"Remove it." David cleared his throat. "But we'll take him on base to get a new one in."

Two feminine gazes pinned him with questioning looks. It was not the most comfortable he'd ever been. "The microchips for MWDs are more robust than the average pet chips linking a bar code to an owner's name, address, and phone number. All military working dogs have GPS too."

Medicci nodded. "We're going to need to restrain him. This won't cause major pain but it will be more than a pinch."

"You don't need to put him out, do you?" Lyn sounded concerned.

He didn't blame her. Anesthesia wasn't something to do lightly. He'd never seen Medicci do it, wasn't sure she could on an on-site visit like this.

Medicci shook her head. "Normally, it'd be something I'd recommend an office visit for. These chips are intended to be permanent and even though they're inserted to sit below the skin, they can sort of migrate over time. If they do, I'd need to make a bigger incision and maybe even tease apart the tissues to get a good hold of it. "

She spread the fur to expose the bump David had pointed out. "This one is easy to locate, obviously. It'll be a pinch. Just enough of an incision to retrieve the chip. Should be fine to restrain and muzzle him. But you two should probably leave the room so he doesn't associate any negative experience with either of you."

CHAPTER TEN

"Come in." David closed out a few spreadsheets and directed his attention to Medicci as she walked into his office.

"All done. Lyn is with Atlas now, fussing over him." Medicci smiled. "Good to see a softer touch for these dogs sometimes. You all do a great job with them; don't get me wrong. But the battle weary deserve a dose of spoiling here and there."

David didn't plan to argue since he agreed. "Small doses. Anything I should know about aside from what we talked about before?"

The amusement fled from Medicci's face, her gaze darkening and the corners of her mouth turning downward. "A couple of things. First, once I shaved away the fur around the area, it looked to me as if the chip had been placed fairly recently. The skin had newly healed from an incision. It definitely hadn't been there for several years. Which was odd because I thought the size of the bump was indicative of scar tissue forming around the chip. There *should've* been more scar tissue around it under the skin, developing a sort of sheathe. That wasn't the case."

Medicci placed a wax-covered object on his desk. Her expression was completely blank. "This is not the microchip any vet anywhere implanted. Military or otherwise."

David touched the wax. The right length, but flat and rectangular instead of cylindrical. It was a micro SD card, for shit's sake. What was it doing in Atlas?

Of course, he'd seen something like this before in animals and in humans. Hell, people had been known to bury the damn things in open sores on their own bodies, letting the wound scab over. It was scary what a person would do in the face of necessity . . . or desperation.

He had no idea what to say but Medicci definitely didn't need to know everything. "This is—"

Medicci held up her hands. "It's out. As long as there is no threat to any animal's health under my care, I don't need to know. It's best if I don't, isn't it?"

David nodded, grateful. He'd lie if he had to. But the best lie was one he didn't have to tell. Or truth. That worked well, too, in the proper dosage.

"Keep the incision clean and he'll heal just as fast if not faster than the other injury. If you think there's more, we could do an X-ray at my office to locate any other potential implants. I didn't detect any more bumps under his skin, though." Medicci headed for the door but paused. "He's a good dog."

"He is," David agreed.

And all this time, he'd really been carrying the weight of Calhoun's last message on his shoulders.

He pocketed the micro SD and headed down the hall, finding Lyn with Atlas in the examination room. "How's our guy?"

"Acting like nothing happened." Lyn laughed, giving Atlas a hearty rub around the shoulders.

Atlas deigned to give David a doggie grin, tongue lolling out. When Lyn's rubbing migrated over his back to his rump, the dog's eyes practically rolled back into his head as if to say, *Oh yeah, that was the spot.*

Atlas had to really trust Lyn to allow her behind him that way and in a dominant position. Even for butt rubs. Usually military work dogs were too dominant and aggressive to let anyone but their handlers such privilege. In Lyn's hands, Atlas could almost be a normal dog.

"Let's keep things easy for him today. You feel comfortable going for a walk around the property? Forte's still on watch this morning and he's got your mobile in case he sees anything on the perimeter cameras."

Lyn straightened, her expression momentarily somber. "Didn't realize you had video surveillance all around the property."

"Had it on the entrances before and added more to cover the entire perimeter since last week." David and the others had considered it previously and cursed themselves for not already having it installed. No matter how quiet the town was where they were located, forewarned was forearmed and they'd corrected the mistake immediately, each of them contributing to the cost from their own private funds. "We'll all have notice if anyone is even snooping around the fences, much less tries to step onto the property again."

She nodded slowly. "All right."

Atlas had settled down, sensitive to her change in mood. He'd be hypervigilant with her this agitated. Which was even better. The big dog wouldn't be tempted by random distractions like squirrels or rabbits while Lyn was agitated. No running off chasing furry things or coaxing her to play fetch. He'd stay with her and ensure her safety. He shouldn't be running today anyway.

"Okay. Take a long walk then, and I'll get some administrative work done here. Check back in with you both at lunchtime."

Lyn nodded. A minute later she had Atlas on a leash and they were out the door.

Back in his office, David dug into one of his drawers. After way longer than he'd like, he came up with a small toolkit. Armed with those tools, a soft cloth, a firm bristled toothbrush and isopropyl alcohol, he went to work. Removing wax from a micro SD card wasn't fun but it wasn't hard either. He'd done it with fewer tools to hand. This time, though, he wanted to do it right in one shot with minimal chance of further complications.

Once the wax was completely removed and he was sure the contacts on the micro SD were perfectly cleaned, he loaded it into his memory card reader. A few minutes to scan for viruses and he had two files, both video. The first was tagged as highlights and the second was significantly bigger, compressed, and encrypted.

Calhoun had intended for David to find these first. David was going to make a guess that he was supposed to view the highlights to get a clearer idea of the issue at hand, then take the time to absorb the other video over more time. First things first. He made copies and backed them to his secure storage, then made secondary back-ups to his cloud storage. Encrypted.

Then he took his computer offline and double-clicked the video file to watch it.

"What's Calhoun's status?" a voice offscreen asked.

"Stable, sir. He'll live. Unconscious for now." Only the legs and torso of this speaker were visible.

The camera was low—around waist height or lower. Meaning it was likely a camera attached to a canine tactical assault suit. Probably Atlas's specifically. Nor-mally those cameras were used to give human handlers and the rest of the team knowledge of what lay ahead as the canine took point. In this case, it looked like Calhoun had been injured and Atlas was still in use. Not recommended, but there was usually a backup on the team able to take over the working dog if some-thing should happen to the handler.

"Just as well," the offscreen speaker said. "Not sure our teammate has the stomach for what we need to do here."

Not likely. Calhoun had had the balls for anything that needed doing.

The unseen man continued, "We'll use the dog to ter-rorize the prisoner. Damage to extremities is acceptable but try to keep it limited. We want to be able to patch him up if we need him alive past this evening."

David set his jaw. It went against his morals to use a dog this way. But war wasn't noble. He'd done things he'd have nightmares about for the rest of his life. He was only sorry Atlas had been commanded to do similar.

The video skipped. Highlights reel, after all.

A man was secured to a chair. He'd been worked over already and there were several more men in the room. Once in a while, a face came into frame and David paused to capture the image of the face. Only a couple; the camera hadn't captured all of them. But he was going to need those for later, especially since the SEALs had covered the name tags on their uniforms for the interrogation.

"Wait! Wait! You want this man? I can give you his location. We can do business."

English. Fairly well-spoken and with the kind of accent that indicated a higher level of education. David listened more carefully.

"You want him. I want him dead. Kill him for me and I will make sure you and your future company have exclusive business once you are established."

David stopped the video and replayed. If he'd heard correctly, this wasn't an interrogation anymore. It was evolving into something uglier: a conspiracy.

"It's what you do, isn't it? Once your career is complete with the US military, you go private. Establish a private military company. Mercenaries." The man was sweating, could barely see out one swollen eye, but no one was stopping him or redirecting his discussion to more pertinent information. They were all listening. "Mercenaries need work. The best work is here. Will be here, for decades to come."

True. Even once the war was officially over and troops were brought home, the area would be ruled by unrest. Mercenaries had job security in those sorts of hot spots all over the Middle East and surrounding regions.

"I will be the head of my organization. Not some middleman. Don't just capture and interrogate the man you are looking for. Kill your target for me. We will do business for a long time to come."

An unseen man—probably the commanding officer based on the authority in his tone and the way the men in camera view deferred to him—spoke. "You make a very interesting proposition. We can make a deal."

Son of a bitch.

* * *

A sunny morning with blue skies and a light breeze went a long way toward banishing her worries. Lyn didn't want to live a paranoid life. Walking with Atlas had been a lot easier than she expected, relaxing even. She babbled about random things like the trees around them and the squirrels she spotted. He listened. He was good like that, being a dog and all.

People made things way the hell too complicated.

This trip, she'd spent far more time than usual pondering her childhood. Contrasting and comparing her experience to what she was learning about David specifically, and Brandon and Alex by virtue of their work at the kennels. They were so very different from the wealthy clients she normally worked with in terms of their knowledge of dogs and the way military life had influenced their life after. They were complex men with simple desires: build a good life, train good dogs.

And they were all single. It hadn't required a morning shopping with Sophie to figure out why, though the woman had provided some interesting insight. Every one of the men, including David, had serious issues to work through.

Lyn's parents had lived walking on eggshells. Too many secrets between them, unresolved misunderstandings, and unaired grievances. They'd remained married but they'd fallen out of love. Lyn had trouble believing maintaining the appearance of propriety had been worth the misery in a loveless marriage. But then, her mother had been married once before and probably preferred the security marriage afforded her.

Lyn's stepfather could've been worse. He could've been abusive, for example, but he hadn't been. He'd just never had a use for Lyn's mother or for Lyn. There'd been so much more important away than there was to pay attention to at home.

She should steer clear of David for those telltales. He preferred to work on a need-to-know basis, and he was the person to decide what she needed to know. It was something she could work through on a professional level but in a personal relationship they were going to slowly deteriorate. She wouldn't be able to stop herself from resenting it over time.

The memory of his kiss stirred up fluttering sensations in her chest and brought heat to her cheeks. He was good. Really good. And the chemistry between them was more intense than anything she'd experienced with anyone else. No way was she going to regret the kisses last night. But what she needed to decide was whether she wanted more.

"Lyn." David came striding across the grounds.

David standing still was a striking figure. The man in motion was enough to make her stop in her tracks and stare. He had an economy of motion, neat and efficient, but covered distance faster than she imagined a man could just walking. She wondered what he was like running an obstacle course. Actually, she'd pay to watch him traverse one of those. Maybe there was one of those traveling challenges coming through the region in the near future. Sophie would help her enter him.

Plans for another day.

"Change in plans." David came to a halt a few yards short of them. His jaw was set and he wore a decidedly grim expression.

"For the day?" She considered him. "Or in general?"

"This project with Atlas could be closed out a lot sooner than we planned." He frowned. "It's not the way I want it to work out, but it might be for the best. You don't want to be involved in what's probably coming next."

"I'm capable of deciding what I want, given the full picture." Oh, he was not going to toss her to the curb.

"It'd be safer for you."

She held up her free hand. "I was attacked in my own hotel room the night I arrived. One of those attackers showed up here the next morning. Now that man is on bail and no one ever found the other guy. Last night you told me I could feel safe here. And now you're telling me it's safer for me to go out there. Make up your damned mind."

Anger and frustration welled up inside and this time he was not going to dispel it with a kiss. He'd dismissed it, distracted her from it, and done everything to take her attention away from the cause but now he was trying to push her away and this was the limit.

"Why don't we go inside and—" Not a single sign of his truly comprehending showed in his face. He was still focused on getting her to do what he wanted.

"No." She widened her stance, figuring he couldn't possibly make her move. Atlas came to heel at her side, watching the exchange between her and David intently. "We can talk about this right here. Give me good reasons, supported with real information, and I will make a decision based on those."

David sighed. "It's better if you—"

"This is not a military operation." She cut him off. "If we are truly partners working for Atlas's best interest then we share information. Nothing less."

She shut her mouth then. Interrupting him twice was already beyond rude. She wanted to resolve this, not antagonize him into throwing her off the property for real.

David worked his jaw, obviously reining in his own temper. "Anything to do with Atlas is looking to be complicated."

The dog in question glanced over at the sound of his name but stayed where he was.

"His previous handler wasn't only lost in the line of duty." It sounded like a struggle for David to share even that much and he looked all around them.

They were yards from the perimeter fence and even farther from the main house. No one was near enough to overhear.

David continued, scowling. "Atlas's previous handler's name was Calhoun and we served together when I was still active. We were friends. So receiving texts from him wasn't unusual."

She wasn't sure where this was going so she waited.

"Any communication from deployed military is monitored." David shoved his hands into the front pockets of his jeans. "His last text was out of character for him. Odd. But what I read into Calhoun's last text to me could be discounted as paranoia."

He looked at her, braced. Waiting for a reaction.

She considered it. Considered David. He wouldn't be worried over something that wasn't an actual threat. "Just because a person is paranoid doesn't mean they're delusional."

That won her a ghost of a smile. Nodding, he continued. "Text was weird as hell. Typically any bar on base would only issue two drinks in a night over there. But we drink so infrequently, two is more than enough. I figured he was in between missions, low on tolerance and sleep, and drunk texting me."

Lyn snorted. "Better than texting an ex."

"But a drunk text still has a purpose behind it." David pulled his hand out of a pocket and rubbed his face. "Dramatic, I know. But he was going on about Atlas and carrying the answers on his shoulders."

Lyn raised her eyebrows. "So he could've been referencing a book I read in college or mythology."

David snorted. "We do a lot of reading deployed, believe it or not. But Calhoun wasn't into that kind of fiction as much as mythology, especially as it applied to strategy and the art of war."

"So we're thinking the Titan Atlas, then. I remember he was supposed to carry the celestial spheres on his shoulders but that's all I've got." She'd had a phase as a kid reading up on Roman and Greek mythology. Atlas was one of the only Titans she remembered at all. If they got into Nordic gods, she was going to have to start running Internet searches.

David held up both hands. "The message meant exactly what it said: Atlas carries the answers on his shoulders. There was a micro SD card in his shoulder instead of a locater chip."

"Oh." Well, her overactive imagination could take a break, then.

"I've got some of the data running through a decryption now but I'm not sure which encryption he used. It's going to take a couple of days." He gestured back toward the main house and his office. "But Calhoun left me a highlights reel to give me an overview of the issue. It's bad."

"Is this where the conspiracy theory starts?" She wanted to laugh it off but she was afraid it was real.

Lyn studied David. He was agitated, tiny muscles in his jaw jumping beneath the skin as he clenched and unclenched his teeth. As fantastic as this story sounded, it was serious.

David tilted his head to the side briefly. "It's contained and involves plans of a small group of people for after they leave active duty, at least as far as I know."

Relief swept through her and her knees wobbled a bit. She'd worried it was one of those impossible, reaching-up-through-the-ranks kinds of things they showed in action hero movies. "But it's not the peaceful, quiet life sort of retirement, I'm guessing."

"Nope. Some men come home and want to build a life." David looked out over the kennels. "Others want to find a way to go back and keep doing what they did, for more pay and less red tape. The problem is, this is someone's golden parachute, a way for them to make insane amounts of money after they retire from the military and go private. It means deals and contracts and connections that have nothing to do with protecting our country anymore, and everything to do with making profit off of other people's chaos. Anyone planning to go this route has no issues taking out anyone who might get in their way."

She wasn't sure if she understood the latter but she did the former. It was what Brandon, Alex, and David had done here. They were putting their lives back together. Finding their way back from whoever they'd become overseas.

"You need to find these men, don't you?" For his friend, Calhoun. For Atlas.

"They're responsible for Calhoun's death." The one statement held so much conviction. "I need to know why and how. And I need to see them held accountable."

"Do you know where to start looking for them?" She wasn't sure how she could help, but she wanted to. Because David needed to do this for his friend, but she wanted to do this for David.

"I saw one, yesterday. Shouldn't be hard to find him again," David commented. "He's keeping a close eye on Atlas."

And her by association.

"He was in New Hope yesterday. That's why you told us to come back here." Her anger had been settling but it sparked back up. "You could've told me."

David held up his hands again. "I knew he was following but I didn't have the connection until we found the micro SD today. I don't have the full picture yet, just a bunch of pieces to the puzzle, and I'm going to have to dig for the connections to assemble everything."

It was her turn to rub her face with her hands. "What about the men who attacked me?"

"Not military. Hired thugs, most likely. But they've got to be connected." David drew in a deep breath and let it out. "I'm going to find that connection, too, and see them held accountable for what they did to you."

"You sound like a man about to turn into a caped crusader." She regretted the words as they came out. It was the wrong thing to say and she didn't mean to make little of what he planned to do.

He shook his head. "I'm not a superhero. But there's something wrong here and it's got a cascading effect. Hurting people like you and probably others. This is about doing the right thing, and seeing to it Calhoun didn't die for nothing."

She'd always thought of honor as a word on a plaque or written under a crest. David was teaching her about the meaning of it.

"I'd like to help, however I can." She put every ounce of sincerity she had into it, to make up for her previous statement. "It'd bring a lot of attention on if you took me off Atlas's case. I can work with you still, and help track down the rest of the information you need."

"You don't have the training for this." But he didn't sound adamant.

"Any time you leave the kennels, you're going to be watched, aren't you?" She tried to think as quickly as possible. "Just like me. They're less likely to think something is off if we're together and working with Atlas. It could just be another approach to his rehabilitation. Without me and Atlas, it'd be obvious you're up to something."

"You have a point." He wasn't happy about it. His shoulders sagged.

"I said it last night and I still mean it; there's nowhere I feel safer than with you and Atlas." Truth again.

His gaze locked on hers, searching. After a long moment he sighed. "Okay. We work on this together, but anything starts to go sideways and you listen to me. No arguments in the midst of shit going down. Understand?"

She bit her lip. Not a small thing to ask and he'd hold her to it. "Agreed, so long as I can ask my questions once we're someplace safe again and you promise to give me the full, unedited answers."

"Agreed."

CHAPTER ELEVEN

Is it horrible to ask for a rest stop?"

Cruz glanced at the digital display on the dashboard. Only an hour and a half into their road trip. Granted, they'd been caught in some traffic getting past Philadelphia but they hadn't even made it through Delaware. Traveling through it on I-95 was almost literally a blink-and-you-miss-it sort of thing.

Atlas chose that moment to let out a brief whine from the back seat. Dog probably sensed her discomfort but damn, it seemed like Atlas was always going to take her side in awkward situations.

He sighed. Well, he'd decided to bring the two of them along. If this was an indicator for the rest of the trip, he should be glad there were rest stops at regular intervals the whole way there and back. "There's a big rest stop just up here."

"Thank you." She fidgeted. "Have we gotten at least close to halfway there?"

Nope. "Is this your way of asking if we're there yet?"

"No!" She huffed. "It's been a while since I've been on a road trip instead of a flight. I guess I've been spoiled by the availability of a restroom en route."

"You don't ever get stuck in a window seat with someone sleeping?" The image of her squirming in a coach seat, too polite to wake somebody up, amused him.

"It happens, but usually people want to get up at least once during a flight and stretch their legs, too." She shifted in her seat again. He increased his speed some to get them to the rest stop faster. Entertaining as it might be, he didn't actually want her uncomfortable if he could do something about it. "The longest I've ever had to wait is the twenty minutes or so during takeoff or landing."

"And you've never been caught having to go then?" The rest stop came up on the left-hand side and he slowed as he took the exit.

"Murphy's Law kicks in once in a while and I have to go just because we're not allowed to leave our seats." Lyn laughed—a self-conscious, sort of embarrassed sound. "I try to always time it so I go right before we board and right before we land so I don't have the issue."

He could see her milling around at the airport, timing her visit to the rest room perfectly to boarding. "What do you do if the flight has a delay after you've boarded?"

"Hope I can make it." She sounded serious, grim even.

He went over a speed bump nice and slow. No need to aggravate the full bladders in the car. A parking spot opened up right up front near the entrance to the welcome center building. He pulled in smooth and dropped the car into park.

"Thanks!" She popped out of the car.

He got out and called after her. "I'm going to take Atlas a ways down so he can do his business. When you're done, come down this way and meet us."

She waved in acknowledgment, hurrying into the large building.

Cruz chuckled. She really had to go.

Honestly, he didn't mind. It was a long way down to Richmond, Virginia, and the Navy SEAL he'd located. Sheer luck the guy was stationed close enough to seek out with a casual day trip. A long one, but doable in a day and a night.

The man had been one of the soldiers in the highlights video and it'd taken some creative digging to figure out who he was. Cruz was still waiting on the decryption for the full-length video, hoping to get better face shots of the others in the room for identification. In the meantime, Cruz was on a mission to get information from the one he'd located but doing this with Lyn and Atlas put a different spin on the trip. He was willing to take some time and go at an easy pace for this ride. Serious as things were, he couldn't help but smile with her around.

Maybe it was her way of enjoying things all around her. The outlook was contagious. She'd been looking out the window the entire trip and commenting on the greenery or buildings or whatever she saw. The world hadn't gone to crap when you looked at it through her eyes. Not that she was naïve, because a person blinded to the bad all around them would irritate the hell out of him. No.

She was aware of the awful things in life. But she took them, dealt with them, and still came through with a positive outlook. It took a different kind of strength than the obvious and he admired her for it.

Atlas walked beside him on the lead, relaxed and mildly interested in the people around them. The big dog had watched Lyn go until he couldn't see her anymore but had come along with Cruz without resistance. He was alert as he should be, but relaxed in his own way. He even stopped to sniff a weed.

They both had it bad.

And Lyn? She didn't even know the power she had over them.

*   *   *

David had no idea how attractive he was.

Lyn paused to take in the scene. David and Atlas had reached the end of the long walkway leading away from the welcome center building. Maybe they'd even made it to the plot of grass marked for dog walking and come back. But currently, they were surrounded by a pack of teenage cheerleaders and a smattering of moms. No doubt the moms were every bit as interested in catching the surly man's eye as the teens were.

And David had on his best grouch face, scowling and generally attempting to brush off any attempts at conversation.

Only when it came to questions about Atlas, his armor had chinks. His answers might be curt but he still answered. And the teens peppered him with more questions. She could see the girls pointing to the big dog.

From a distance, Lyn couldn't make out what David was saying but his dark, growly voice sent delicious shivers across her skin.

The man gave good voice.

Of course, the moms weren't in a hurry to lead their girls away either. They added their own comments and laughed, tossing their hair salon-perfect hair. Lyn tugged at a loose lock of her own hair self-consciously. She'd caught a look at herself in the mirror in the bathroom. Tidy but not exactly looking like a supermodel. Every one of those women was made up, done up, and looking fabulous. How did women manage it on road trips and *why* would they bother chaperoning a bunch of cheerleaders?

Because leave a man like David out on his own within five hundred yards of those teenage girls and they'd flock to him. It was hot-guy radar. Had to be.

Lyn hung back, unwilling to break it up. Insecurity was an ugly beast and she readily admitted she was succumbing to it. Rather than show it to David, it'd be better to wait at a distance. Instead, she observed Atlas—which was her job, after all. Atlas was standing at heel, trying to keep all of those waving hands in sight. Generally, dogs didn't like all those grasping hands coming at their face. So far, though, Atlas had managed not to get defensive. He was wary but not upset. Under control. David was doing his part as handler, keeping the girls at a minimum distance to allow Atlas to feel safe.

They weren't rehabilitating him to be friendly.

Social, yes. Able to pass calmly through anything and still follow commands, absolutely. But he wasn't a pet and he wasn't expected to play with random people. He wasn't a PR dog.

He could play, if he wanted. He did play with her and with David. Most of his games revolved around a much-loved tennis ball and fetch. She loved seeing Atlas happy. And once in a while, the perpetual tension left David's shoulders. His face relaxed and the worry lines fell away. David was even more handsome when he was happy, too.

But neither of them was the domesticated male those women and girls expected. It was unfair of them to demand either David or Atlas be safe, perfectly behaved, even submissive to poking and prodding and unwanted attention. But if they made one move to try to shoulder their way out of there, they would go from military hot to scary dangerous. If David even tried to be more assertive about insisting they leave Atlas be as a service dog, they'd decide David was mean rather than respecting Atlas's space.

Not fair.

Suddenly, Lyn started walking. Neither David nor Atlas could be rude to get away. They were essentially trapped. And it'd reflect badly on them if they snapped to be free of the twittering attention showered on them. Fine. She could be a bitch on their behalf.

"I bought us coffee for the road." She plastered a broad smile on her face as she shouldered her way right through the other women and girls.

Passive–aggressive whispers and mean girl giggles surrounded them. Ugh. She didn't miss high school. And really, what was it about people losing all respect for personal space or someone working? Lyn remembered similar gaggles forming around hot police officers or firemen when she'd been on school field trips, more years ago than she cared to count.

The center of attention—be they a man or a woman—always had an awkward time extracting themselves while leaving a positive impression.

David looked like he'd seen salvation. Atlas's ears swiveled forward and his tail even moved side to side once. *Tock, tock.*

One of the girls said something. Lyn ignored it. "Hope you weren't waiting too long. Ready to go?"

"Yup." David wrapped an arm around her shoulders like she was a lifesaver and he was drowning. They headed back to the car as the girls made sad pouty faces. The grown women shot looks that could put Lyn six feet under. David dropped a kiss on Lyn's hair.

No blushing. None. Nope.

Damn it.

Delighted warmth ran through her. Even if it was for show, he filled her with a happy glow.

Once they all got in the car, David let out a long sigh. So did Atlas.

A person would think they'd been through days of combat instead of surviving minutes with hungry ladies. Well, the latter might've been worse. Depended on the type of guy and his preferences.

David started up the car. "Let's go."

Lyn smiled at him—a genuine, happy smile.

* * *

"It should be the next right and up the street on our left." Lyn hoped the GPS was correct. Otherwise, it'd be an incredibly awkward conversation when they knocked on the door.

Actually, it was going to be awkward no matter what. At this point, how awkward was more an order of magnitude.

"We're going to drive around the block first," David said, passing the right-hand turn and continuing onward. "Never hurts to get a good look at what cars are parked on the street and nearby."

"Did you get a look at the car the man was driving in New Hope?" She wondered if she should've been keeping an eye out for it this whole drive.

Of course, they'd seen a lot of cars on the drive down from Pennsylvania to Virginia. It'd been a solid road trip. Atlas had settled into the back like a champ with very few issues. Come to think of it, Atlas probably had more experience than she did with road travel. The military working dog had also been trained in para-jumping and rappelling, so he was a lot more experienced in traversing distances in every direction. Officially, the purpose of this trip was to socialize Atlas in a variety of environments and record his reactions. She wondered what sort of other environments they were going to take him into today.

"I did get a look at his car." David scanned the street as he drove, parking around the corner from the house they wanted to visit. "But the man used to be a Navy SEAL. He'll have switched cars by now. Either gotten a rental or maybe a cheap used car from a local dealership. Something easy to acquire and even easier to get rid of."

Lyn shifted in her seat. The man could be anywhere, still following her. "Why didn't we call the police?"

David hesitated. "No solid proof he was following you. It would've been my word against his. At most, they'd be able to bring him in for questioning but would've released him again. And he'd have gotten more careful."

"Oh." The word sounded quiet, timid, to her ears.

"This way, he's still confident and hopefully underestimates me." He reached out to brush her cheek with his knuckles briefly. "Which gives me an advantage in keeping the bastard away from you."

His touch gave her more reassurance than she thought possible and she tucked his words away to think about later. There'd been a lot of information to process in a short period of time.

He gave Atlas the order to stay and left the car windows cracked for airflow. It was cool outside so Atlas would be safe in the car waiting for them. As they walked toward the house, they kept a casual pace.

"Do you think he's home?" It was late afternoon on a weekday. The entire neighborhood was quiet, though.

"I think he will be home. He works day shift right now, based on my intel. Should've gotten home about twenty minutes ago so long as he didn't get caught up on base." David didn't seem concerned and he didn't elaborate on his sources of intelligence either. "If his family is home, he's less likely to get overexcited."

She didn't like causing trouble for the man's family. It was one thing to search out a bunch of soldiers in her mind but now that they were here—about to talk to one—the ramifications were widening in scope. By a lot. "We're just here to ask questions though, right?"

David was silent for a second as they turned and

walked up the driveway. "For right now, yes. But we all make choices and the reasons behind them get complicated."

She didn't have a chance to pursue the topic because they'd reached the front door and David knocked.

The sound of small feet stampeded toward the door before a feminine voice called out, "Let your father answer the door."

The man who answered the door was lean and dark, and intimidating. Lyn wondered what it was like living with a father like him, but then the man gave them a ready smile and laugh lines creased the corners of his eyes. "Can I help you?"

"Sean Harris?" David asked, extending his hand. "I'm David Cruz. I'm reaching out to some of the teams who worked in co-op with the Air Force military working dog teams. Wanted to get some feedback if you can spare a couple of minutes."

The man's smile quickly disappeared. Perhaps David's approach was too transparent. Which unsettled Lyn because she'd considered his introduction pretty circumspect.

"Seems unusual." Harris's voice maintained a neutral and significantly colder tone.

David spread his hands out at his sides. "I'm retired from active duty, working on consult with the three-forty-first training squadron. Doing some informal research on how we can improve interactions with co-operative teams. Particularly the SEAL teams since you do have dogs of your own."

"Not every unit, as I'm sure you're aware." The ice melted a fraction but Harris didn't step back to invite them inside. Beyond him, Lyn caught sight of three curious children. None of them could've been older than maybe ten years old. "My team has worked with several Air Force pairs."

David nodded. "Did any of them stick out to you as particularly difficult to work with? Any of the dogs have behaviors incompatible with the primary objectives of your team?"

"Not that I remember." Harris wasn't buying it. Lyn noticed he hadn't done more than glance at her the entire conversation but she got the sense he was keeping an eye on both of them.

"Any of the teams memorable at all?" David asked.

"I don't know what you think you're doing digging into things no one should know about." Harris was done with pretending. "But you both need to walk away. Now."

David dropped the pretense, too. "There's a man dead and no one knows the real reason why either."

Harris's gaze swept the street to the right and left before filling the door even more, blocking Lyn's view of his children. "I can't talk to you. You should know this."

Which meant there was something to talk about. Lyn couldn't believe they were in the middle of something so dire that a man as tough as this one obviously was could be frightened into silence.

"I'm trying to do right by my friend," David said quietly.

Harris didn't even flinch. "I have a *family*."

Then he closed the door in their faces.

CHAPTER TWELVE

It's hard to hold it against him." Lyn climbed back into the car.

Atlas sat up from the back seat and touched her cheek with his cool nose. She reached up to give him a scratch on the side of his head and he leaned into her hand.

David finished buckling himself in and started up the car. "You think so?"

He'd been silent on the walk back to the car. His jaw set but otherwise his features were neutral. Blank, almost. Only to her, he could never be a blank, forgettable face.

"Well, family is a reason a lot of people do a lot of things, even things that aren't exactly the right thing." If someone had asked her a few years ago if she'd ever request a favor of her stepfather, she'd have ripped their head off and told them where they could shove it and the very thought of asking. She'd been determined to show him she had the intellect, talent, and determination to make it on her own in a field he'd dismissed as unimportant. But here she was, because she'd swallowed her pride and decided the chance to work with Atlas was worth her stepfather's patronizing oversight. It'd been a compromise of her principles. She wasn't sure what David would've thought of her choice but chances were he'd made difficult choices of his own.

David didn't respond to her statement, though. Instead, he was looking straight ahead and guiding the car onto the road.

She sighed. So did Atlas. It would be a really long drive back up to Pennsylvania if David stayed withdrawn. On the other hand, she could understand his wanting to be left to his own thoughts. She could imagine—and it wouldn't be even close to the reality—what he might be thinking about the dangers his friend had faced without the very men he was supposed to call his teammates guarding his back. If everything around you was likely to kill you, having the team you're with willing to leave you exposed had to have been terrifying.

Only some didn't show fear, not in the way she or other people might be expecting to see it. Everything they presented to the world was very possibly different from what was actually going on inside their heads. David was hard to read in general and in this instance completely shut down. He might be angry or upset, sad or scared. But there wasn't much body language for her to go by. All she had was Atlas and the big dog didn't seem concerned by David at all as the dog leaned into her. She rubbed her forehead with her right hand since Atlas still had a monopoly on her left.

Humans were complicated. It was why she preferred working with dogs.

"Atlas, *af.*" David gave the command as he pulled onto the main highway. Atlas looked at him for a long moment, then turned and settled down to lay across the back seat. The delay in obeying commands was still there, but it was getting shorter. At least in response to David.

She turned her head as she mentally did a little happy dance. Baby steps with Atlas. Every improvement, however subtle, was worth celebrating.

Lyn continued to look out the windows and watch the world zip by. No need to reinforce the command for Atlas since the dog had obeyed. In fact, if she'd tried it would've undermined David's authority anyway. Besides, she agreed Atlas shouldn't be standing up between them on the higher speed roadways. If something happened, the big dog would fly right up into the front seat with them or even possibly through the windshield. Technically, they should have him secured in the back and not just free to lay back there.

"I should consider getting an SUV with one of those cargo nets to partition off the back for dog transportation." Thinking out loud wasn't a bad thing. Hopefully.

"Huh?" David didn't turn to look at her but his response was louder than expected.

"Well, this probably won't be the last time I need to transport a dog in my career. I should provide a good example. Maybe be ready to make recommendations to dog owners." Made sense to her. It'd take more saving, though, and a couple of good clients.

"Oh." David nodded. "I was worried there for a minute."

She blinked. "Why?"

There was a hesitation. "Well, you know Atlas needs to go back to Lackland. Even if he's retiring, there's a process for adoption and applicants are considered in a specific order."

"Oh." She'd read about it in her research. "Yeah, I know. Usually handlers or their families have priority, right?"

Another nod.

"But..." She bit down on what she was going to say next.

"Calhoun doesn't have family. At least no one in a position to take Atlas." David addressed the difficult topic anyway. She admired his ability to take things head on. 'Course, she liked a lot of things about him. Too many.

"So who would be next in line?"

"Other military or families. There are several variables under consideration."

"I figured." She didn't look back at Atlas but she was tempted to pull down the vanity mirror so she could see him in the reflection. "Things have been moving so fast with him. I hadn't thought about where he'd go next. Hard to imagine what it'll be like to see him go."

She felt a sinking feeling in her belly. She wouldn't just be saying good-bye to Atlas.

"You might be able to visit him," David offered. "Depends on who gets him. I plan to try to stay in touch."

With her, too? She didn't ask. Maybe later, but things were too... new. She wasn't sure where they stood yet.

"Maybe. I think he'd like a new forever home with a family. It might be awkward for me to pop in, though."

She struggled to put the empty feeling into words then gave up and tried for a different direction. "Did you ever want one?"

"Want what? A dog? I have all the dogs I can fit into my life back at Hope's Crossing." There was happiness in his voice. Pride. It made her smile.

"I meant a family." Now that she'd said it, she sort of wanted to take it back. The good humor left his face.

Damn. Just when he'd started to come back to a cheerful mood.

"No. Not in a conventional sense." He said it slowly. Carefully. "While I was active duty, I had my own demons. Every deployment was another chance to work through them. Only I picked up new ones every time I went out there. I figured it'd be the worst idea in the world to have a wife and kids waiting for me at home, wondering and never knowing if I was going to make it back. And depending on the wife, my kids might never understand why I was always away. She might not understand it either. I've seen too many marriages filled with constant fighting over that. I didn't want that for anyone."

Had her stepfather? She tried to remember. But her perception of him from her childhood had been of a stoic man. Stern. Immovable. She'd spent a long time thinking he hadn't cared at all.

This was the first time David had said so much about his past, though, and she wanted to know more about him. "What did you do in between deployments? Go home?"

He snorted. "Nah. Not because it was bad or anything. I just didn't fit in."

"Oh." She didn't know what to say. "That's hard."

"Well, my parents divorced while I was a teenager. High school angst doesn't get much worse than what I had. I was angry. At my dad. My mom. Myself. Just always angry." He opened and closed his hands on the steering wheel. "Mom left. Dad remarried. I got angrier."

She reached out, touched his thigh with her fingertips. Not sure if it'd be welcome but it seemed more than trying to come up with words. He dropped his right hand from the steering wheel and took hers in his. Warmth enveloped her hand and tingles ran up her arms and along her skin.

Wow, it didn't take much. His touch had her so finely tuned to him. Aware.

"I enlisted right out of high school. Basically took my diploma in hand and went straight into the Air Force. Some of my other friends went Army or Navy, but I knew what I wanted to be."

She cocked her head to the side. "And you've always gone to do what you set out to do?"

He squeezed her hand. "Basically. It took a while, but becoming a PJ was worth every second of hell to get there."

"A PJ?" Her favorite pajamas popped into her mind. And then she wondered what he tended to wear to bed.

Bad Lyn. Bad.

"Para rescue jumper."

That made more sense. "Ah. Must've taken a while."

He lifted one shoulder and dropped it in a half-shrug. "Longer than I wanted, not as long as most."

Not too prideful, not too humble either. She smiled.

"Any time I did go home, the house was full of half-brothers and -sisters. All way younger than me. Dad had rebooted his family life. He didn't make me feel unwanted, but it was awkward." He paused. "His new wife was nice enough but we never clicked."

"I'm sorry."

"It's not even a thing." He lifted her hand and kissed the back before placing it back down on top of his thigh. "Mostly, the kids like me just fine while I'm buying them video games or whatever is on their online wish lists for birthdays and Christmas."

But he didn't have a home to go back to. "Didn't they even think about it, though? Sure, you made it comfortable, easy for them. But they left you outside their world."

That made her furious.

"My choice to leave," he reminded her. "And I don't need to be angry with them. Plenty of other things to work through all on my own."

"You mentioned demons." She said it quietly. Not sure he wanted to talk about it. Her father had always sent her to her room if she asked about his deployments, what he did.

"Yeah." David fell silent for a while. His hand was a comforting weight on hers, though. A sign he wasn't pushing her away. "It's a weird thing, being over there. You become...institutionalized. And when you come home, you feel out of step. Hard to back down from the level of hyperawareness you need to maintain overseas. People want you to be a hero. But they want you to be the perfect citizen, too. The problem is, to be out there and survive, you become a rough man...ready to do violence."

It was a part of a saying. It swam up from her memory as one of the things her stepfather had repeated often at the dinner table.

People sleep peaceably in their beds at night only because rough men stand ready to do violence on their behalf.

The line was attributed to George Orwell. Her mind brought up the source she'd researched. The words had always stuck with her but some of her Internet research had said it wasn't a direct quote, more an interpretation of what the man had said. She'd looked it up in the hopes of impressing her stepfather. But he'd pinned her with a stare and asked her if she truly appreciated what the words meant or the men who stood ready to defend her sleep.

Until now, listening to David, she hadn't.

"It's not fair to expect you to switch gears when you come back." It was hard to know what to say so she went with what she thought, felt. Honest.

He barked out a laugh. "True. I try not to think about fair. Life's generally not."

"But some people try to make it that way." She would, moving forward. No matter where tomorrow took them. Mostly because she'd always been told life wasn't. And seriously, it wouldn't ever be if no one ever tried.

"Yeah." David shook his head. "I thought Forte was crazy when he said he was going back to his hometown to open up a kennel. But he'd saved every penny from the day he enlisted. And it added up. Then he got me and Rojas to come out to look at the place. It was huge. Right in the middle of a decent-sized town and close to a couple of different cities, but still private."

"Perfect?" She could imagine. All the different environments to fit a wandering soul. They could go to whatever surroundings their mood needed in a day trip. Or night.

"Absolutely."

"I can see the draw." They'd even come several states away and were still going to make it back in one day. She wondered if he'd even considered stopping for the night.

"Besides. Working with the dogs helped." David lifted his chin to indicate the rearview mirror. Looking up, she could see Atlas in the mirror too. "Look at him. He loved unconditionally."

Hearing the word come from David, easily, tugged at her. Too many men wouldn't say the word even about somebody else. Like the word was somehow a worse curse than any other four-letter word in existence.

"Dogs do." And she loved them back. Every one she'd ever met. Because they were so worth it.

"A dog like him—one with a heart that big—he loves without question once he decides to give it," David continued. "He laid his life on the line for his handler, because to him, it was worth it. But sometimes half the team doesn't make it back."

David paused.

"It wasn't his fault." Never. Not even knowing what had truly happened, she wouldn't believe Atlas had failed his handler.

Sometimes, no matter how hard anyone tries, lives are lost.

"No. And I thought maybe he'd pine away. Some of them do. And it would've hurt Calhoun worse than dying all over again if his dog had died of heartbreak. Calhoun would've wanted somebody to help Atlas through this. And someday, maybe Atlas will choose somebody new to look to." David glanced over at Lyn.

Her heart leaped. And then she squashed the happy dance. Atlas wasn't hers. None of the dogs she worked with were actually hers.

Atlas stirred in the back, having heard his name. He gave a quiet whine.

Her own bladder decided to alert her to the amount of time they'd been moving. Glancing at the clock, she couldn't believe how much time had already gone by over the course of their conversation. "So how close is the next rest stop?"

"Not far." David released her hand and picked up his phone. A quiet command and the phone's GPS kicked in. "There're stops all up and down this highway. If not actual rest stops, then exits to get food or gas."

No sooner had he said so than a sign came up for a rest stop in a couple of miles. They sat in companionable silence as they approached and he pulled into a parking spot to one side, closer to a patch of grass and some trees.

"You go on ahead and I'll let Atlas take care of his business." David gathered up Atlas's leash from the console between them.

"Okay." She popped out of the car, the call of nature too urgent to even care about dignity. Atlas, apparently, was feeling the same way, considering how fast he hopped out of the back of the car and sat to have the leash attached to his collar.

She hurried to the building and took care of business.

On the way out, she bought three bottles of water and some beef jerky.

David and Atlas were standing next to the car as she returned, both looking in her direction but not actually watching her. Or at least it didn't seem like it, because David didn't return her smile or even react to the bag of beef jerky she waved at him.

As she approached, David put a hand to the small of her back and rushed her back to her side of the car. "See anything odd inside?"

"No." She got in quickly and didn't protest when Atlas hopped in after her and scrambled over her lap to get in the back seat.

As David closed her door, headlights turned on suddenly from the row ahead of them and blinded her. Tires screeched. David rolled across the top of the car's hood. She got the impression of a dark car screeching past them, so close they clipped the side-view mirror.

Atlas let out a deep bark, lunging back up to the front seat. Lyn turned and grabbed his collar as David yanked the car door open and dove in, slamming the car door shut as he turned on the car. "Seat belt!"

"*Af.*" Lyn gave the big dog a nudge and Atlas returned to the back seat as she reached for her seat belt.

David didn't wait, throwing the car into reverse. Her head almost hit the dashboard but they turned sharply and she was slammed back into her seat as they went into drive. Desperately, she fumbled the seat belt until she got it buckled as David sped back out onto the highway.

"Sit tight." Whether the grim order was for her or for

Atlas, she didn't know. But she was guessing it was for her since he hadn't said Atlas's name.

More screeching as a car came up on their right and cut in front of them. David decelerated sharply to keep from running off the road and then poured on the speed, getting ahead of the other driver again.

"Is this a good idea?" The bottles of water were rolling around by her feet.

"Sure it is." He sounded *cheerful*.

They barreled down the highway in the left lane and she watched the streetlights flash by as streaks across the windows. Somebody had tried to run him down and force them off the road. Maybe even were trying to kill them. Her heart pounded through her chest and in her ears. There wasn't anything she could do.

"Reach into the glove compartment." David's instruction was urgent but calm. "There's a flashlight in there. Point it back over your shoulder before turning it on. Do *not* look into it. Do *not* point it in Atlas's face. It's way more intense than your average flashlight."

She did as instructed.

"Handy high-powered flashlight for heavy weather conditions," David explained. "It might as well be a hand-held spotlight. If we're lucky, it'll shine in the bastard's eyes and blind him some. At minimum, it'll be a distraction. Just hold on to it and turn it to the left and right a couple of degrees."

The small, black cylinder fit into her hand, heavier than she expected, and the power button was easy to find. Making sure Atlas was laying down low, she followed David's directions. A veritable spotlight poured out the back of the car.

David nodded. "Good."

Suddenly, David turned right, barely making an exit and slamming the breaks to slow down enough not to flip them over on the curving ramp.

"Turn off the light." The words came through gritted teeth as he picked up speed again.

She did.

They twisted through several smaller roads until they were in a nondescript neighborhood, parked among a few other cars in an equally nondescript apartment complex.

He shut everything down and made sure all the lights were out, even on the dash.

"All right?" His voice came low and calm as his hand touched her shoulder in the darkness.

She nodded, hoping he could see her because words weren't coming at the moment.

"Hang in there for a few minutes until we know for sure we've lost whoever that was."

She swallowed hard. "Okay."

"Atlas." There was a stirring from the back seat, low in the foot wells.

David released his seat belt and turned in the seat to check on Atlas. "Keep an eye out the windows. Tell me if you see anything."

She peered out into the dark but there was nothing. No cars. No people. It was really dark in this parking lot. "Apartment complexes should have better lighting in their parking lots."

The thought popped out of her mouth.

David chuckled, returning to his seat. "They should. Most don't."

"Good for us in this case?" She clutched the flashlight as if it was a weapon. And maybe it could be. If someone came up, maybe she could blind them until they could get away. She should get one for herself.

"Very good for us." David paused. "Change of plans for the evening. Best thing for us to do is be unpredictable."

"Which means we're sleeping here tonight?" Outside. Exposed. She shivered even though the car was still warm. With Atlas and David, she could do it if it was necessary. She might not actually sleep, though.

"No." David was silent until she turned to look at him. Her eyes had adjusted so she could make out his face and his gaze caught her, reassured her. He wouldn't let anything happen to her. "Let's get you someplace safe tonight. Then we'll head out again in the morning."

CHAPTER THIRTEEN

This... was not what I expected."

Cruz turned to grin at Lyn, happy to see some color returning to her previously pale face. Her tone was more of hesitant surprise than dismay, which was good. "Exactly."

"And you just happened to know about this place tucked away in a little town off the highway?" She sounded dubious.

Okay, he'd be asking questions too if he were in her place.

He chuckled. Her mind was always working as she studied every conceivable angle of a situation. Kept him on his toes and made messing with her fun. "In fact, yes."

She planted her feet at the end of the walkway and crossed her arms. Next to her, Atlas came to heel, then sat. "Seriously."

Cruz kept walking, unhurried, until he reached the

top of the walk and tapped a discreet, stylized sign. It had the silhouette of a German shepherd and a concise warning—not enough to scare away potential guests but enough to assure likely thieves that the property was guarded. "Not every puppy is suited for military or police service. We try to be sure to find good homes for the youngsters who don't make it all the way through training. We've got clients all up and down the East Coast."

The shadows cleared from her expression and curiosity sparked in her eyes. Easy as that. For all of her wariness, she believed too quickly. Somebody, someday was going to take advantage of her. The thought tightened his chest. It wasn't fair of him to want a person to be both wary and trusting.

But then his expectations of people hadn't ever been fair. It was why he worked better with dogs.

"I guess they'll have no problem with Atlas coming inside with us, then." The big dog, sitting next to her, looked up at her then at Cruz and voiced a short bark.

Dog was getting more talkative than Cruz ever remembered him being, even with Calhoun. As a rule, the military working dogs were trained to be silent most of the time. Her habit of conversing with him was changing Atlas more than Cruz had initially considered. The question would be whether Atlas reverted to a more stoic behavior pattern once he was working with another military handler.

He should if he was going back overseas.

Time spent with Lyn was nothing to regret but Cruz was more than a little worried about the impact her moving on would have...on both of them. Lyn's caring heart had softened them. If times were peaceful, it might not be as much of a worry but they'd just been given a taste of combat conditions in a place where there shouldn't be any. Now, more so than ever, they needed to be vigilant. "Shouldn't be a problem." He waited until they'd joined him before climbing the few steps to the landing of the historic bed and breakfast. "And I should be able to handle any introductions to their dogs to avoid any potential issues."

Her gaze settled on him, one eyebrow raised in an eloquent expression.

He nodded to her. "Not saying you couldn't, but since these bruisers know me it'll go faster if I do it."

Subtle tension went out of her shoulders and the corners of her lips turned up in a rueful smile. "You have a point there."

Any animal was more responsive with a familiar person. No matter how skilled the trainer, familiarity helped things go along more quickly. He'd met a lot of people with too much pride to acknowledge this simple practicality. As if admitting it made their skill less somehow. Or because they had to prove their abilities could overcome the advantage.

Lyn could be competitive. He had no doubts there. But she'd worked alongside him, burying her pride for the common goal. It'd made it easier for him to set his own emotional baggage aside and focus on Atlas.

Tonight, though—he was going to start taking more of a lead in the situation.

Almost getting run down did that to a man.

"Hopefully, they've got a room open for us." He reached out and knocked on the door.

"Will they hear that? There's a doorbell." She pointed.

He shrugged. "Don't want to wake up any other guests. There's rooms on the ground floor. The dogs will hear the knock and alert them to someone on the property."

Sure enough, Atlas stood. His big ears swiveled forward and nose twitched as he watched the door. The big dog stood ready and alert, every line the perfect balance of tension and listening. He was waiting for the barest whisper of a command.

Lyn huffed out a soft breath. "That'll work."

Quiet footsteps came to the door and paused. An older man peered out the tall thin window beside the door. A moment later, the deadbolt turned and the door opened. "David Cruz? What brings you to our door tonight?"

Cruz held his hands to his sides, palms open. More for the benefit of the big dog behind the older man than the man himself. Unarmed. Nonthreatening. The breeze at his back would carry his scent inside for the German shepherd. "How are you, Thomas? We were driving up north and got tired. Thought we'd stop in for the night if you've got the room."

"Always room for you or any of the boys from the kennel." The older man nodded to Lyn. "Hello, miss. Welcome."

Lyn gave him a shy smile. "Hello. This is Atlas."

Atlas had eyes only for the German shepherd. Until they were introduced, neither of them would relax. David planned to get it done as soon as possible. For the meantime, he shifted enough to block direct eye contact between the two dogs.

"Don't think I've ever seen David here in the com-

pany of a lady when he's working with his dogs."
Thomas gave Cruz a significant look as the older man
stepped back and opened the door wider, giving his dog
a quiet command to stand down. "You remember old
Brutus."

"He's looking good." David stepped inside and ran
his hand down Brutus's back as the dog's tail waved side
to side once in greeting. Gray around his muzzle and
eyes showed his age. He had a couple of good years in
him yet, though. "You mind if I put on his lead and take
him outside? I've got another dog to introduce him to
and it's best to do these things out on neutral territory,
off your property."

Thomas nodded, reaching for one of two leather leads
hanging from a hook on the wall. "Not at all. I'll go get
Caesar. We'll introduce 'em all at once. Kathryn will get
your room ready. You're lucky tonight. Master suite is
the only room empty."

Cruz shrugged. "Ah. Any room would be fine."

"Maybe for you. We give hospitality to ladies here."
Thomas tipped an imaginary hat toward Lyn.

Lyn laughed. "And it's appreciated."

Cruz opted out of the conversation and instead spoke
quietly to Brutus. Immediately responsive, the dog sat
for him and turned his head to make it easy to clip the
leash to his collar. "You've been keeping up on their
training."

"More like they've been keeping us up on ours."
Thomas chuckled as he stepped away. "It's the way you
and the boys changed our lives by helping us with Brutus
and Caesar. Couldn't have done it without you."

Cruz smiled, suddenly awkward and embarrassed. It

was what he did, training dogs. A job well done meant a happy owner and a content dog. It meant a dog was more likely to have a home for the rest of his days. Comfortable. Belonging.

Lyn called to him quietly. "Let's get them all introduced and then head up for some rest. It's been a weird night."

Yeah. Tomorrow wasn't going to get any more normal.

* * *

Lyn wandered around the room—suite, really—and took a moment to simply enjoy. She stayed in hotels all the time and they were most definitely *not* all made equal. In fact, even hotels in the same chain varied to a certain extent, depending on location. She hadn't spent much time in bed and breakfasts or inns or even boutique hotels but seeing this place, she might need to do research to start including these in her accommodations for the future.

This room was decorated with Old World charm, overlooking a garden with a formal fountain elegantly lit for nighttime viewing. As Lyn wandered past the queen-sized bed, she ran her hands over the sheets and pillowcases. Cotton woven so fine to the touch, she couldn't wait to get into bed. Okay, and she was a sucker for a thick down comforter, too.

Peeking into the bathroom, she bit her lip. "Hey, David?"

"Yeah." She heard David walk into the suite and shut the door. He must've unleashed Atlas, too, because she heard the sound of the big dog shaking himself.

"Mind if I take a bath?" Who knew what he'd think but damn it, there was a real Jacuzzi in there. "A real bath."

David chuckled. "As opposed to a pretend one?"

She tore her gaze from the Jacuzzi, and shot him a pointed look. "It's been an interesting road trip. I'd be stiff from the hours in the car alone. But then we had some insanity." She held up her hand when he was about to say something. "A lot crazier than I think I can process all at once. I'd like a long soak because I don't know how anyone is supposed to stay loose during that kind of driving and I will be sore tomorrow. This'll at least help it from being worse."

A long moment of silence. "It would be good. Go for it."

Lyn started into the bathroom and halted. Leaning back out of the bathroom she studied David. "We are safe for the night, aren't we?"

David tipped his head to the side. "Like I told you before, I don't have all the answers. But yeah, we should be safe tonight."

Should be? It was one thing to go searching for pieces of a puzzle. This had all gotten exponentially more real. David's reserved personality was somewhat frustrating all on its own but the way he hadn't talked to her more about what had just happened or any precautions he might be taking wasn't helping her relax any either. She *did* have faith that he was taking them, but she'd appreciate being part of the decision making. Which wasn't exactly fair because she didn't have the knowledge or the skills to be able to help in any sort of planning for this kind of thing. It was only for her pride, really.

She should be on equal footing with him. She should be actively a part of deciding their next move. Instead, she was asking if he minded if she took a bath. Her hard-fought independent nature had evaporated at the sight of a Jacuzzi tub.

She sighed, consciously relaxing her jaw and wondering if he'd been aware of her grinding her teeth. It wasn't good for her to think in circles and wouldn't be constructive to talk to him about it because he'd be damned one way or the other with the way her current thought process was stuck in a loop.

She just...needed to be away from all the strong personalities for a while.

"Okay." She looked at Atlas. "You, stay out here and be his wingman."

Atlas dropped his jaw open and let his tongue loll out.

She stepped inside and closed the door.

David's voice called to her. "Better lock it; he can open doors."

She turned and responded through the closed door. "You know, this is like a scene where a velociraptor looks down at the doorknob and..."

"He can do it a couple of ways. Use a paw, use his nose. He can even spring himself from most crates on his own." David didn't sound serious.

Nah. None of the dogs she'd worked with had ever turned a round doorknob. Maybe if it were a handle, something for him to get a paw on and pull down—like the velociraptor did in the movie—but this wasn't likely. She left it unlocked and turned the hot water taps to start filling the tub. It wasn't as if David was going to come peeping.

She trusted him not to. And to be honest with herself, the thought of locking herself away from the only other friends she had in a strange place triggered a tightness in her chest. Probably a reaction to the freaky car chase. She wanted some distance from them but not actual isolation.

All the more reason to soak in a nice tub and relax, work through some of these weird nerves, and get back to steady ground.

There was a lovely wooden tray on a small table next to the tub, maybe teak? A few packets of bath salts were arranged in a glass jar, labeled with ingredients. A small handwritten card warned to read ingredients carefully in case of allergic reactions.

"Wonder how many times that's happened," she muttered.

"You need something?" David's voice came through the door.

She straightened and studied the door thoughtfully. How close was he to the door if he heard her? "No. Just reading a few labels out loud."

"Okay. Holler if you need anything."

"Thanks." She was guessing she wouldn't need to raise her voice by much. He must be sitting right next to the door. Odd...

A snuffling sound came from under the door. Atlas.

She paused and thought that through. No. David wasn't lurking by the door listening and damn, she should know better. Atlas must be by the door waiting for her and had reacted to hearing her mutter. David was a very perceptive trainer. He must've been watching Atlas and seen the cue.

Mystery solved and significantly less creepy. But then, David wasn't the type of guy to do such things.

Sighing, she picked out lavender bath salts and poured the contents of the little packet into the water. Definitely not thinking straight and a good thing she hadn't lingered out in the bedroom to talk with David like this. She felt bad enough about the way she was jumping to conclusions inside her own head. It'd be horrible if he heard her.

Turning off the water, she tested the heat before getting in. About right. And when she turned off the main light switch, the little porcelain night-light on the wall above the vanity provided just enough to see by. She undressed, leaving her clothes in a heap on the floor and stepped in carefully. She'd gather her clothes up later and hang them up to air out. Right now, she wanted to soak. Desperately.

Lowering herself into the tub slowly, she smiled. Really hard to find mid-range, reasonably priced hotels with a tub deep enough to enjoy a truly good soak. Most tubs, you could sit about waist deep or bend your knees and neck. Not exactly optimal. But here, she was settled comfortably in the deep tub with the water line right up to her shoulders. The heat immediately started to seep into her limbs. Oh, this was so good.

Inhaling the lavender-scented steam, she started to systematically tense and relax her body a part at a time. First her toes, then her feet, then her calves... and on up. Tension released in areas she hadn't realized had been seized up. It didn't take more than ten minutes, but the relaxation exercise helped immensely, more so in combination with the hot soak.

She'd probably still be sore tomorrow but not as bad as she might've been.

Come to think of it, the whole night had turned out better than what could've been.

She'd reached for her car door handle when the other car had almost run down David. Stupid. Even if she'd have managed to get the door open it would've probably been too late to do any good or she might've hit him with it and slowed his escape. She hadn't been thinking so much as horrified. Actually, if she'd opened her door and the car had collided with it, it could've hurt her pretty badly, too.

Swallowing hard, she wrapped her arms around herself.

David had been quick and avoided the danger far better than she could have. And then the drive...

At those speeds, would any of them have walked away from a crash? Atlas hadn't been secured. He'd have bounced around the car like a ping-pong ball. Even with the seat belts, she and David could've been seriously hurt.

Visions of the car running off the road, flipping over and rolling, flashed through her mind. There was a chattering noise and it took her several seconds to identify the sound as her own teeth. The water around her was still warm but she was shaking all over. She'd drawn her knees up without noticing and she sat in a semi-fetal position in the tub trying to hold herself together.

But it was too late. The panic attack was in full swing. More images streamed through her mind of the dark, the bright headlights. The sounds of engines and screeching tires echoed in her ears. Her heart beat harder and she couldn't catch her breath.

Then the sounds changed to words.

...she won't see our faces.

There was a sharp bark.

"Lyn? You okay in there?"

But we can show her a couple other things before we leave.

She held her breasts, trying to protect them from the painful pinch. Squeezed her eyes shut and tried not to see his face. *No. No. No.*

Another bark, deeper, and a scratching sound.

There was a soft creak as the door was opened and Atlas was there, leaning over the tub, licking her face.

"Lyn! I'm coming in."

She didn't protest, glad for Atlas and relieved as she realized David was there.

David reached in and lifted her out of the tub, cradling her against his chest. "It's okay. You're okay."

"S-sorry. S-sorry!" She couldn't stop shaking, couldn't stop her teeth from chattering.

"It's okay. We're here." David carried her out of the dimly lit bathroom into the warm light of the bedroom and set her on the bed.

She wanted to cling to him, ask him not to let her go. But he was back in seconds and wrapped a soft blanket around her.

David sat next to her then, his arm open in invitation. She tipped right into his chest, burying her face in the hollow of his shoulder. He stilled for a minute. "Just this once. *Over.*"

She looked up in time to see Atlas jump onto the bed and give her a quiet, concerned whine. The big dog stared into her eyes for a long moment, then lay down pressed up against her other side. His heavy weight against her hip helped settle her jangling nerves.

"I love baths. I don't know why I'm like this. I hate this." She was babbling and she had no idea why.

His hands rubbed up and down her upper arms, warming her through the comforter. "Could be a lot of factors. These things sneak up on you."

He was matter-of-fact about it, accepting. None of it was weird to him. She was so glad he wasn't calling her crazy. She was a little worried that she was, in fact, losing it.

"I don't understand what's wrong with me."

He kissed her forehead. "None of this is wrong. You've been through awful things. They'll come back and bite you once in a while."

She considered his words. "You get these...moments. Panic attacks?"

"Yeah. Not often. More nightmares than these, but I've seen it enough." His voice turned rough. "It's nothing to be ashamed of."

Leaning into him, she breathed in the scent of him. He smelled like clean air and woods. "How do you make it stop?"

"You don't." Simple. Matter of fact. Gruff but not callous. "You figure out how to work your way through it each time it happens, but don't try to avoid it and don't convince yourself it won't happen, because that's when it'll catch you with your pants down. Accept it. Work through it."

It was what he did. She considered his words. Short, to the point. But not without caring. His understanding helped more than lots of talking. He'd gotten through these kinds of things. Nightmares? He woke up every day and walked out into the world and she couldn't ever remember a moment she'd thought he was anything but capable and confident and on top of it all.

He'd shared a weakness with her and somehow, it made her ridiculously relieved to know she wasn't alone.

David's arm had closed around her and he used his free hand to clear strands of wet hair from her face. "Take your time and get your bearings. Look. Listen. Smell. Everything is different. You're safe here. It's all good."

It was his face she looked at. His chiseled features and dark hair, his steel blue eyes. She etched it into her memory and drove away the other man's disgusting leer with the warmth and concern of David's expression. Here was safety, strength. This was what she wanted to remember.

She leaned up and pressed her lips against his. He held still for a long moment, not pulling away but not reciprocating. Then his lips parted and he returned her kiss gently.

But it wasn't enough.

"More," she whispered against his lips.

David lifted his head and tucked her against his shoulder again, resting his chin on her head. "You're really upset right now. It'd be better to tuck you in and let you get some rest."

No. No sleeping. She didn't want nightmares.

"There's too many things crashing inside my head. Too many bad memories." She needed him to understand. "I'm terrified and I don't want these things to keep ambushing me in the dark."

His arms tightened around her. "It takes a while to work through these, sometimes a long while. When they happen, you've got to find your way through. Breathe. Look around you." He paused. "Maybe see a professional to talk through it. You've been through a lot in less than two weeks."

She shook her head. "A shrink isn't what I need right now."

"Well, I'm not sure of one who's got office hours at this time of night anyway but soon. Everybody handles these things their own way. You'll find your way."

She huffed out a laugh. Maybe. Probably. So far, she liked his method of dealing. The panic had receded to a faint jangle in the back of her head and she was grateful. It'd be even better to replace it with something positive.

"To be honest, I want better memories." She pulled away from him just far enough to look up into his eyes, catch his gaze. It was important for him to know she meant every word she was about to say. "Make love to me? Not because I'm upset. But because you're wonderful and I'm insanely attracted to you. Because I want to make memories with you. Good ones. Can we do that?"

CHAPTER FOURTEEN

Oh boy, did he want to. Cruz struggled with his raging libido.

"This isn't right, Lyn." He needed to get off this bed and out of this room. Stat. What she was offering would test the self-control of a saint and he wasn't one. Not even close.

"You've already insisted we do the right thing once." She reached out of the cocoon of the comforter he'd wrapped around her and snagged a handful of his t-shirt.

He could break away easily, but because it was her holding him, he wouldn't. Did she even know?

"I'm completely awake and in full control of my mental faculties." Her gaze held his with a steady, smoldering burn.

Every part of him was waking up in response to her. Woman knew what she wanted. "You are extremely upset and vulnerable."

Part of him wanted to pounce on her, press his

lips against every delicate part and run his tongue along her body until he found sensitive places even she didn't know about herself. Curled up as she was, completely naked under that comforter, she was definitely vulnerable.

His damsel in distress narrowed her eyes at him and pressed her lips together. "There's a whole lot of life going on and it doesn't make sense to me to wait for happier times or calmer days."

She had a point there. She was also shrugging out of the comforter some and the smooth skin across her exposed shoulder was insanely enticing.

"Besides, there's a certain excitement about the last twenty-four hours at least." Her cheeks warmed to a rose flush. "I've never felt more alive than now."

He could understand her reaction. Extreme danger, potentially life-threatening. One of the ways people could deal with coming through those kinds of situations intact was to celebrate life. And hell, as far as he was concerned, enjoying it with another person was even better.

Buying himself some time to clear his head, he straightened and looked Atlas in the eye. "Let's get you settled for the night."

Lyn leveled a smoldering stare on him, letting him know she definitely didn't plan to cool off while he was stepping away, and caressed the big dog's head. "Good night, Atlas."

Of course she'd sound happy, all sorts of sweet and innocent. None of them was fooled, though. Atlas was probably more than aware of the pheromones floating around the room.

Atlas reluctantly followed him off the bed and out of the bedroom into the sitting room. There was a large crate for guest dogs set up, complete with water and food bowls, freshly laundered blankets.

"*Hok*." Cruz motioned to the crate.

Atlas studied it, then Cruz, for a long moment before entering. He sniffed around for a few seconds, then lay down with an audible huff.

"Sorry, bud." Cruz had a small amount of brotherly sympathy for the big dog. Besides, depending on how he answered Lyn, he might end up out here bedding down next to the big dog. "We've both slept in strange places. At least this is comfortable."

Besides, if circumstances were reversed out in the field, Cruz wouldn't have begrudged Atlas. Well, things were different for dogs.

Moving on.

Lyn was still curled up at the top of the bed with the comforter gathered around her when he returned. He strode across the small room and paused. The lights were all on but in their vintage fixtures, the glow they cast was soft.

*   *   *

"Stay with me, David." She rose up out of her comforter when he came within reach, pressed a kiss on his jaw.

His control frayed and dissolved. Heat rushed up through his body and up into his head despite the few moments of clarity he'd gained earlier. Nope, he hadn't had a chance.

As her lips found his, he angled his head to give her

better access and opened for her. Their tongues danced and explored. He drank in her sweetness, her lips touched with a hint of salt from the bath. He wondered if he'd get the same complex flavors when he ran his tongue over other parts of her.

When, not if.

Oh, he was going to hell.

"Are you sure?" He wanted to give her every opportunity.

Her gaze was steady, though, and her smile was warm, intimate—a visual caress just for him. "What's taking you so long?"

He chuckled. "Oh, you have no idea what you are getting yourself into."

He climbed onto the high bed and stalked up to her on hands and knees.

"I have high hopes." She reached out to him, caressing the sides of his face.

Her lips were soft, welcoming. He kept the kisses light for the moment, playful. "Do you want the lights out?"

She froze for a moment and he drew back so he could catch her gaze. Shadows and fear flickered in her eyes.

He made a soft hushing noise. "I like the lights, if they're okay with you. I like seeing you."

The tension eased throughout her body and he let his weight settle over her as she gave him kisses as her answer. Her body was pliant under his, her curves pressing against him and tempting his control. He'd burned out most of it trying to resist her at all.

He ran a hand along her side, enjoying the silky smoothness of her skin and the curve of her hip under his hand.

She nipped at the corner of his mouth and tugged at his t-shirt. "No fair."

He sat up long enough to pull the t-shirt over his head, enjoying her touch as she sat up with him to run her hands over his chest. "I haven't had a chance to shower yet. I could—"

She shook her head, tugging at his belt. "Uh-uh, I've waited long enough."

Okay then. He helped her with undoing his pants and both of them chuckled as he got out of them without leaving the bed, mostly because she wouldn't let him. Once he was naked, she ran her hands over him, hungry and greedy in the best of ways.

This was another aspect of Lyn he enjoyed, the way she met him in every activity. She didn't just sit back and let him do all the work or always take the lead. She met him head on.

As her fingers wrapped around the length of him, he shuddered. "Careful."

"I'm done being careful."

The heat of her mouth closed over him and he almost lost his balance, his control, and everything right then and there.

He buried his hand in her gold hair. God, she was doing things to him and he'd have all sorts of catching up to do. And he would.

She sucked and licked the head of his shaft as her fingertips teased the tender skin under his balls. He groaned under the onslaught of sensations, almost blinded by how good it felt. He gritted his teeth and reached for whatever willpower he had left not to thrust or rush her in any way.

A moment later, she released him, looking up the length of him with wet lips and a very saucy expression. Growling, he pushed her back on the bed. He settled himself between her legs and ground his hips into her, rubbing his erection along her slit. She was already wet, ready for him.

"There's so much I want to do for you," he groaned. Then he kissed her neck, tasted the slight salt left behind by her bath mixed with the natural sweetness of her skin. "But I want to be inside you now. Right now."

"Please." Her whisper tickled his ear and her hands gripped at his hips.

He drew back and reached to one side, pulling open the drawer of the nightstand and fishing out a condom from the box thoughtfully hidden there. It'd been Kathryn, not Thomas, who'd pulled David aside before settling them into the room to tell David she kept the master suite well stocked with amenities for all sorts of needs. He sent the saucy old proprietress silent thanks.

After unwrapping the condom and rolling it on, he was back to Lyn as fast as he could be. He nuzzled her breasts until she giggled, her arms wrapping around his shoulders. Capturing one taut nipple in his mouth, he suckled until her breath caught.

"Tease." Her voice was husky now with a tinge of impatience.

Good. That made two of them. He took one of her hands and guided it south, placing her hand on his rigid shaft and letting her guide him in. He watched her, kept her gaze locked with his. Any moment, any fear, any doubt, and he'd stop. But he didn't want to miss this. Wanted to enjoy every bit of it with her.

As she positioned him at her opening, he pressed inside her, hot and slick. Tight. Her eyes fluttered shut and her neck arched as he filled her. He fisted the comforter on either side of her as he pulled back out and slid in, rocking against her in a slow rhythm.

Her breath changed to heavier panting and he drank in the sight of her gorgeous breasts rising and falling as he continued to move inside her. She groaned and grasped his forearms, trying to angle her pelvis for even better penetration.

He bent his head low to catch her mouth for a hot kiss. "More?"

"Oh, yes." Her face was flushed and her hair spread out all across the bed under her. She was beautiful.

And he planned to give her everything she wanted.

He coaxed one of her knees higher against his side, then hooked his arm underneath. The new position allowed him to go deeper. She called out brokenly and her inner muscles convulsed around him.

She was close. He was closer. And damn it, he was going to hold on until she got there.

He dragged in breath after breath, slowing his pace and savoring every slide in and out of her. She clutched at his shoulders then shifted her grip to his hips, urging him deeper and faster. Every time he rocked into her, she made fantastic sounds of pleasure. Her breasts bounced beneath him and he couldn't deny her what she wanted.

Increasing his rhythm, he drew out and plunged back into her faster.

"David! Yes! Harder!"

Yes. Pleasure gathered low and tight, his balls even

tightened, until every other thought left his brain and his focus was only on the feel of being inside Lyn.

Her thighs tightened and her hips thrust upward as she gasped, then she came apart beneath him. He pulled out and slid himself back in tortuously slow as her inner muscles convulsed around him and she came, hard.

They held on to each other in the aftermath, both breathing hard. Every few moments one or the other of them twitched, sending a cascade of sensations through both of them. Hypersensitive, it was agony to leave her and clean up in the bathroom. But when he came back, she'd moved over on the bed and pulled down the sheets to tuck them both in.

He climbed into the bed next to her and tucked her up against his side. "Is it okay with you if we wake up early tomorrow?"

She snuggled into his shoulder. "Mmm. Sure."

There was a beat of silence as he pondered turning off the lights in the room. It wouldn't hurt to leave them on, for tonight at least. Given time, she'd work through her triggers.

"Fair warning," Lyn whispered, her lips brushing his lower jaw. "I'm very partial to morning ambushes so we might be waking up a little earlier than you planned."

His lips stretched into a real smile. "Yes, ma'am."

CHAPTER FIFTEEN

Cruz didn't enter the neighborhood this time until buses had gone through for just about every age group. People in suburban areas like this took notice of a lone stranger walking through when children were headed to bus stops. He didn't want the attention and he wasn't interested in the kids.

What he wanted was to catch Sean Harris at home, alone. Or at least without his children around, amping up his need to protect his family.

Lyn and Atlas were back at a small coffee shop with the car parked outside. He'd tucked them in the back corner of the place away from windows and in direct line of sight of a security camera. Safe as he could make them without being there. Then he'd headed back to Harris's home on foot. He didn't want the possibly familiar car tipping Harris off to this visit before he could confront the man face to face. And he didn't want Lyn involved in case things got ugly. Besides, the less she knew about all this, the better.

It'd been one thing to bring her along the first time. She'd added to the impression of a friendly visit. Just a few questions. No danger to anyone.

This wasn't likely to be a friendly visit.

Harris was home. His car was in the driveway. The minivan wasn't. Good. Likely his kids and his wife were out of the house.

Cruz wasted no time heading straight for the front door and ringing the doorbell.

It took no more than a minute for Harris to answer. "I already talked to you. We're done."

Before Harris could close the door, Cruz shoved his booted foot in the doorjamb. "Someone tried to run me down last night. Then they tried to run me and my friend off the road. You know anything about that?"

Surprise flashed across Harris's face, then his mouth pressed in a grim line. "I told you I can't talk to you."

"Considering someone knew where to find me to make a go at me, I'd say they know I was here yesterday." Cruz tipped his head. "They might even know I'm here again. Could be they're planning on asking you what I wanted to talk to you about but I'm guessing they haven't yet. Either way, they're going to be making some assumptions. How much you want to bet they'll err on the cautious side and assume you talked to me anyway?"

"How stupid are you, threatening me?" Harris's face had turned a ruddy red.

"I'm not. I'm making some educated guesses." Cruz kept one hand on the doorjamb and the other loose at his side. Nonthreatening, but ready to bring up to guard if Harris decided to throw a punch. Harris was probably in good shape. It'd be a challenge, but Cruz had been keeping up his conditioning, too. "And I'm going out on a limb figuring you're a decent man who didn't try to turn me into roadkill last night."

The other man was definitely angry, but he wasn't homicidal.

"Look. I was home all night. It wasn't me." Harris worked his jaw and then shook his head. "Why did you come back here? You don't have enough evidence to convince you to stay out of this?"

Cruz shook his head slow. "Just getting started. Whatever this is, my friend died because of it."

"It's not espionage or a threat to the country or any of that shit." Harris was loosening up, eyes darting past Cruz up and down the street.

Cruz was keeping an eye out himself, using the reflections in the small windows to either side of the door.

"This was just a business deal." Despite his claim, Harris sounded like he was swallowing glass talking about it. "The kind of business that takes years to complete. We all needed to keep our mouths shut. Some of us didn't."

"Calhoun knew about this...deal?" No way. Calhoun had been a man of honor and he wouldn't have gotten caught up in any shady dealings. He'd wanted to come home with nothing on his conscience, no guilt and no regrets.

Not likely to happen for any of them. A person had to make choices out there. Some of them weren't black and white, right or wrong. But if a soldier could make the best decisions possible, then it made coming home easier.

Harris shook his head. "Nah. Your friend took a hit to the head from a stray piece of wall in a rundown building we were entering. He made it through the initial incursion but was down and unconscious while we were mopping up the site."

"You call interrogating someone mopping up?" Cruz raised an eyebrow.

It might not be wise to let on how much Cruz did know about what was in those videos, but obviously Harris was still playing it safe. Cruz needed him sharing more. Give a little to get to what mattered.

Air rushed out of Harris in a whoosh, as if Cruz had sucker-punched him. "How much do you know? Forget it. Look. Your friend wasn't awake when we interrogated that son of a bitch and didn't make a deal. The rest of us, what the fuck were we supposed to do? Once some of us were in, we all had to be. None of us was willing to risk being the only man standing back from it."

And now they were getting somewhere.

"What was it?" Cruz asked.

Harris held up his hands. "Doesn't matter."

"My friend thought it mattered enough to keep evidence," Cruz growled. "Hiding it was a gamble with his life and he lost. I want to know why."

"Evidence got your friend killed. Knowing too much gets a lot of people killed," Harris shot back. He worked his jaw for a moment and then sighed. "But you know too much already. Look, it was a trade of services. Okay? We were asked to kill our target instead of taking him into custody. In exchange, our new business partner would take over the insurgent cell and after official military units were pulled out of the area, there'd be a need for private contracts. Those choice contracts would be offered to us first, once we'd retired from active duty and went private ourselves."

Cruz raised his eyebrows. "Going for a long-term retirement plan."

"If you call going private retirement." Harris's voice was grim. "I don't. What matters is after we were done and came back from that mission, we were split. Our unit was reorganized and each of us was reassigned."

Not good. Someone high up was involved then. And whoever it was wanted these men alone and constantly on edge. Even if their new units weren't a part of it, there'd be no way to know who could be trusted. Who was involved, who wasn't, and who would stand aside and let a hostile sniper take you out just to make life simpler for the rest of them.

"One of us wanted to talk anyway—and maybe he talked to your friend, Calhoun—but he took a shot to the back on an easy search-and-retrieval mission a few weeks later. Message came across to the rest of us loud and clear. Back out or talk about the deal and we wouldn't know when a hostile bullet would take us out. Our own team wouldn't have our backs. Or worse— we'd take out some poor innocent bastard who'd have no idea why one of us was being left to die." Harris swallowed hard. "I'm not willing to have that kind of blood on my hands. You don't need to know more details. I wish I didn't know. But I'm going to see this through to the end or until I can see my way clear without harm to my family."

"Could take years." Cruz understood. The position this man was in was a waking nightmare. Any mission could be the one: the time when a teammate stood aside when they should cover him. No way to know, and no man could be completely vigilant a hundred percent of the time.

"This was always going to take years." Bitterness flavored every word from Harris's mouth. "And for people who believe honor is an outdated concept, it isn't a problem. But some of us are still burdened with a sense of things gone to shit."

"Calhoun was going to blow this open; I get it." Cruz fished for more. "But who was he going to tell? How?"

"I don't know." Harris shrugged. "Does it matter? This needs to be zipped up tight. No way to know how news of this could impact the future. For now it's a business deal."

"Later, it could be a political skeleton." Cruz continued the thought. Never knew when a military veteran was going to run for office. This kind of thing could play havoc with a campaign for senator or the presidency, or however high the main person wanted to go. "How was the other SEAL going to opt out?"

Silence. Harris obviously didn't want to continue. But Cruz's foot was still in the doorjamb and the man had already spoken more than intended. In for an inch, in for a mile and all that.

"He reached out to all of us first and said he didn't want to be a part of it. Swore he wouldn't tell a soul, just didn't want to be involved any longer." Harris sighed. "E-mail went out encrypted."

Not easy to intercept then. And not as likely to have been read by just anyone.

Cruz nodded. "So one of you either eliminated him or passed on the information to make it happen."

Harris didn't respond. His face was grim. The anger simmering behind his eyes wasn't for Cruz anymore. Otherwise, Harris would've shoved Cruz off his front doorstep already. No. The anger was directed someplace else, toward the people responsible for holding all of this over Harris's head.

Good. Talk more. Give up a way to get to the real people responsible for Calhoun's death.

"When you're out there, you have to make the best choice out of the options you've got. And they're not good. Ever." Harris glared at Cruz. "Who do you have out there in the world to worry about? Who will be hurt based on the choice you make today? Who could pay the price if you make the wrong one?"

Cold washed over Cruz. He pushed words through gritted teeth. "No one."

Harris raised his eyebrows. "You and I both know better. There's a certain kind of person that's alone with no one to care if they live or die. You might've been one of them in the past, but it's been a good while since. You've got people who will get caught in the blast radius if this explodes in your face. Family isn't just by birth."

It was Cruz's turn not to respond. Lying would only insult both of them. He had shown up with Lyn at his side. And he could pretend hers was a friendship but their connection was something more even if he hadn't admitted it to her directly. Didn't surprise him to have Harris hint at it. Man wasn't stupid. He was just a man caught in a foxhole with no way out.

"Think hard about how much further you want to take this." Harris wasn't threatening. Hell, there was some sympathy in his voice. "We all want to do the right thing by our brothers and sisters in combat. But our first priority is to look to the living. Don't bring down the kind of shit storm that'll hurt the people you care about. Calhoun wouldn't want that."

Anger burned away the hesitation. "What do you know about what Calhoun would've wanted?"

Harris's expression turned sad. "He was a good guy. Didn't have long to get to know him when he and his dog were attached to our unit. But you know how it is. You get a feel of a person pretty quick out there. He tried to do the right thing."

"Then it shouldn't be a surprise I'm out here, trying to do right by him." Cruz couldn't help the rumble in his tone.

"Maybe." Harris drew the word out slowly. "But then you have to think about what the right thing is for the living first."

And Harris had family. Cruz got it. He did. But someone needed to answer for Calhoun's death and the others'.

"At least give me names of the other soldiers in your unit. Give me something to go on." Cruz tried again. He'd find a way through this mess to see Calhoun didn't die for nothing.

Harris shook his head. "I've already said too much. I could be a dead man already. Maybe. No more."

Cruz ground his teeth but didn't press harder. Harris was right. It'd already been too much.

"Thanks for this, at least." Cruz figured any additional words were over the top so he walked away.

It was time to get Lyn and Atlas back home and for him to find another angle to go at this entire issue.

CHAPTER SIXTEEN

Lyn walked in and dropped her travel bag on the bed. She'd need to do laundry. Soon. Like in a couple of minutes, before she forgot and tried to go do something else. Like maybe flop down onto the bed and take an impromptu nap. The cabin was starting to feel like home, complete with cozy nap-inducing temptations. Blankets. Pillows. Bed.

Of course, her thoughts were scattered. Had been since she'd gotten out of the car.

"That is one potent male," she said out loud to the empty cabin.

And she wasn't talking about Atlas.

Memories of last night had kept popping back into her head in the car, making her blush. Damn her fair complexion. It was such a giveaway.

And David, the bastard, had noticed every single time and given her a knowing smile so sexy, the rest of her heated up, too. She'd even been tempted to instigate a make-out session at one of the rest stops, if a car full of kids with a puppy hadn't pulled up right next to them. Probably a good thing she hadn't. It would've been downright mean to Atlas.

At least they'd made it the entire way up from Virginia to Pennsylvania without further...adventures. This whole case had been one crazy occurrence after another. Even without the insanity, she hadn't caught her balance in regard to David Cruz since she'd arrived. Working side by side with him—seeing him every day—and the more she learned about him, the more she wanted to know. He'd taught her a few things about herself, too. And she was all for continuing education.

But a tiny worry niggled at her, now that she was away from him and truly alone for a few minutes. This warm, happy sensation was a temporary high. It had to be. This sort of thing wasn't sustainable, and she knew this from witnessing it in her mother and dozens of military wives growing up. This was either going to fade or end abruptly. In fact, it'd be just like any of her other dating experiences since she'd become a training consultant. Wouldn't it?

Temporary.

Eventually, she was going to move on to the next client and the next dog. Maybe they'd keep in touch. Or perhaps they'd cut it clean when she left. The latter was actually the more practical so she could easily see David opting for that.

"Ouch." She sat on the edge of the bed abruptly.

The thought burst her bubble of happy effectively. In

fact, she was quickly dropping into a serious need for fudge brownies. David hadn't even said a single word about the future or end of one, when it came to them. Her own brain had decided to take the trip on its own. He wasn't to blame at all.

Maybe she still had a bag of those dried cherries dipped in chocolate she'd bought in New Hope with Sophie.

She stood and walked back out into the main living area. Movement was good when she was thinking too hard even if she didn't find her remembered snack. Truly, this was her problem. Too much worrying, too much dwelling on things out of her control, and too much agonizing over things that hadn't happened yet. This was a project with real exposure and Atlas was a great dog. This thing she had with David was chemistry like *whoa* and better than she'd imagined even when she'd been daydreaming about it and him, specifically. Neither was over yet.

Maybe both were a chance for her to live in the now. Focus on the project and do better than she'd ever done in the past, for Atlas. And enjoy her time with David. At the very least, there'd be memories to savor for a long time to come. And if she stopped worrying for a few minutes, even, maybe something would surprise her.

Maybe.

There were a lot of uncertainties and most of them weren't under her control. She'd never been good at handling such situations in the past and she didn't want those frustrations or disappointments to ruin what she had now. Been there, done that. Regretted it.

This. Here. Now. She'd shoot for no regrets.

Her phone rang. It was her stepfather.

Of course. Because he had a sixth sense for when she was implementing positive changes in her life. And would call—not to support or encourage either.

"Jones speaking."

"You have caller ID. You know it's me." Her stepfather sounded irritated.

"Our last phone conversation didn't start off on the best of notes so I thought I'd try answering the call in a different way." There. Perfectly reasonable. And she thought she'd managed a positive tone too. Sort of.

Okay, at least neutral. She didn't do fake cheer and he'd have recognized it for what it was anyway.

"You are late on your status reports." He sounded distracted.

At least he hadn't insisted she call him "Father" before he'd gotten to his point.

"We took Atlas on an extended behavioral training trip, socializing him in multiple public environments with varying crowd types." Truth was always the best way to start these things, but it was so much easier to leave out the bits she didn't want to share via an e-mailed status report as opposed to phone conversation. Spoken out loud, she lost some of her confidence with her stepfather, always.

"An extended trip takes more than a day?" And there it was, the doubt and inevitable censure in his voice.

"Multiple." She would not waver on this. "We stopped at various places both with suburban surroundings and crowded city areas. Indoor and outdoor. It's good to see what he's still sensitive to and what kinds of crowds he'll need further exposure to in order to get him back to his former level of training."

There was a long silence.

"I see." And the hesitation this time—if she could believe it—was doubt on his part. "I'll admit I haven't paid this close attention to the military service dog training program in the past. I've only recently become responsible for public perception on high-profile veterans within the last several years. The majority have been of the human persuasion."

Somehow she was surprised, actually. Her stepfather was detail-oriented if nothing else, and she assumed he'd keep himself thoroughly informed on the particulars of any project. Most especially one in which her performance, or that of any other contractor, could and would reflect on him. After all, he'd provided the extra support she'd needed to get this contract in the first place. Otherwise, David Cruz and his partners made much more sense in working with a high-profile military service dog regardless of background.

Of course she'd made her arguments but to be honest, she'd understood her chances were slim initially. It'd been why she'd swallowed her pride and coordinated with her stepfather in the first place. She'd completely expected to be in the red with her stepfather for something close to forever for this particular support from him. His hesitation was unexpected.

She pushed her advantage. "Atlas is a multi-purpose trained dog. He's not just explosives detection or search or drug detection. He's got to be flexible and adaptable to step up to anything the team needs him to do. His missions could take him through crowded populaces as much as remote locations so he needs to be able to move through those and anything in between while still being able to focus on the task he's been given. I want to be thorough about his rehabilitation."

"Of course." Her stepfather had recovered apparently and managed to get irritable in the bargain. "I'm aware of the value this asset represents. The steps required to return him to full working status, however, seem to be unorthodox."

She counted to five, figuring she didn't have until ten to get back on firm footing with him. "An unusual approach has proved effective, as my previous status reports demonstrated. Wouldn't you agree?"

"He's made progress." Not complete, but he'd allow at least that much.

"Rehabilitation has renewed Atlas's drive in a way simple retraining wouldn't. He's eager to work again and almost one hundred percent responsive." Her pride for Atlas's progress seeped into her tone. "David Cruz has also been very generous in sharing his expertise in training technique. I've found the information he's shared valuable as well."

In a whole lot of ways.

"According to his records, David Cruz is a creditable trainer. He wasn't directly assigned to a military service dog while he was on active duty, though. I find it interesting that he's chosen this profession now." Her stepfather would have access to David's service record. Somehow that was downright predictable.

Come to think of it, though, she didn't know exactly why David had come to Hope's Crossing Kennels. Funny. Each time he'd shared with her, she'd thought she'd learned so much about him. And then a moment like this demonstrated how much of his background was completely undiscovered.

She'd ask, though. Because it was something she did want to know.

"Cruz was a para rescue jumper." Her stepfather must've opened David's service record right there, on the spot, based on the pensive note in his commentary. "Air Force. Obviously not much ambition for himself, since he left the service without advancing as far as his records indicate he had the potential to achieve."

Of course it was always about potential. What her stepfather never understood was that people measured success in different ways. Their goals weren't the same as what he'd expect. What satisfied a person—made them feel whole—wasn't something quantifiable or repeatable in each individual the way following a recipe to bake a cake would be.

"Self-worth isn't always measured by promotions or advancements." She should've kept her mouth shut but nope, the words had slipped out dry and disapproving as you please.

"Your opinion in this case may be biased," her stepfather snapped. He had no tolerance for her opinions, especially when they were expressed with "attitude," as he'd made a point to tell her back when she was younger.

He couldn't know, though. Not about her and David. Her stomach twisted. "How so?"

"You're working side by side with the man. Obviously you're pleased with the cooperative arrangement." Her stepfather huffed. "Any partnership introduces bias. You're too close. You can't see the forest for the trees.

This is why I insisted you give me *timely* status reports so I can ensure you have the objective perspective this requires. That asset is too valuable to ruin with sentimentality."

This, she could address. The idea of him knowing about her and David was too many levels of complicated. No way was she going there until she absolutely had to.

"I've demonstrated repeatedly my ability to accurately assess and rehabilitate dogs of a wide variety of breeds and temperaments." And her record demonstrated it in glowing personal recommendations from her clients. "No matter how cute the tiny toy breed or how intimidating the larger breed, I approach each case with objectivity. As soft as some might consider the psychological foundation to the rehabilitation approach, it is by no means compromised by sentimentality."

It also turned out this way. Conversation ramped up until the big words drowned out the practical meaning of the discussion. It was a contest to see who could speak with greater formality and not get caught at a loss for words. It wasn't about the original topic anymore.

"In this case, it's not you I have concerns over."

Oh. Lyn rocked back on her heels. Almost uttered the gut response and ruined the whole conversation. "I see."

"David Cruz is obviously working with Atlas in honor of the memory of his deceased friend. They served together." Her stepfather cleared his throat. "I can sympathize to a certain extent. It's not easy to lose the men you've fought beside. But at least it was overseas and in combat, as opposed to some sort of overdose or home and asleep in bed."

Because passing away at peace in bed was the most horrible way for a person to die.

Some people were willing to put away their uniforms. Maybe not her stepfather, and she could respect him or the choice, but she also wondered if he ever gave any sort of consideration to the alternative choices people made.

"I want your status reports expanded to give me insight into how Cruz is reacting to Atlas's progress." Captain Jones made a clicking noise with his tongue. "My concern is that he is chasing ghosts better laid to rest instead of focusing on the task at hand. I do not want this asset put at risk because a man couldn't leave well enough alone."

There was an interesting way to put it.

"What would he be looking into?" Because now she wanted to know why her stepfather was coincidentally concerned with David's investigation of Calhoun's death. It wasn't a secret as far as she could tell. David had mentioned openly going to the nearby military base to look over the reports.

"Every friend is convinced there are suspect circumstances around the way a man has died in service. They're looking for a reason. Call it a form of grieving. My concern is that Cruz could become delusional, depending on how much he's indulging in other bad habits veterans occasionally pick up once they leave the service. While you are the contractor I've engaged to work with this asset, he is also involved in the project and could reflect on it negatively."

Ugh. And it was always about how things could reflect back on his reputation.

Anger had been slowly building through this latter part of the discussion. "Why single out David Cruz? There are several trainers here on site and there've been handlers involved with Atlas since he returned to the US. Did you keep close tabs on every one of them?"

"Once this asset came under my sphere of influence, everyone involved with it was scrutinized, yes." Captain Jones huffed. She could almost picture him tugging the front of his uniform straight in his annoyance. "Cruz is of particular concern both because of his service record and his direct involvement with the asset."

She bit back an ugly retort.

Her stepfather was judging a man he'd never met and assuming the worst about him based on the unfortunate outcomes of other people's lives. She wouldn't deny things happened like this. Truly. It happened a lot. And she understood that.

But the men of Hope's Crossing Kennels had built something so much better here with their energy after they'd left active duty. To suspect any of them of having succumbed to delusions or alcoholism or drug usage— any of the things her stepfather was alluding to—was so completely wrong, she couldn't ignore it.

"These are good men here." She said it slowly and clearly. All pretenses of friendly conversation dropped. "I would stake my reputation on the quality of their training and the kennels they've established. They build a safe haven and are continuing to give to the community in their own way. It's not the Service, but it is still incredibly admirable."

Silence. Then her stepfather cleared his throat again. "All the same, I would like reports on his approach and activities while he's working with you and the dog. All influences on the asset are of interest to me at this time."

"He has a name. Atlas is doing well." He could acknowledge David as a good man and Atlas as a living soul, not a simple thing to be inventoried.

"He has a designation number and responds to the name 'Atlas's." Her stepfather made the clarification. "If you want to work with more military working dogs, you should ensure you refer to them as both their designation and their name."

She didn't know how to respond to that. He was right. And it killed her to admit it so she kept silent.

"This could be the first of many contracts for you and you would do well to look at it as a key objective to come out as the lead trainer in this." There he went, setting goals for somebody other than himself. Maybe it worked for the people under his command. It didn't suit her. "I didn't mention this at the beginning because you have a stubborn tendency to go in exact opposition to my suggestions in order to spite me. However, I hope you've matured enough to realize this is counterproductive to your career development and I would like to think you wouldn't jeopardize the career you've worked hard to establish against my better judgment in order to spite me again."

Of course not. He'd trapped her in logic. Go against his recommendation and she hurt her own career. Follow his suggestion and she'd be following his lead, doing exactly what he wanted her to do. He won either way.

"Working independently is admirable, Evelyn." And there was her full first name.

She gritted her teeth.

"What it doesn't give you experience in is leadership." His voice took on a distinctively patronizing tone. "Only by working with people—actual humans—and earning their respect, can you learn leadership."

"Not everyone respects you." As soon as she said it, she snapped her mouth shut. Now she sounded petulant even to herself.

He remained unperturbed. "No. You are correct. Let's clarify then and say you become a true leader when people follow you even if they don't respect you because they have no choice but to acknowledge yours is the better judgment."

Like this particular situation.

"I'm sorry you don't like this." He paused. "And I would like to remind you that life isn't about getting people to like you. It's about ensuring that what needs to be done, is. They can hate you and it wouldn't matter so long as they do what needs doing."

She sighed. "I'm not in the military."

It wasn't so much the status reports. She gave those to her clients regularly as a standard practice. Being able to see the progress of their relationship with their dog over time positively reinforced the hard work involved and illustrated the value of her services. But she didn't work with people or dogs who didn't like her. If she wasn't able to build a rapport, she refunded the money and dissolved the contract.

"No, but this would be true in any corporate environment." She didn't hear it but she could picture him shrugging.

A key reason she'd chosen a profession with the flexibility and freedom she had now. It hadn't been the easy path by any means. But it had been truer to the way she wanted to spend her time.

"All of this complexity is only conjecture and words." She'd had enough of both. "For me, it boils down to a simple truth. I like dogs better than I like people. I will continue to work with Atlas because I want to see him happy."

"A working dog is happy working. Not so different from a worthwhile human being." Her stepfather continued with his inexorable logic.

God, was he never wrong?

"I think we've beat this conversation into the ground." She was definitely worn out from it. He always did this to her. Give him another ten minutes and she'd have a raging migraine.

"Fine. I want your agreement, though, that you will update your status reports in accordance with my request."

She sighed. Anything. Anything at all to end this. "You did not make a request. You instructed me. Understood. I'll have a report ready tomorrow."

"Tonight."

She'd accuse him of needing to have the final word but he hadn't terminated the call. He was waiting for her to acknowledge him. Damn it. Forget time in the Service. Her stepfather alone was enough to drive her to heavy drinking.

A brisk knock scared her right out of her thoughts.

"Lyn?" David's voice came through the door.

"Fine. Tonight." She ended the call before her stepfather could hear anything more or say anything to put her in an even worse frame of mind.

CHAPTER SEVENTEEN

David let himself into the cabin, scanning the room more out of habit than any suspicion of someone in there with Lyn. She'd have found a way to warn him. His girl had a good head on her shoulders, after all. The last couple of days had proved it.

Something was off, though. Lyn had a deer-in-headlights look on her face and while it was adorable, he didn't think she intended for him to read her so easily. She was used to reading the dogs and people around her, not the other way around. Her ability to detect bull-shit seemed as fine-tuned as any delicate instrument, but he'd developed his perception around some of the most closed-off personalities a person could come into contact with and remain sane.

So to him, her expressions and body language were an open book. One he enjoyed reading as he ran his hands over her, kissed her into quiet desperation.

Her current tension wasn't anticipation and nothing

about her posture was an invitation. He was a little disappointed actually, but more immediately he was concerned.

"What's wrong?" And whatever it was, he wanted to eliminate it.

She blinked. Panic flashed in those big blue eyes for a second before she got hold of herself. "Oh. Nothing."

Uh huh. Try again, darling. "I could guess, but we both know this would go a lot faster if you told me so I could help you."

She laughed, a short huff of dry humor. "If it's all the same, I'd like to avoid introducing you to even the concept of my stepfather."

His stomach dropped. Guess introducing him to the family wasn't high on her list of priorities. Funny, the idea of introducing her to his hadn't occurred to him but the idea of not hit him in the gut. Hard.

Her gaze was on him now and she took a step toward him. "I'd love for you to meet my mother someday. If the idea of it doesn't make you want to pack your bags and head someplace far, far away. It's just introducing you to my stepfather would mean I'd have to *see* my stepfather and I try to avoid him pretty much all the time."

The sucker-punched sensation eased up a bit and he took a slow breath. "Okay. I take it you talk to your stepfather on the phone, though."

Had to be who he'd heard her talking to if the man was at the forefront of her mind. He'd not wanted to eavesdrop though. It'd been why he knocked and waited for her to tell him it was okay to enter. Suddenly, he was more careful of her personal space than he'd be with normal people. He honestly couldn't care less if he got other people upset but her—well, things had evolved.

"Yeah." She drew out the confirmation as she looked away, out the window. Obviously she had a lot on her mind when it came to her stepfather. "Recently more so than the last several years."

And not in a good way, apparently.

"Yeah?" In his experience, family had a way of coming in and out of life, sort of the way comets were gone for years then back in the night sky. Signs of the Apocalypse, too. "Any family trouble?"

Lyn shook her head. "More of a disagreement."

She scrunched up her face, the tip of her tongue showing.

Damn, she was adorable and sexy simultaneously. He had no idea how she managed it but he liked it. A lot.

"Most of my discussions with him are disagreements, really. So it's not a surprise. It's just frustrating."

David didn't know what to say. He waited and when her weight shifted forward as if she was about to walk toward him, he opened his arms in invitation.

She came to him without hesitation and snuggled deep as he closed his arms around her. Warmth spread through him and he dropped a kiss on her hair. She might never understand how much it meant to him, the way she'd come to him. No hesitation. No fear. No reservations. Every time she did it, he came unhinged. "Family always seems to know the exact buttons to push."

She nodded, her face pressed against his chest. "Mmm hmm."

After a moment, her arms slipped around his waist. He was pretty happy to stand there and enjoy.

But Lyn wasn't the type to be silent for long. He grinned when her head popped up, almost catching him in the chin. "What buttons does your family push?"

Oh, hell. "There's a heavy answer to what you probably meant to be a light question."

She leaned back in his embrace so she could gaze up at him, her expression somber. "I'll take the heavy with the fun. I'm guessing it requires a lot to get under your skin when it's people who matter. You're incredibly patient once you've decided someone is worth your time."

He grunted in response and she giggled and rose up in his arms to press a soft kiss against his jaw. Embarrassed, he tucked her back against him and thought hard. He wasn't sure what to do with her.

If he wanted to keep her, he owed her answers to her questions. And the intent might not have been clearly thought out before, but he did. He wanted to keep her near, like this.

"I enlisted pretty young and I didn't have a handle on how much it'd changed me my first time out. When I got home, I wasn't good at compartmentalizing yet, or pretending to be...normal."

He remembered the change in their expressions, the moment when real smiles froze into polite horrified masks.

"They expected you to be normal? What was normal in their eyes?" Lyn's questions were murmured against his shirt and her arms remained around him. No hint of her pulling away.

He tightened his arms around her anyway, because she wasn't trying to get away.

"I was rough around the edges, rude." He shrugged.

"It was embarrassing to them. They felt I'd developed bad habits, and I had. I smoked. I drank. I cursed at everyone, even the kids, without meaning to."

Lyn nodded and he absorbed her acceptance like a balm on his memories. Funny how they were still raw. He'd thought he'd made his peace with the reality of it.

"It wasn't the habits that were the problem, though. Those were...manifestations. I needed, craved a change in my state of mind. Whatever could do it for me, I went after it. It was all to take me out of the numb and help me feel something different than the shit place I was in most of the time." He cleared his throat, suddenly thick with emotion. "Next time I came home, my father quietly said they didn't feel comfortable leaving the kids home alone with me. Never been so ashamed in my life. I'd never hurt those kids. Never."

But his being near them was a bad influence and maybe even a danger. He'd accepted it. Taken accountability.

Lyn's arms tightened around his waist. "You respected their wishes."

"'Course."

"But did they ever come to you, try to understand you?" There was a thread of anger there in her voice. For him. And he found himself holding onto it like a man drowning. No one had ever been angry on his behalf, not a civilian. Not someone outside the service. Not someone who hadn't lived it. Lyn was, though, for him. "They were concerned about the kids and themselves. Fine. But did they make any effort at all to be there for you?"

"I was a grown man. Fighting for my country. I could take care of myself."

It's what he'd told himself over and over. He'd never had this part of the conversation with his family.

"They had expectations of you but didn't stop, did they, to ask you if they were fair?" Lyn was working up a temper now. Her hands had fisted the back of his shirt.

"Life isn't fair, darling. I'm okay with that." He'd felt he deserved it.

"I'm not!" Her head popped up this time and he captured her mouth in a kiss.

He was more than hungry for her. He wanted to drown in her sweetness, the way she made him feel whole and cared for. As he kissed her, he continued to hold her close and urged her body to meld against his. A needy whimper escaped her lips and he nipped the corner of her mouth before settling his over hers for another deep kiss.

Bitterness, disappointment—it had all sat ignored and festering for a long time and finally it had washed away in the wake of this tidal wave of . . . whatever the hell she made him feel.

God, she made him happy.

He finally let them both up for air and she was clutching at him for balance. Which was all good as far as he was concerned. "Let it go. It's okay now."

"How is it in any way okay?" She was a little breathless. He'd have to work on making her more so. But she was still riled up.

She was hot when she was mad. Sexy hot.

"Because it's past and gone now and wouldn't do anyone any good. It'd hurt them to know but not be able to go back and fix it." The truth of it settled in his bones as he spoke it out loud. "I don't want to cause them any hurt or regret. I just want to find happy on my own."

He smiled down at her, his happy, and wondered if she'd understand. She could be dense about the impact she had on the people around her.

She was still hung up on the issue, though—had it between her teeth and wouldn't give it up.

"Let it go," he said again, putting more force behind his words. "I want to so I need you to as well. Deal?"

Defiance was still there, a fire in her eyes. But she sighed and relaxed in his arms. "Okay. But only because you've built so much here for yourself now. This place is good for you."

"You're good for me." There, he'd said it. Out loud, directly to her. Not to the air or to Atlas; to her.

She bit her lip. "You mean that?"

He'd said it, hadn't he? He could say the obvious but he'd rather kiss her instead. So he did. And when he pulled back, he brushed his lips over hers, teasing, until she rose up on her tiptoes and claimed his mouth with her own insistence.

She did get demanding when he teased her enough. He should tease her more often.

* * *

Lyn couldn't get enough of David. Really, she couldn't.

Kissing him was everything she could ever want and not enough all at the same time. She loved the feel of his mouth on hers, the taste of him, and the way his hands roamed over her body. He let her pull back and brush her lips against his, playing, and nip at his lower lip. He bit her back gently in kind and then settled his mouth over hers in a deeper kiss to steal her breath away.

He caught her by surprise, dipping low and hoisting her up in his arms, and she squealed. Embarrassed, she buried her face in his shoulder but he only chuckled as he strode into the bedroom.

"I like the sounds you make." His voice was rough, deepened with a need she'd only recently started to get to know.

She clung to him as he lowered her onto the bed, coming down on top of her. "I like the things you do to me."

"Yeah?" He smiled against her lips and pressed his pelvis into hers.

"Mmm." She nuzzled his neck and then set her teeth against his skin.

He paused, his hands tightening on her body. "Do that again."

She did, this time sucking a little as she bit him.

He groaned and kneed her legs apart. When he pushed his thigh higher between her legs, she let her eyes flutter shut and her head fall backward. "Tease."

He chuckled. "Oh, this? Not this."

His weight lifted off her then and her eyes flew open as she looked for him. But David hadn't left, only rolled off the bed to chuck his clothes off. He gave her a challenging look, his eyebrow arched, and she smiled and pulled off her own shirt. She was wriggling out of her jeans when he rejoined her on the bed and helped pull them down her legs.

Fun. Lighthearted. She couldn't help smiling. This

was different from her other experiences with men. Those had been short, to the point, and just about the sex. With David, there was give and take, fun and moments of passion to steal her breath away. She learned about him when they were together like this, in ways that didn't involve conversation. And she learned new things about herself, too, parts of her personality he brought out in her.

He caressed and kissed his way up her legs, bringing her thoughts back to exactly what he was doing. When he reached her panties, he ran a finger under the edge until she squirmed. Grasping both sides, he pulled those down and tossed them over the edge of the bed to join her pants.

"Pretty." His gaze ran over her from her toes, up her legs, and lingered over her sex before traveling up her belly to her breasts and finally finding her gaze, holding steady there. "So incredibly pretty."

Heat filled her everywhere his gaze had gone, and that was all over. She bit her lip.

His gaze still holding hers, he cupped her sex in one hand and reached up to caress one of her breasts. His touch was so intimate, comforting and compelling at the same time. When his fingers parted her, exploring and teasing her entrance, she let her eyes flutter closed and arched her back.

One of his fingers entered her and she bucked, the pleasure of his touch already driving her crazy. Then his other hand, caressing her breast as it was, shifted just enough for him to brush her nipple with his thumb. She cried out.

"Wet and hot." He slid his finger in and out of her

in a slow rhythm. "Is this the way you like me to touch you?"

She panted. If he wanted her to use words, he was a cruel man.

Then he pushed two fingers into her and she arched for him again, fisting the sheets.

He chuckled. "I'll take that as a yes."

Oh good. She'd keep breathing and words could come later. Because the way he continued to touch her, play with her, was sending pleasure coursing through her body until it coiled low in her abdomen. When he found her clitoris with his thumb, adding pressure in time with the slide of his fingers inside her, she lost ability to think at all.

He petted her through the orgasm, prolonging it with gentle strokes. And when she opened her eyes again, he climbed over her, putting on the condom as she watched. Then he leaned forward until his forehead touched hers. "May I?"

She loved the way he asked, didn't presume, each time. In answer, she twined her legs with his and looked deep into his eyes, then nodded.

He reached down with one hand and positioned himself, then entered her in a smooth slide. She gasped as he filled her, her muscles stretching to accommodate him. This was another way they fit, so, so well.

Once he was buried to the hilt inside her, he paused, his breath hot in her ear. Then he began to move, firm and steady, pulling out and sliding back into her in a deep steady rhythm.

She groaned, her already sensitized body rising to a crest again. "David, please."

Not even sure what she was asking for, she clutched at his shoulders, tried to encourage him. He drove into her faster, harder, his hands reaching around her to cup her behind and angle her for an even better fit. Every stroke pushed her closer to the edge until she arched under him helplessly, gasping.

He buried his face into her shoulder and growled as he came too, shuddering with the power of his release.

Lyn kept her arms wrapped around him as he slowly relaxed, lowering his weight onto her. His breath was hot against her skin and after a few moments, he rolled to one side and rose up to give her a quick kiss on the bridge of her nose.

"Be right back." He went into the bathroom and returned a few moments later with a cool, damp washcloth to help wipe her down.

This was a gesture she appreciated, too. His care, and the way he wanted to see to her comfort, took their time together beyond sex to something much more intimate. She wanted this.

Once he settled back onto the bed with her, she snuggled up against his side, content.

"What's on the agenda for Atlas's training later today?"

He froze next to her.

Unsettled, she rose up on one arm so she could see his face. "I didn't mean to break the mood. No work talk in bed?"

She'd said it in a semi-teasing tone, but lost even that as his brows drew together.

He sat up. "I'd wanted to talk to you about this, but I didn't plan for us to get distracted."

She raised her eyebrows. "Us sleeping together is getting distracted?"

He reached out and ran his hand up her arm. "You are absolutely a distraction, in really good ways. Please don't take this wrong."

She drew in a slow breath. "Okay. I'll try not to, but let's get back to what you got distracted from."

"This is going to be bad timing." He eyed her with trepidation.

Oh, great. "Better bad timing than not talking to me at all."

He nodded, ran a hand through his hair, then got started. "I was coming over here to talk to you about how we were going to move forward with Atlas's training schedule."

She nodded. So far, nothing to be worried about.

"You've done incredible things with his rehabilitation. His socialization is up to par based on the last couple of days of travel." He paused and she waited. His words came out faster. "I wanted to suggest we adjust your participation in his training to intermittent sessions while I focus more on his specialized skill sets for explosives detection and human search."

It was her turn to raise an eyebrow. Dogs like Atlas searched out humans for other reasons than the search-and-rescue dogs trained in the United States. There were other reactions built into Atlas's training, other behaviors expected. He was expected to act more independently in the search and respond differently on locating said human. She could understand how she didn't have the experience in the training technique to work with Atlas for those behaviors.

Still, this was more than two trainers talking about techniques. She gathered the sheets up around her, suddenly vulnerable.

"Intermittent." She said the word slowly. "What sort of intervals?"

"Well, maybe twice this coming week, then we could move to once a week or even once every other week. You could go check on your other clients and come back for his sessions." David's voice had gone neutral, the way he did when he wanted to distance himself from a situation. Compartmentalizing.

"You want me to leave." Oh God, and they'd just slept together. "This was good-bye sex?"

"No!" He tried to reach for her but stopped when she flinched back.

"Sounds like it is." Embarrassment and anger burned through her.

"I don't want to say good-bye, Lyn, but I want you safe." David didn't sound neutral anymore. In fact, the urgency in his tone drew her gaze back to his. "Atlas and me, we're in this. We're going to find out exactly what happened to Calhoun and we're going to make sure this video doesn't get buried. The deeper we get into this, the more likely shit is going to rain down around my head. I want you clear of it all."

She couldn't argue with the danger. The car chase the other night had frightened the hell out of her.

"When this is over, I'd like to come to you." David leaned toward her. "Or you can come back here, whichever you want. I'd like for us to see where this thing between us goes."

"But you want me to give up my work with Atlas. Just

leave." She gritted her teeth. "I think you need to grab your clothes and step out."

"Lyn—"

She shook her head. "You want me to think about this with a cool head, you need to take yourself out of here."

He studied her for a minute, then did as she asked.

CHAPTER EIGHTEEN

What's wrong?"

Cruz scowled at Rojas where he sat at the breakfast bar playing some game on his smartphone. "Who says anything's wrong?"

"You've been glued to Lyn's side since she got here." Forte pulled open the fridge and peered inside. "If you're not with her, you're with the dogs or in your office at your computer. Since you walked in here and sat your ass down in a chair, I figure Rojas's got a point. Something's wrong."

"True." Cruz took the beer Forte offered him and took a swig as he thought about how to fix the mess he'd made. He didn't hide anything from Forte or Rojas. It was part of the reason they were able to live with each other. Trust.

In fact, he'd sought them out. Staying inside your own head for too long resulted in spinning wheels. He needed their perspectives to see his way clear.

"So where's Lyn?" Forte asked, leaning against the counter.

The three of them lingered like this sometimes. It wasn't as if they were lifelong friends. They'd served together and in a lot of ways they knew more about each other, because of that intense period of time, than most people ever found out in a lifetime. It'd been Forte who'd told Cruz and Rojas to come to Pennsylvania. And hell, Cruz hadn't had anyplace in particular he'd wanted to go right out of the service. Neither had Rojas. The man had only had one prerequisite: a safe place to raise his daughter. Hope's Crossing Kennels had been a place to start, and if Cruz hadn't been a fit he'd have moved on. Only, Forte had made it the right place to be for all of them. Expectations were straightforward. Life was pretty simple. And it was a life.

Cruz hadn't realized he'd been missing anything until Lyn came along, and now he'd told her to leave.

"Packing." Cruz sounded sullen and he didn't want to. It'd been a solid decision. Logical.

The other two men froze.

After a moment, Rojas started playing his game again. "You get into a fight or decide things were getting too complicated?"

Of course the other two had noticed. They'd spent their military careers taking cues from body posture, subtle signals, and the smallest gestures. Either of them could've noticed the new intimacy in the way Lyn responded to him from the moment they'd returned. Maybe even as soon as they'd stepped out of the car. He'd have noticed if it'd been one of them.

"Complicated." Cruz scowled at the beer. It was

cold but not cold enough. Or he was too irritated to enjoy it. "This thing with the video Calhoun sent me. There's too much shit involved. She'd be in the line of fire."

Cruz glanced around. Rojas's daughter was likely over at the cottage they shared but he should've checked before shooting off his mouth. They all tried to keep the cursing to a minimum around the Boom. Unfortunately, the kid walked around quiet as a cat and hell, they all cursed worse than sailors.

Rojas shook his head without taking his eyes off his game. "Woman's already been attacked twice. At the hotel and right here on this property."

Forte growled.

"Not a one of us is happy about how that happened and it won't happen again," Rojas continued. They all had reasons to ensure the security of this place. It'd become a haven. It needed to stay that way. "But what I'm saying is this: she's already been yanked directly into the middle of whatever is going on. You're not going to save her any issues by sending her away."

Forte nodded. "Whoever tossed her hotel room thought she had information and it was before we even knew what Calhoun had left with Atlas. They think she's a part of it and she is at risk no matter how far away you send her."

Cruz scowled. "I can keep focus on me. I've got lines on at least one more of the SEALs on that team. One of them is going to give away more than they intend to. We're all good, but over enough time we all develop cracks in our stories."

He hadn't been a SEAL but he'd been Special Forces.

And he'd been a man with secrets to keep. The trouble with need-to-know information was if you knew, you didn't want to. Secrets lived with you forever and eventually you were desperate for a way to purge them. One of these guys wished he was out but he had family to protect. There had to be at least one or two more who wanted out.

"Maybe so." Forte spoke slowly. He had a tendency to think as he spoke and random brilliance occasionally fell out of his mouth. Most of the time, though, it was bull-shit. Still, the rare jewels of wisdom were worth it. "I'm thinking anyone with enough influence to have SEALs afraid on domestic soil, not just on a mission, has a far enough reach to cause her harm the minute she leaves this property."

So this time was one of those one in a million moments where Forte's point was so true, it should've been obvious to David from the beginning.

Cruz cursed again.

"It's too dangerous here. They've got eyes on her already." Cruz couldn't see a way to get Lyn out of this mess. "She's got clients on the West Coast, a business to run after all this is over."

"And she planned to be here until this project was complete, right?" Rojas asked.

"Yeah. It was open-ended, though. No idea when Atlas is going to be declared recovered." Beckhorn had Cruz's back on that. It was the way any of them worked. They took as long as the dog needed to be ready for the work it had to do. And every dog was different.

"I'm guessing she didn't have clients scheduled any time soon because of that." Rojas could be so damned reasonable. "She's not going to have an immediate job to pick up where this one lets off."

Great. More guilt to add to the weight in Cruz's chest.

He shook his head. "You've both got good thoughts. No disrespect here, but I've got a gut feeling. She needs to get out of here. I've got no logic to go up against the reasoning you've put out there. It's just a feeling."

And even as he admitted it, he hated it. Because it wasn't a logical decision. He didn't have good reasons even if he'd convinced himself he did. And Lyn was a smart woman. She'd have refuted his reasons every bit as effectively as Forte and Rojas had just done if Cruz had given her a chance. Only he hadn't. And he'd probably damaged whatever it was between them in the process.

She was very mad at him. And when she had time to cool off and really think it through, she was going to be over here to tell him exactly what his two best friends already had.

He raised his gaze and looked each of them directly in the eyes. "Something isn't right. She needs to get someplace safe."

They got it. He could see it in their expressions. Sometimes it wasn't about logic. They'd all learned to follow their instincts when everything else in the world told them to do different. Following those gut feelings had seen them through hell and back, through multiple deployments each. Sometimes the world didn't make sense.

"You could lose her if you push her out of here." Rojas's warning was almost inaudible. He would know. He'd lost a wife by pushing her away. "If she decides to move on before you catch back up with her, are you ready to deal with that?"

No.

Cruz swallowed. "I'm going to have to."

This was the right thing to do. And if nothing else, each one of them did his damned best to do the right thing.

* * *

When Lyn came through the door, both Forte and Rojas made a break for it.

"Good luck, man." Forte gave him a parting slap on the back.

Great thing about brotherhood: they were willing to leave a man to the inevitable without any witnesses to see him ripped to shreds. Cruz appreciated it.

Lyn strode into the kitchen and came to a stop outside of arm's reach. The distance she left between them hit him like a brick wall. She'd changed into a fresh pair of jeans and a soft knit top. Its fabric clung to her curves and he wanted nothing more than to run his hands over her. Her hair was gathered up in a knot, looking suspiciously wet. She must've taken a shower. He should've stayed and joined her.

But no. He'd gone and pushed her away, so he needed to clear his head of things he shouldn't be caught up in thinking and focus on what she had to say. Thing was, she muddied up his brain process without even trying.

She lifted her chin. "I've been thinking about what you said. Not one of your reasons holds up against good, solid reasoning."

Here we go.

He was hoping she'd listen to him once he let her blow off her steam. Maybe she'd understand if he explained. He was willing to give it a try. She was the most instinctual trainer he'd ever met and if anyone could understand what was driving him to risk this thing they had, it'd be her. He hoped.

"I'm listening." He turned toward her in his seat, giving her his full attention because she deserved it.

Maybe she wasn't used to it, because she hesitated. It took her a full minute to recover, visibly gather her thoughts and open her mouth to speak.

"Sorry to interrupt." Forte was back. "Beckhorn has been trying to get ahold of you and you haven't been answering your phone. We've got company waiting at the main gate and neither of you is going to be happy with what they're here for."

Atlas.

He'd gotten pretty good at reading her expressions. Same thought crossed her mind and there was a hint of fear, too. They'd both been ready for a scuffle but neither of them had been prepared to let Atlas go. He'd brought them together.

They moved for the front door in unison.

* * *

Lyn nabbed her laptop bag on the way out the front door, letting David get a step ahead of her. He'd outdistance her regardless, with his ground-eating stride and longer legs. When he didn't, she was silently grateful. The partnership between them wasn't gone, despite his telling her to leave earlier.

Please don't let this be over yet.

They'd barely started to explore what was between them and had only made partial progress with Atlas. She wasn't ready to leave either of those unfinished.

The two men at the front gate were standing next to a blocky SUV, bare to the point of utilitarian. But then, she was used to the rental SUVs with frills and extra features. It wasn't obviously a military vehicle as far as she knew but it didn't look like the usual thing an average person would buy, either.

Add to it their stance and general attitude and Lyn figured they had to be military. Spending time around David, Brandon, and Alex had gotten her used to the body language. Neither appeared to be particularly intimidating and, in fact, wore such neutral expressions she studied them even more closely.

David probably saw more than she did. Whatever this situation was, and she had her suspicions, she was glad she was side by side with him. Standing up to these men alone would've been a lot more of a challenge.

The men waited for them to approach rather than coming to meet them. When David came to a stop, so did she, at a distance slightly farther away than would normally allow for comfortable conversation. Already there were irritating undercurrents being exchanged between David and the strangers. Glances and minute frowns. Dogs and cats weren't the only ones that got into pissing contests.

"David Cruz and Evelyn Jones?" the older man asked, but it sounded more like a statement than a question. He knew he had the right people. "Sergeant Zuccolin. I have orders to retrieve the military asset known as Atlas. Came through early this morning. Captain Beckhorn has been notified."

Lyn preferred straightforward souls like David, Alex, and Brandon. This man talked more like a politician despite his brevity. His tone was too pleasant. He spoke as if they were all good friends and this wouldn't be met with any protest of any kind.

"I'd like to see a copy of those orders, Sergeant Zuccolin." David's tone was flat.

The older man clenched his jaw. "I'm sure Captain Beckhorn has forwarded them to you electronically."

"To be honest, there may have been a lag in communication." David made it sound as if that sort of thing happened all the time. "He only called as we were informed of your arrival. I had to choose between coming out to greet you and speaking to him. If you men wouldn't mind waiting a few minutes, I'd be happy to call him back to hear what he has to say."

"There's coffee up at the main house." Lyn regretted mentioning it immediately. Both strangers gave her the once-over and dismissed her from consideration. The look was so incredibly familiar from her childhood and the occasions when her father had brought guests to the house. She cursed herself for not choosing something with more impact to say first.

A person has seconds to establish an impression. In terms of appearance, she was slight and definitely a civilian. On opening her mouth, she hadn't had any great contribution to the conversation. Anything she said from here on out would barely be heard.

Damn it. She had better social skills than this.

The only reason she could think of for being this off-balance was the discussion with her stepfather directly followed by her aborted faceoff with David. Too many thoughts were churning inside her head and she hadn't had a chance to resolve anything. She'd need to shove all that aside and quickly.

"Waiting won't be necessary." Sergeant Zuccolin glanced at his companion, who stepped over to their car and retrieved a folder from the passenger side. "We brought a hard copy."

"Appreciated." No irritation in David's comment or expression. These men were all going on minimal auditory or body language cues. Poker would be torture with any of them.

David read through the orders. It took a few minutes and they all waited. She cheered inwardly as he took the time to look for the loophole. There had to be one.

Then as he looked up and met her gaze, she realized it was because he couldn't find one. The men had come here and could afford to wait because there wasn't anything David could do. She stared at him. Opened her mouth.

He shook his head once. Brief. Barely a movement. He was giving up.

Well, she didn't plan to.

She lifted her chin and stared directly into the sergeant's eyes. "You know who I am, I assume, other than my name."

Throwing around her identity—actually her stepfather's—irked her to no end, but in this case it was the only card she had in her hand. She'd use it.

Practicality.

Sergeant Zuccolin nodded with reluctance.

She didn't blink or turn her head. She kept her gaze steady on his. "Good. Then you'll see the wisdom of sending your colleague there over to the guest cabin to gather my belongings and place them in the vehicle. I'll see to Atlas and prepare him for the trip."

"Wait a minute." Anger was starting to show in David's demeanor and she didn't dare make eye contact with him. "I want to know what business you have accompanying our dog off this premises. We are supposed to be working on his retraining together."

"Atlas is the property of the military, as I have been reminded multiple times, even by you, Mr. Cruz." It hurt to use his formal name this way. She wondered if he'd ever forgive her. Considering what was going to come to light next, probably not. "My contract is to *rehabilitate* him, not work with you. I go where he goes."

This would be for the best. It was becoming very clear whatever was going on around Atlas, her stepfather hadn't been keeping tabs on her for his reputation's sake. He'd been using her to keep up to date on David and how much he was learning about the circumstances around Calhoun's death. If she went with Atlas, David could be free to continue investigating without her stepfather's scrutiny.

Sergeant Zuccolin didn't step in. Man must be wiser than she'd initially given him credit for. Instead, he leaned over to his fellow soldier and murmured a few words.

The man nodded sharply and approached Lyn. "Ma'am, if you'd show me where to go, I'll accompany you to gather both your belongings and the asset."

She nodded.

David wasn't finished, though. "Enlighten me. Who are you that you can amend their orders to go with them?"

"It's not about who I am." It never was. She'd struggled for years to build her own identity and it still boiled down to this. "It's about who my father is. Captain Francis Jones of the US Navy. I get the impression he's a few pay grades higher than your Air Force Captain friend in San Antonio. He sponsored my request to be allowed to work with Atlas. I'm sure he'll confirm upon request."

And she was sure she hadn't made any friends for making the comparison in ranks between Air Force and Navy.

But it was worth it. David's jaw tightened and his eyes narrowed slightly. There might've been a vein popping across his forehead but she might've imagined it. Either way, he was angry, not hurt. And his anger was much more preferable to leaving him visibly hurt in front of these men.

"Jones is a common name." David had his calm well in hand. In fact, his tone had gone cold. "I'd thought it was a coincidence. I stand corrected."

"Well, then, there's just a few things left to do then." Lyn was at a loss for anything else to say so she walked past David and headed for the cabin.

It took moments, since she was packed anyway. The soldier who'd accompanied her didn't comment. Good, because she didn't owe *him* any explanations. She was too busy hoping someday David would give her the chance.

Atlas was on his feet and happy to see her when she approached the kennel. She almost cried when he eagerly sat and turned his head so she could attach the leash to his collar. He must've picked up her mood, though, because on the walk back, he remained at a precise heel position. He took notice of the man walking with them and Sergeant Zuccolin when they approached. They were unknown and Atlas regarded both of them as threats in relation to her.

"Load him in the crate." Sergeant Zuccolin gave the order to the man next to her.

"I'll take care of securing him." Lyn made her statement firm and didn't give anyone time to argue with her.

She led Atlas around to the back of the SUV. The soldier hurried after her with her bags and juggled them for a minute in order to open the door for her.

"Atlas, *over*." On her command, Atlas jumped easily up into the back of the SUV. "*Hok.*"

Atlas obeyed her immediately, entering the crate and turning to face her as he lay down. His ears were cocked backward, though, and his head tilted to one side as he regarded her. This wasn't like the previous road trip and he had to be sensing her stress. It was a good thing these men weren't watching him and probably didn't care to use him to guess at what was going through her mind.

David, on the other hand, had moved around to a vantage point where he could see both her and Atlas. Carefully keeping her eyes on Atlas, she leaned in and gave the big dog a caress on the cheek. "Hopefully you'll understand one day soon."

Words for David, not Atlas.

"Miss Jones, we'd like to get going." Sergeant Zuccolin had lost whatever patience he had initially.

"Will there be stops along the way? I didn't have a

chance to take Atlas to relieve himself before sending him into the crate." She didn't want to leave. Everything about this was rushed, off, and for once she desperately wished she could call her stepfather.

It wasn't likely he'd ordered this. Maybe he hadn't even known. His last instructions to her indicated he'd expected her to be around David for a while longer at least. This didn't fit.

"I assure you, we'll be stopping before you know it." An odd quirk popped in the sergeant's voice as he spoke. Or maybe she'd imagined it.

She nodded and closed Atlas's crate door. No bungee cords or anything to secure the latch so she left it. Atlas was well-behaved now so she doubted it'd be an issue.

"Good-bye, Mr. Cruz. It was a pleasure to work with you." She met David's gaze this time but it was still frigid.

He only nodded. "Miss Jones."

And that was it. She turned back toward the SUV. The other soldier had the front passenger seat door open for her and she climbed in without looking back. As they drove away, she tried to unobtrusively watch David in the side-view mirror.

He never moved.

Then they turned onto the main road and trees hid him from view.

CHAPTER NINETEEN

It didn't take a genius to catch the hint that she wasn't wanted. Her two military companions were stoic and noncommunicative as they pulled onto the main road headed for the highway.

Oh, she hadn't expected them to be friendly and chatty or even make small talk, but they could at least answer her questions. So far, they'd been mute and possibly pretending to be deaf. She'd figured it was because they were concentrating on getting on the road so she'd subsided.

Now that they were picking up speed and headed on a major road, it could be worth another try.

"What's the next step for Atlas?" She tried to sound friendly, positive, yet professional.

Nothing. If anything, the only response from the man driving was a deepening scowl. Maybe he'd been hoping she'd be quiet the whole ride. Not that this SUV was particularly quiet. It was utilitarian, absent of the padding and console treatments she was used to seeing in vehicles. As a result, there seemed to be something rattling in the center console, the doors, pretty much everywhere.

There was a radio but no one had turned it on and she wasn't ballsy enough to reach out and start fiddling with it. She didn't know the local radio stations anyway since she and David had alternated playlists on their phones for their road trip. David and Atlas had been much better driving companions.

But that adventure was over. In a whole lot of ways, most likely.

She tried communicating with her current travel companions again. Simple question. Perfectly reasonable. "Which base are we headed to?"

Zilch.

In the back, Sergeant Zuccolin might have shifted in his seat a bit. Maybe.

There was an awful cold creeping across her skin and through her insides as the situation forced introspection. She probably wasn't wanted back at Hope's Crossing Kennels either. Maybe David was moving back into his cabin at that very moment.

It might be a while before she could work up the courage to call him. Try to explain. He might not even take her call. And if he didn't, would an e-mail be opened or immediately deleted? What about a text?

There were so many ways for her to reach out to him and he could ignore each and every one of them.

There was no telling how long she'd manage to stay attached to Atlas once they got to whatever military base they were heading to. She'd most definitely be going through some challenging conversations. Ideally, she wouldn't have to reach out to her stepfather directly to keep herself a part of the project. Maybe she could apply what she'd learned from working with David, Brandon, and Alex to her approach for reasoning with the military men she'd be encountering once they reached their destination. Get started on a more positive note with a better impression.

Sergeant Zuccolin had most definitely formed an opinion of her already. It might be good, but probably the best she could hope for was neutral. Possibly bad. He'd been a direct witness to the surprise she'd sprung on David and it hadn't been a nice one.

Betrayal came to mind. *Stabbed in the back* might be a good way to describe it, too. David had looked like he'd been smacked.

She owed David an apology no matter what. It hadn't been something she'd set out to do to him, but she should've talked to him about it sometime earlier. The unsettling feeling had snuck up on her and she truly hadn't recognized it as keeping a secret from him until the moment she told him. Maybe he'd understand. Things had happened so quickly, she'd spent very little time thinking about any role her stepfather played in all of this or why he might want reports on Atlas.

Stupid.

But it was the truth. And if there was anything David valued beyond excuses and apologies, it was honesty. Simple, bare, sometimes brutal. He gave it and appreciated it in return. She should tell him. Whether he believed her or not was up to him but at least she could give it to him to do with as he chose.

The scenery was passing by as a blur outside the window. She barely took notice. They'd be getting on Interstate 95 soon if they took a similar route to the one David had on their road trip. At least, if she remembered it correctly. If this was a long ride, she was likely to lose her mind wondering about what she should do. To be honest, there was no time like the present. Later she might be too busy to keep her thoughts clear and it'd also be too easy to push it off repeatedly until she never reached out to him. Now was better.

She took out her smartphone and swiped the screen to unlock it. Tapping the message icon, she started to text David.

"Time to end this farce." Sergeant Zuccolin's hand shot over her shoulder and grabbed her phone out of her hands.

"Hey!"

She didn't have time for more as the sergeant grabbed for her hands, starting to wrap duct tape around her wrists.

Panic blinded her and she thrashed.

"Fuck!" The SUV swerved as her flailing hands contacted with the man's shoulder. The hell was his name? She should know both of their names so she could report this.

If she survived.

Atlas was barking and growling. The metal crate crashed in the back.

Her brain had gone into overdrive as she struggled against the sergeant. He was too strong, though. In seconds, he'd captured her hands and wrapped the duct tape around her wrists. Once. Twice.

Metal screeched and clanged. The sergeant shouted as Atlas came flying into the back seat.

"Shit! How did he get loose?" The enlisted man started to pull over.

"No!" Sergeant Zuccolin shouted even as he struggled with Atlas. "Keep driving, you idiot. I've got this."

Not likely. Another minute and Atlas was going to get through the sergeant's defense with a kill bite. It would be bad. Atlas killing a US soldier would be bad. He wasn't on duty. He could be put down.

And he was doing it for her.

She needed to get him out—safe, away.

Desperation pushed Lyn to wrench the door handle. The door opened and the ground shot by as they started to accelerate again. Quick. Had to be quicker. She jammed her foot against the door to keep it open as wide as she could.

"Shut that door!" the driver shouted.

She ignored him. "Atlas! *Hier!*"

Atlas left off the sergeant in the back and jumped into the front seat, into her lap.

"No you don't!" The sergeant grabbed her by the shoulder, his forearms bloody and ripped up from fending off Atlas.

Not what she had in mind anyway. "Atlas! *Over! Over! Zoek* David!"

Atlas whined but obeyed. He launched out of the SUV, clearing the dangerous pavement to hit and roll in the grass past the road's edge. A normal dog might've been hurt, but Atlas had jumped out of planes and helicopters in his career. She'd had no doubts he could make the jump and get to David.

The sergeant yanked her shoulder painfully and she let her leg off the door. It slammed shut and she desperately searched for Atlas in the rearview mirror.

Her heart leaped when she saw his rapidly shrinking form get to its feet.

The vehicle slowed. "Do we go back for the fucker?"

"We got gloves? Any gear to keep him from ripping us up?" The sound of rummaging came from the back of the car.

"No sir."

"Bitch doesn't have any in her crap either." Sergeant Zuccolin let out a long string of curses. "No. We'll never catch the bastard out in the open like this and even if we did he'd rip chunks out of our hides. Let him disappear. Long as he's not with anyone who can connect him to us, he should just end up in a shelter. He's been erased from the system so they'll come up with jack if they scan for his chip and that bastard will scare any shelter into destroying him instead of holding on to him for adoption."

Never. Lyn was sure Atlas had understood her. She'd told him to jump, to track David. Atlas hadn't ever misunderstood her since the day they'd met. He'd have understood her this time.

"You sure? Orders were to secure the dog."

Zuccolin paused. "Could use the girl to tempt him back."

Lyn kept her expression as blank as she could. She didn't think Atlas would come back if she didn't call him. But if they got ahead of him, into his line of sight, and tried to do something to her... she wasn't sure what decision Atlas would make.

"Fuck that. Dragging her out to bait the dog would

take too long, catch too much attention and we'd still have to restrain him." Obviously Zuccolin didn't want another encounter with Atlas any time soon. "I'm going to need stitches everywhere. Goddamned lucky he didn't break my forearm. Call Evans and have him intercept in case the mutt makes it back to those kennels."

So many people involved. David needed to know. Atlas would get to him and then David would know something was wrong. She twisted her wrists, trying to work at the duct tape around her wrists.

Pain exploded on the left side of her head, blinding her. As she sucked in air, her vision cleared slowly.

"The fuck did you think you were doing, bitch? Think I didn't see you? Something must've tipped you off." Sergeant Zuccolin was screaming. "Did you think you could message your boyfriend? Jump out of the car? We'd have run you down in minutes. Around here, by the time anyone called that in—if they saw it at all—we'd have been long gone. And trust me, it's no issue ditching this vehicle."

Lyn swallowed hard against the fear churning in her stomach. Bad, this was so incredibly bad. She'd figured she couldn't get away. But Atlas? He was fast, too fast for them to go after even in a car. He'd find his way back to the kennels and to David. He would.

"What did you say to the mutt?" Obviously her new favorite sergeant wasn't an actual dog handler. "Waste of time. You're not military and not his real handler. Soon as he gets clear he's going to go do whatever the hell he damned well pleases. This isn't the movies. He's not fucking going to go find help."

Yes, he was.

Though he wasn't a Collie with a little boy for a best friend; he was a Belgian Malinois and one of the US military's best. He'd track the man she'd named because Atlas knew him, trained with him, knew she'd worked with him. Atlas would track his way back to him and bring David back to her.

CHAPTER TWENTY

Cruz tossed the hose to the side and stomped over to the spigot to cut the flow of water. He should've brought the damned thing with him, but instead he let the metal nozzle drag across the concrete floor of the kennels screeching and setting his teeth on edge.

Great. He was making his own temper worse. Next thing, he'd head into Philly and look for a good, wholesome brawl.

Because that would be such an incredibly constructive use of his time.

Cleaning out Atlas's kennel was supposed to have been constructive, actually. It only made him miss the big dog, and by association, the woman who'd helped work with him.

It was easier to focus on the dog.

Cruz had to admit Atlas had been one in a million. An optimal combination of the kind of intelligence, drive—

and yes, aggression—a trainer looked for in a military working dog intended to support special forces units in the worst hellholes humankind could create.

There'd been a quiet air about Atlas that demanded respect. His pining for Calhoun had been a final expression of a kind of loyalty rarely found anywhere, in man or beast. It'd been honorable, simple in its expression and enough to tug at the toughest heart strings. And it'd taken a wisp of a blonde with a heart just as big as Atlas's to bring him out of it.

Lyn had coaxed Atlas—and Cruz, too—to live again. Not merely exist.

Maybe Cruz had been mourning the loss of a good friend, but he hadn't been struck as hard as Atlas. Nothing so noble. Because he'd never let anyone in that way. He'd been coasting along, trying to find a place to fit in again. Lyn had caught him up with her conviction and her good intentions and wound Cruz around her finger every bit as much as Atlas.

And now they were both gone.

Finally finished pulling in the hose and looping it on its hook, Cruz left Atlas's empty kennel to dry and went into the shed where they kept grooming tools and the various dogs' gear. Lyn hadn't taken Atlas's gear. But then, they hadn't practiced much with it in their training sessions to date. Most of what they'd covered had been leash work. Cruz had been planning to take the lead with Atlas more before getting Atlas into his harness for some of the more specialized training.

Might be just as well. Who knew what Lyn would've done with the knowledge? Whatever information she'd been passing along all this time had to have been fragmented. Cruz cursed himself for sharing anything with her at all.

He picked up the harness, working over the chest strap and other parts, searching by feel for something out of place. He'd done it a hundred times before and after they'd found the micro SD card under Atlas's skin. Too obvious for Calhoun to have hidden something in Atlas's gear and others must've searched the same way. But until the bigger video finished going through Cruz's decryption program, there was nothing else to go on.

Harris had ended up being a dead end, confirming what Cruz already knew but providing no further leads. The other man was probably subject to dangerous scrutiny for his trouble, too. A pang of guilt hit Cruz at the thought. The man *did* have a family—one that wanted him—and he seemed to be a genuinely decent guy.

Doing the right thing wasn't as straightforward as it'd seemed before going down there.

Nothing was, actually. And it'd started getting cloudy from the minute Lyn walked onto the kennel property. He should've dug further into her story when she'd first shown up. Should've followed up with Beckhorn to find out who had approved of her assignment to a military project. Hell, he should've paid closer attention. Because she'd played him and he had only himself to blame. Idiot. Jackass. Stupid. A few of the possible ways he could describe himself at the moment.

He'd fallen hard for Evelyn Jones and all along, she'd been reporting back to Daddy on his progress with Atlas. He didn't know which hit his pride worse: that he hadn't even suspected her or that it'd always been about the dog.

Not fair to Atlas. Everything came back to him and none of it was his fault. Atlas was the catalyst in all of this, in so many ways it made Cruz's head hurt.

Cruz placed Atlas's harness back in its storage crate. He'd pack it up for shipment tomorrow. Today, he didn't have it in him. He needed to get outside and do something more constructive.

Rojas was outside, working with one of the big German shepherds they'd rescued recently from a shelter. Three of them had been abandoned after their wealthy owners decided to divorce and leave, too concerned with their own affairs to worry about the futures of the very expensive dogs they'd ditched. Purebred, none of them older than six months, and all of them solid with basic obedience and the beginning of Schutzhund training in them. Not a one of them socialized for human interaction, unless you counted chasing intruders off private property.

The shelter hadn't had the resources to rehabilitate the dogs for normal family homes. The aggression they were already showing, their training, and lack of socialization resulted in the shelter labeling them unadoptable. If Rojas hadn't pulled them, they'd have been destroyed. Instead, he was working to see if they could be directed to a better life.

Cruz came to a stop and watched the dog watch him. Intelligence there, and suspicion. "How's it going with this new batch?"

"Promising." Rojas had a good hold on the leash, relaxed but ready to get control if the big GSD lunged unexpectedly. "This guy definitely has potential but he's got trust issues."

"I can see that." Cruz noted the way the dog let loose a whisper of a growl as he took a step closer.

"*Fooey*." Rojas gave the correction and deliberately continued to talk with Cruz in a pleasant tone. "These boys were all trained in German."

Point was to demonstrate to the dog that Rojas would indicate when aggressive behavior was okay and when it was not. Trick was a dog had to trust his handler to let him know. This one, not so big on the faith yet.

"Huh." Cruz kept his posture loose and nonthreatening, his gaze locked with Alex's. "Not unusual for guard dogs. Track down the breeder yet?"

"Sent them an e-mail. They may not have the resources to place these guys, as old as they are." Rojas shook his head. "But any breeder worth anything is going to want to know where their dogs went."

And if they didn't care, Hope's Crossing Kennels would take note of it, too. They worked with breeders across the country to get the best dogs to train for military, police work, and rescue. No way did they want to support a breeder who didn't care about where their dogs went. Said a lot about those sorts of establishments and none of it good.

"Any of the three likely for multi-purpose work?" Cruz figured this particular dog wasn't likely. Not yet. Maybe after a couple weeks' rehabilitation.

There he went thinking with Lyn's line of thought.

Rojas shrugged. "Maybe one of the other two. This guy's got a chip on his shoulder. I'm trying to work through it but he responds to Boom better than me."

Cruz raised his eyebrows. "Is it a gender thing?"

"Maybe." Rojas scowled. "But he's too rough. Nipped at her hair and ears, shoved her around a little. She can hold her own most times but he's got to learn better manners across the board."

"Ah." Cruz paused. "Maybe I'll start an assessment on one of the other two."

"Sure. Check them out. I'm figuring they'd be solid for police work but one of them might have the knack for multi-purpose." Rojas led the GSD away. The big dog kept craning his neck to keep Cruz in his line of sight for as long as possible. Definitely not looking to Rojas as a handler yet.

Atlas had begun to look to Cruz. Definitely looked to Lyn. It'd been an important step in his retraining. A dog needed to look at his handler to receive a command. But more than the literal meaning, a dog well-bonded to his or her handler was aware of the human on multiple levels. It was the establishment of a strong rapport that made a team effective.

If he wanted to poke at a sore spot some more, he could admit it'd been Atlas's willingness to acknowledge Lyn—trust her—that'd made Cruz relax. In Cruz's experience, dogs had better judgment than humans when it came to character.

Made it doubly shitty the way she'd betrayed them both. Now she was riding along with Atlas back to a military base to continue preaching her rehabilitation philosophy to someone who might not give her two seconds' notice. It'd serve her right, but it wouldn't be in Atlas's best interest.

He needed to stop thinking about Lyn. He still had to track down the people responsible for Calhoun's death and see to it they paid for what they'd done in the way it'd hurt them most.

The real question he should be asking was whether Lyn's father was involved. Seemed likely. Maybe that was the lead Cruz needed to follow. He headed for his office.

"*Fooey!*" Not a quiet correction this time. Rojas was yards away and straining to hold an eighty-five-pound GSD on a leash.

Growling low and throwing all of his weight against Rojas, something had set the dog off. Cruz followed the dog's line of sight to the front gate and saw a sleek Belgian Malinois running at top speed up the driveway.

What the . . . ?

"Atlas! *Hier!*" Cruz called, reaching for a leash—any leash—off the wall.

Atlas didn't need to change course. He was already headed directly for Cruz. Then a lean figure cleared the tree line in obvious pursuit, weapon up and aimed at Atlas.

CHAPTER TWENTY-ONE

Cruz yanked out his smartphone and activated voice recognition.

"Incoming. Single gunman. Opening fire on Atlas."

The text went to Forte and Rojas as a pre-set group.

Something was wrong. Very wrong. If Atlas was here, where the hell was Lyn? And what could happen to make Atlas leave her? Cruz could imagine several scenarios, none of them good.

Cruz bent to retrieve his gun from the hidden holster at his ankle. Staying close to the main house for cover, he moved to meet up with Atlas.

The intruder opened fire on Atlas as the dog approached, but the man had taken the shot on the move. Dumbass. It went wide, kicking up dirt to one side of the dog's path. Not a surprise.

Thank God the only people at the kennels currently were Cruz, Forte, and Rojas. Gunfire wasn't new to them. But shit, Rojas and Forte would be irritated as hell if any of them caught a bullet. Cruz was already pissed. Worse, any of the dogs on the property were at risk.

Gunshot or no, Atlas wasn't deterred or distracted. True to his training, he headed straight for his objective: Cruz.

Another shot fired. Cruz cursed and took aim. He didn't want to put a bullet in a person if he didn't have to, even if he was on Hope's Crossing Kennels property, but the asshole was shooting at *his* dog.

Suddenly he heard the sound of other dogs barking on approach and he grinned. Atlas reached him as three German shepherds streaked past them toward the intruder. Rojas must have set them loose. Perfect distraction and with three of them, the gunman wasn't likely to have time to single out a target and hit any one of them.

Handy to have rescued Schutzhund-trained guard dogs on hand. Socialization was not a primary concern at the moment. They had the experience and training to do exactly what was needed—intimidate the hell out of the intruder and potentially neutralize the threat.

The man stopped in his tracks and even from this distance, Cruz could see him go pale at the sight. Hell, Cruz wouldn't be thrilled in the face of the oncoming canines either. He'd be looking for a tree or wall to climb. Fences weren't a safe bet because most German shepherds and Belgian Malinois could climb those even without specialized training.

Backpedaling, the man tripped and fell on his ass, his baseball cap falling off to expose more of his face. And he looked incredibly familiar.

Cruz put a leash on Atlas as Rojas and Forte arrived, armed and looking grim. The three men advanced on the man cowering in the center of three GSDs. Now that they had him at bay, if he so much as moved, they'd be on him ripping and tearing. Two of them were holding position—barking and snarling—making one hell of a racket. The third and largest was bristling and baring his teeth, but he was silent.

Dangerous, that one. He was the likeliest to break and attack the man physically.

Rojas must've shared the assessment, striding around to leash the biggest dog first. Forte took a position between the other two and leashed them.

"I wouldn't relax if I were you." Cruz figured it was only fair to warn the man. "There's enough slack in all these leashes to let these dogs ruin your day."

Possibly his life. It all depended on how far things went. The three GSDs were trained to rip and tear, possibly break bone. Atlas was trained to go for a kill bite.

Speaking of Atlas, now that the intruder was essentially neutralized, Cruz turned his attention to the big dog. Panting heavily, Atlas must have run a decent distance at high speed. If he'd known his way, he might've gone as fast as he could. No telling where he'd been freed and how familiar he'd been with the area. Lyn and Cruz had taken Atlas for long walks as far as five to eight miles away in both directions along the main road next to the kennel. So chances were, Atlas had been close to home when he'd gotten loose.

Taking a knee, Cruz ran his hands over Atlas checking for injuries. No blood, no bullet holes or grazes.

"Any damage?" Forte made the question curt, expressionless. No need to give the prisoner any impressions to go on.

Cruz shook his head. "No. He's run hard though. He'll need to be cooled down."

Not an immediate need but soon. There was a higher priority and Atlas would agree.

Forte nodded sharply, then focused on the intruder. "You want to tell me why you are on my land, opening fire on a dog under our care?"

"Dog's not yours." The other man's answer was sullen, belligerent.

"And you would know, wouldn't you?" Cruz jerked his chin at the man. "This is the guy who was following our lady friends in New Hope."

The man knew Lyn's name for sure but he might not know Sophie's. No need to give him information.

Still, at the mention of Sophie, Forte's grim expression darkened and chilled. Not a good combination for the intruder. "I think we're going to have a little chat while we wait for the police to arrive then."

"Get up." Rojas barked out the words.

"Fuck that. Damned dogs will eat me." The intruder grimaced, but didn't move a muscle. He was staring at Atlas.

Seemed the man had seen what a working dog could do. Maybe he'd witnessed what Atlas specifically could do.

"Stay where you are and we'll let them loose." Forte sounded almost cheerful and let up on the leashes of the two smaller GSDs just enough to let them loom closer. "Do as we say, you have a better chance of walking away with your skin intact."

The man swore and scrambled to his feet, holding out his hands palms open. His gun lay forgotten a few feet away where Rojas had discreetly shoved it with a foot.

"Not fond of dogs?" Forte didn't even bother sounding nice about the question. "Maybe you should get to know these a little better since you tried to shoot one of them."

* * *

"Sit the fuck down and don't make a sound or I'll gag you 'til you choke." Zuccolin's mood had only gotten worse during the drive.

They'd broken speed limits getting here but seemed like everyone did on the main highway. Their car had only gone with the flow of traffic and there'd been no lucky police stop to give her the chance to scream for help.

Lyn stumbled to the chair and sat. When the other man grabbed her arm, she jerked free and pain blinded her again as Zuccolin struck her across the face.

"Don't hit her again." The voice echoed inside her skull as she blinked to clear her vision.

"Sir, she's caused a shit-ton of trouble." Zuccolin's tone had changed abruptly. Being around a commanding officer would do that to a man.

"She was not your objective. Her presence is going to be a serious issue and you will answer for this problem." The tone was flat, cold, and horrifyingly familiar. "Do not ever hit her again, for any reason. Is that understood?"

"Yes, sir." Zuccolin stepped away as the other man finished duct-taping her elbows to the arms of the chair. Her wrists were still bound.

But she wasn't gagged yet and she craned her neck to get a look at the officer. "Captain Jones."

Her stepfather sighed and stepped farther into her peripheral vision. "Insisting you use family titles at this moment would be useless. You should not be here at all."

She knew that tone. Her stepfather was in a cold, quiet rage. The kind that snuck up on the cause and exploded in ways a person never forgot. What made it scarier was not knowing when he'd actually snap and lash out.

Had he thought she wouldn't get tangled up in this mess? "You backed me. Made sure I got on this project."

"You were to do what you do best: rehabilitate the dog. Get close. Report back to me." Her stepfather clasped his hands behind his back and shook his head. "If you stumbled across the video, I took steps to ensure you didn't have time to understand what it was you had. I could assure my business partner that you didn't know enough to be a danger to our business interests. If you'd have followed your instructions you'd have moved forward in your career none the wiser of this situation and the better for it."

"Well, good to know your reasoning was logical." Lyn let the derision creep up in her voice, not caring about antagonizing the person currently keeping her safe. She was tired of letting him hold her well-being over her head. "And here I was worried I might owe you when really, I was doing you a favor. I was spying for you."

"Yes." He didn't even have the grace to express guilt over it.

But for her, it washed over her and drowned her. She provided her clients with status reports as a standard practice. Fine. And providing them to her stepfather had been an irritation because he'd turned them from a professional courtesy into a way for him to control her. But somewhere in there, she should have recognized when they hadn't felt right anymore. When she'd started avoiding telling David about them. That was when she'd stopped being naïve and started betraying him.

"What are you going to do with me now?" She wiggled in the chair and raised an eyebrow at him. There was a certain level of ridiculous to her current position but she also wasn't delusional. He wasn't going to let her go. Not now.

Silence.

"Sergeant Zuccolin."

The sergeant snapped to attention. "Yes, sir."

"Where is the animal?"

Well, at least she wasn't in the current spotlight. She listened as Zuccolin gave a halting report of what had transpired from his arrival at Hope's Crossing Kennels to the warehouse. And she was going to hell in a hand basket because she took some pleasure out of listening to the bitterness in Zuccolin's words as he had to describe how an itty bitty lady civilian let loose their target.

"I see." If anything, her stepfather's tone became more monotone. He was not pleased.

"Sir, Evans set out to intercept. He'll bring back the dog." Zuccolin definitely had lost his confidence.

"Evans is as likely to kill the animal as anything else." Her stepfather began pacing. "This has escalated into a complete clusterfuck and I'm holding you directly responsible."

Apparently, Zuccolin had some experience with her

stepfather's arctic anger, too, because the man had gone pale.

It took a minute for Lyn to realize she was the one laughing. Okay, maybe she was going into shock or sliding into hysteria. Neither was good because she needed to use her brain. She focused on her stepfather. "Whatever this is, did you actually expect it to stay all neat and tidy the way you planned it?"

His jaw tightened as he studied her. "If it had been my plan in the first place, it would have been executed efficiently and without complications. Unfortunately, I joined this particular project in later stages, once the dog was already back on domestic soil."

Well, it was good to know her stepfather hadn't been a part of David's friend's death. A tiny relief in the midst of this insanity. She wasn't even sure why, but she was glad.

"But you're not on the right side of lawful, either, are you?" Maybe she was hoping.

Her stepfather only held her gaze, a sadness in his eyes she'd never seen before.

Nope. He wasn't going to suddenly neutralize these two men and rescue her. He really was a part of all this.

"I don't even want to know why." And her voice sounded empty in her own ears.

"I'd have been disappointed if you approved." Her stepfather walked toward her. When he moved to touch her face, she turned away but he grabbed her chin. "Even if we get ice on this, it's going to be bad."

"Why bother?" She was tempted to ask if he was going to kill her but she really didn't want to die, and why tempt fate. She'd learned a long time ago not to ask her stepfather questions if she didn't want to know the answers. And she was pretty sure she didn't want to know yet.

He huffed this time. "You are never going to grow out of this pig-headed stubbornness. It's not a phase. It's a character trait."

"I prefer to consider it perseverance. Maybe tenacity." Talking seemed to be a good idea. Keep everyone talking.

Give David as much time as possible to come find her.

CHAPTER TWENTY-TWO

Cruz stood with his back to the wall in the room they used for on-site veterinary needs, Atlas sitting at his side. The old dog was seeing the inside of this room more often than most of their canines did. All things considered, though, Atlas was in good shape and practically trembling to go into action.

So was Cruz, but they needed to know where they were going and what they were getting into first.

"How do you want to handle this?" Forte leaned against the examination table, currently not in use. Might be before all this was over but thankfully, it wasn't yet. If that ex-SEAL had stopped to take a steadier shot, Atlas might've been hit.

Heat coursed through Cruz's veins, pushing at his already frayed control. Thinking on the possibilities didn't help his temper. Wherever Lyn was, she probably wasn't out of reach yet but every minute could be taking her farther away.

"We can't take much time before we really do notify the local authorities." Rojas threw in his two cents from his seat on the one stool in the room. "We need to stay clean from a lawful point of view if we want to look at this guy through bars and us on the right side of 'em."

"We need to know where Lyn is, what kind of head count we're dealing with at the location, anything useful for safe extraction, and anything additional the shithead knows about Calhoun." Cruz paused. "In that order. Lyn takes priority."

They all nodded in agreement.

"Every minute counts for Lyn." Cruz wasn't just pointing out the obvious in a kidnapping situation. Every second ticking by wound him up tighter and tighter with the need to go out and do something to help her, to get her back. Atlas was no different, taking in all the actions around him, watching with an air of impatience. Cruz got the impression the big dog was evaluating how every action was taken. Right now, they were moving too slowly.

But they needed to approach with a strategy in mind; otherwise they could do more harm than good to Lyn and to themselves and the people who'd miss them. Like Boom and Sophie.

"Question goes back to you." Forte faced Cruz.

Cruz thought hard. Lyn was his and Forte would take his lead on this. What he was about to do was for Lyn and she wouldn't thank him, or forgive him, for becoming a monster to save her from monsters. If he could find a better way, one that would leave their consciences clean—or at least not scar them any more than they already were—it'd be best to try.

"We mess with his head first." Cruz put some force behind his words, as if sounding confident about it would make it the right choice. Sometimes it did. "He's not the brightest light bulb out there for sure. Say the right thing and he'll sing."

"You sure?" Forte's gaze had gone cold, flat. "Mind games are the way you want to go?"

Uglier, more direct options hung in the air between them.

"We'll get the most accurate information out of him this way, not just what he thinks we want to hear." Truth. Plus there was the question of Cruz's temper. This course of action gave Cruz the best control over the situation. "We try to soften him up any and I might be tempted to go too far."

His anger simmered right now, coiled and waiting, familiar. The stranger he'd locked away within himself had been coming closer to the surface of his mind through this whole ordeal. Compartmentalization bullshit. The driving need to go find Lyn was all that saved the man they had in custody from being beaten to within an inch of his life, or worse. Cruz had done it before and even if he already hated himself for it back then, he would do it now if it weren't for Lyn. Everything he was doing and *how* he was going to do it was because he had her in his life now.

Because without her, there wasn't a good enough reason to keep trying to be someone other than the stranger he used to be.

"Beckhorn found the man's service record and sent it over." Cruz owed Beckhorn big for the favor, too. It'd be worth it. "There's a few things in there to leverage."

"That was fast. Beckhorn hasn't lost his touch." Rojas snagged the printout off the examination folder. His eyebrows raised after only a few seconds of skimming. "Yeah, this asshole is easy."

"This isn't just about Lyn." Forte crossed his arms. "The shithead tailed Sophie, too. And we have Boom to worry about. Whatever we do to get the info we need, this guy goes away where he can't hurt any of them anymore. That means we call the police. We can't delay any longer without opening ourselves up to scrutiny and giving this guy loopholes when he has his day in court. If you think you can do this, do it now while I put in the call. We'll be on a countdown."

Last time they'd had to call in the police, it'd taken half an hour or so to respond. Not a lot of time.

Cruz blew out a breath. "It'll be enough. Any more than that and you two will have to stop me from getting physical anyway."

To say he had a short fuse was probably a message from Captain Obvious.

Forte straightened and headed for the door leading to the main house. "Let's get to it then."

* * *

Cruz strolled into the kennel where they'd tied up their man with Atlas on a short leash at his side. The streaming video from cameras on this side of the run would show a cut-off time coinciding with shots fired. Completely believable to say a stray bullet had taken out the security feed.

The guy was covered in sweat and obviously frustrated by his inability to get free of the binding keeping him in the metal chair. All he'd managed to do was tip himself over on the concrete floor. For once, Cruz regretted how clean they kept their kennels. He wouldn't have minded if the guy managed to roll himself in some crap.

They'd all suffered worse.

"Neal Evans. You've really lost your edge, man." Cruz decided to start out conversational but he didn't have to be nice. "You're ex-Navy SEAL. Maybe it's been too long since you got through SERE training."

Survival, Evasion, Resistance, and Escape. Any special tactics personnel would have been required to go through some level of SERE training prior to selection.

"Fuck you." The answer carried a whole lot of ire.

Good. Forte, Rojas, and Cruz were all special tactics, too. Every one of them had pitched in to make sure Evans wasn't getting loose before they were ready. Cruz personally wasn't sure he could even get out of those bindings on his own. Well, not in the short time they'd taken to converse and decide on a course of action.

Give a man enough time and anything was possible.

"Ah well, we could've given you more time, Evans, but we're running low on patience." Cruz strode over and yanked the chair back to an upright position. If the guy's head snapped up at the sudden movement, not a big deal.

"I'm not telling you anything." Evans was sucking air through his mouth, his breathing labored.

Cruz took a good look at the guy's face. Evans might've tipped the chair over and used his nose to break his fall. Maybe. It didn't appear to be broken. "I think you will. It'd be your best shot at getting clear of all this with a chance at a live."

"Ha!" The bark of laughter made Atlas lift his lips in an answering snarl. The man's gaze darted from Atlas to Cruz back to Atlas and he sobered up quick. "I've got a sweet retirement parachute set up for me. Golden. You can't touch me."

Cruz tipped his head toward the man. "Thing about golden parachutes, they're not actually good for saving your life. In the last few minutes, you've managed to make yourself a very visible inconvenience."

Evans gritted his teeth and kept his mouth shut.

Ah, but not for long. "Police are on their way. See, my partner's kid lives here and with the trespass just last week the police aren't likely to think this is unrelated. There'll be a lot of questions. I don't think it'll be easy to convince a judge to allow bail. All things considered, I'm pretty certain your employers will consider you expendable."

"No fucking way."

Yup. Barely any poking and the man was already back to responding. Even if Evans planned to keep his mouth shut, he was one of those guys who couldn't.

"You've demonstrated you're sloppy enough to be made tailing a target. Or didn't you mention our little meeting in New Hope to them?" Cruz shook his head. "Never keep things from Big Brother. You never know who he's got watching you while you watch someone else."

Beady eyes widened a fraction then narrowed. "You're trying to mess with my head."

Yes. But why lie when the truth was so handy?

"You've also trespassed on private property in broad daylight with a weapon in hand, opening fire. All captured on security feed. How much do we want to bet your employers are going to consider you too stupid to live?"

"I know too much for them to just leave me out here." Too stupid just gave an excellent reason for why he wasn't likely to live much longer.

Cruz nodded. "Yeah. And your face is nice and clear in the video I've recovered, too. You know, the one you've been convinced Evelyn Jones was going to find eventually."

"Bitch will give up the video. Probably already has." Evans sneered.

Cruz clenched Atlas's leash in his fist. "She doesn't know anything, doesn't have the video. But I do and I'm here. I also know what to do with it, whereas she wouldn't."

"Trade then." Evans rolled his head in a stretch. "Give me the video and let me loose, I'll make sure you get the girl back."

This time, it was Cruz's turn to laugh. And he did. "There you go overestimating your value again. I already spelled it out to you. You're expendable. I could trade the video alone for Evelyn Jones, no issue. Don't even need to mention your name."

Actually, it'd be best for Evans if Cruz didn't but he doubted Evans would see it that way.

"You need to let me go. I can contact the people who have your girl. Faster than you can track them down. I can arrange for the trade." The desperation was growing in Evans's tone as he started to believe Cruz.

"There's a lot of men featured in this video. You all decided to bring Atlas here into the interrogation, use him to terrorize your prisoner. None of you thought to check to see if the camera on his harness was still capturing video feed. The camera caught your faces." Cruz shook his head. "Unfortunate."

For Calhoun it had been, once he'd found the feed. The entire SEAL team had been in on the interrogation, listened to a man beg for his life and offer something none of them could resist in the moment.

And Calhoun had never made it home to get the video to the right people. It could mean the end of careers for several of them. Some of them deserved it, like this dirt bag. For others, it wasn't so clear, like Harris. Cruz was beginning to understand how alone Calhoun must've felt trying to decide what to do.

In the end, Calhoun had tried to do the right thing and they'd let him die for it.

"Look. We cut a deal, okay? Prisoner wanted the same man dead as we did. It coincided with orders. We did nothing wrong. We just secured a side agreement with the prisoner. It'll make us all rich in another couple of years. The new company's going to get started soon. The prisoner we set loose is the leader of his group and he's giving us exclusive contracts as soon as we're all out and ready to go private." Evans lifted his chin. "You're out now. You ever consider going into the private sector? There's going to be big money contracts with this outfit. Immediate money to be making."

And have this snake at his back? Pass. "I'm not thinking too far in the future right now. I'm just interested in a trade and I'm still not convinced you even know where to find my girl."

"I do!" Evans leaned forward. "We've been using some warehouses down on the Philly waterfront as a base of operations. They were only supposed to retrieve the dog but when she got in the car, too, our guys took her along. When the dog got loose, I was sent to clean up the loose end."

And what would they do with Lyn?

"But you don't have the dog. I do." Cruz didn't dare let his concern for Lyn show on his face.

Evans didn't seem to notice. "Yeah. But they can't have gotten all the way to the warehouse yet. I can call them."

"Or you could give me the number and I can call them."

Evans scowled. "No fucking way."

Well, Evans was caught up in the possibilities of a trade but he wasn't quite out of his mind.

Cruz kept the pressure going. "How many times do I need to explain to you how very expendable you are?"

"Look. You give me the video and whatever the hell it was stored on, then I'll give you everything you need to know about your girl. Where to find her, who's there. Everything." Evans coaxed. "If you give me the video, I can take it back to my bosses and everything will be right again. You can even keep the dog."

Cruz hadn't planned to structure another course of action on the fly, but he hadn't anticipated Evans being stupid enough to think Evans was going to remain valuable to this group either. They'd already been using Evans as their fetch and carry man. Somehow, the man still thought he was going to be in on the full deal whenever it came to fruition. This was an opportunity to make a trade for information that'd be way more accurate than what might come out of coercion.

Time was short. And if Cruz managed things correctly, the video would still end up in the hands of the authorities. If he worked this right, he could get to Lyn, too—hopefully in time. Calhoun would agree Lyn's life came first.

"Deal. You tell me everything I need to know first, then I'll give you the video. Start with the exact location of where they took Evelyn Jones and how many men are there."

CHAPTER TWENTY-THREE

Approaching the warehouse in question hadn't been as much of a challenge as Cruz had initially thought it'd be. Once he'd gotten the location from Evans, it'd been a matter of driving close enough to park his car out of sight and approach on foot.

Pedestrian traffic in the area had been easy to blend into and there were plenty of tiny side streets to duck into as they'd gotten closer. Now, there were just old crates stacked up in a maze between them and the warehouse itself.

He'd waited in the shadows to observe as long as he dared, figuring a man and a dog caught the eye much more readily among normal pedestrians. Taking a moment now to be sure they hadn't been watched on approach could make the difference between bringing Lyn home and none of them getting out of there at all.

Atlas had settled down to wait next to Cruz, the big dog's shoulder barely touching Cruz's left leg in a heel position to keep Cruz's strong-side clear. Atlas's behavior was sliding more into the working attitude he'd been trained to adopt when out on a mission. No suspicious movement in or around the warehouse and no sign of anyone coming to investigate either of them.

Both of them were embracing old habits better suited to action than to civilian life.

In situations like this, Cruz wasn't going to regret it. Of course, he hadn't missed the hurry-up-and-wait aspect. Moving at the right moment was key. But recognizing the difference between patience and paranoia became better with practice and got rusty with disuse. His timing had to be on point today.

He proceeded forward, keeping to cover as much as possible and taking calculated glimpses of the warehouse and its surroundings. The more he was able to see of it, the more likely someone was going to be able to spot him. Taking a full circuit around the building from a distance gave him a chance to choose his entrance and determine whether there were eyes on it.

Atlas paused suddenly—rigid stance, his head up and weight forward—the dog's attention directly ahead of them. His big ears had swiveled forward, catching sound too faint for Cruz to hear yet. Atlas had detected another human approaching, blocks away from normal foot traffic. The only people wandering this area were the ones he was looking for or predators of the streets. Based on information from Evans, accurate thus far, it was more likely to be one of a couple of guards on the perimeter of the warehouse area.

Taking on a guard alone would be a challenge. If the other man spotted him approaching, an alarm could be sounded before Cruz could subdue him. A one-on-one, straight fight would take too long and potentially leave Cruz damaged. He couldn't afford to take every guard head on, by himself.

But Atlas was too fresh from overseas, the dog's rehabilitation incomplete. Atlas hadn't yet been retrained to bite to break instead of his fiercer combat training, bite to kill. Here, on US soil, Cruz didn't want to risk Atlas killing a man.

Torn, Cruz looked down at the dog, considering. Atlas gazed back up at him, waiting for a command. What he saw in the dog's eyes wasn't the ready eagerness of 100 percent obedience. Here, now, Atlas was waiting to see what he would do.

Lyn's safety, possibly her life, hung in the balance and trust had to begin with trust. There wasn't time to wait for human backup and he had a partner right here with him, if he could time things right. Take the lead in this partnership and make himself understood.

Dropping Atlas's leash, Cruz crouched low and murmured a command he'd never taught Lyn to use with Atlas. "*Reviere*."

Atlas sprang forward and streaked around the corner. Cruz darted to the left and around stacked crates, listening as he did. Moving as quickly and safely as possible to circle around, Cruz pied the next corner in order to give himself a chance to bring his weapon to bear and got his eyes on the target as Atlas came around on the other side.

It was the perfect opening and critical moment. Cruz charged forward as the other man began to lift his weapon to take aim on Atlas, oblivious to the danger from behind. Before the man could fire, Cruz threw his left arm around the man's neck in a choke hold and brought up his right arm to throw off the man's aim.

Atlas streaked across the remaining distance and leaped up, taking the man's right arm in his jaws. The man dropped his weapon as the dog's momentum took them all to the ground in a nearly silent struggle. But Cruz's choke hold was tight and in moments the other man's struggles weakened as his air supply was cut off.

A dog like Atlas could exert something close to triple the bite strength of a human. Once the other man began to go slack, it was time to stop the dog before he broke the man's forearm.

"*Los.*" Cruz scowled when Atlas didn't release the man. The dog wasn't throwing his head back and forth to rip and tear, but Atlas wasn't letting go either. Cruz stared into Atlas's eyes, refusing to let go of the man between them.

Atlas stared back.

Cruz set his jaw and it wasn't anger but determination that filled him. Drove him. There wasn't time for this. Lyn didn't have time for this. "*Los.*"

Something changed in Atlas's stare. The challenge in his eyes flickered out, a decision made, and the big dog released the man.

Laying the poor bastard down on the pavement, Cruz reached into his back pocket and pulled out a few zip ties to bind and some duct tape to cover the man's mouth. Securing any guards as he took them out was better than having them come after him again if they came to. And he didn't plan to kill if he didn't have to.

Picking up Atlas's lead, Cruz straightened and ran his hand along Atlas's flank. "*Braafy.*"

Good dog.

With one man down, he needed to move even more quickly. It'd be just him and Atlas. Both Forte and Rojas were holding down the fort back at the kennels—Forte handling the police report and their intruder, Rojas seeing to his daughter as she came home from school. Both would be following to provide backup as soon as he could but it was a toss-up as to which of them could get free first.

He couldn't afford to wait. The situation wasn't optimal but he and Atlas needed to move quickly.

Cruz studied the warehouse and a door tucked away in an alcove set in the side of the building. Security camera was hanging by a hinge and obviously not operational. Could be the best entry point.

He headed for the entrance, pausing to hug the wall and study a large ventilation grate in the same alcove. Cover was rusted almost completely off. The ventilation shaft behind it was big enough to accommodate a full-grown man. But hell, he was heavy. Atlas might be lighter than his German shepherd counterparts but the dog wasn't tiny either. The two of them in a rusted-out metal shaft were not going to get far without making a shit-ton of noise. They were not ninjas.

But he didn't have to pass it by completely. Taking out his pocketknife, he pried the cover the rest of the way off and set it on the ground against the opening to the ventilation shaft.

Then he and Atlas stepped over to the door.

They stayed to one side and listened. Atlas sniffed

along the bottom edge. No sign of danger around or on the other side. No indicators from Atlas that there was either person or improvised explosive device waiting to surprise them.

And Atlas would've scented either.

It took more precious minutes to quietly pick the lock. Not his favorite activity but luckily it was a simple one, old and not particularly secure. This entrance had definitely been overlooked while the hostiles were securing the location.

Once inside, Cruz eased the door closed behind them and immediately took them to one side to crouch under the cover of a set of stairs. He drew in a breath, deliberate and slow. The air was musty, thick with dust and stale. No one had opened any windows or doors on this level for a sufficient length of time to ventilate the place.

What he could see of the warehouse's ground level was covered in more dust. It was a wide open space with random clutter along the outer walls. No places to hide and no places for hostiles to pop out and surprise him.

Atlas turned his nose upward, sniffing, and his big ears swiveled as the big dog studied the ceiling. Cruz strained hard to identify whatever Atlas was hearing in the quiet stillness.

It wasn't complete silence, though. Now that he knew to listen more closely, there was a faint murmur coming from above. Not loud enough to identify voices or what was being said, only enough to recognize the rhythm of conversation.

Up they would go.

Cruz unhooked Atlas's leash. Inside the warehouse with all the crap scattered everywhere, the leash could snag and it'd be best to let Atlas go ahead to react as necessary. In the meantime, letting the big dog loose freed up both of Cruz's hands.

The two of them proceeded out from under the cover of the stairs and along the near edge of the room. Atlas was ranging forward, the way he'd been trained, nose to the ground and weaving back and forth in a snakelike path. Every few steps, the big dog would lift his head to catch any target odors in the air before returning his focus to the floor.

For his part, Cruz scanned the room and listened hard as he followed Atlas. Once they reached the far wall, Cruz put his back to the wall and considered their options for going up to the next level: stairs or a freight elevator.

Thus far, they'd managed not to pause in hallways, doorways, or windows. Riding up in an elevator was asking for attention and unless they both could climb out quickly, it was a kill box. Stairs weren't easy either. In his experience, stairs were where men died.

Cruz approached the foot of the stairs and listened hard, peering up into the darkness. Atlas wasn't any more enthusiastic but both of them could hear the murmurs of conversation more clearly.

Atlas gave a low, eager whine with an upward lilt, his head slightly tilted.

Up was where Lyn was.

A trickle of relief flooded through Cruz. Atlas must've recognized Lyn's voice among the murmurs. The eagerness would only be for her. She was still alive and able to talk then. Which meant she was conscious. Hopefully, she wasn't hurt.

Hang on, Lyn. We're on our way.

They were halfway up the stairs when Atlas froze again, his posture tense. A low, almost inaudible growl rumbled in the big dog's chest. Another guard approaching.

For the second time, Cruz gave Atlas the command to search out a human target.

* * *

"I'm guessing you're not going to share the full scope of your nefarious plans with me." Actually, she was torn between wanting to know what could possibly have possessed her stepfather and being too disgusted with his involvement to listen.

He shook his head. "The more you know, the less likely it'll be possible to convince my business partner to let you move on with your life."

"Promises to forget everything I've seen so far aren't believable either, huh?" Rolling her eyes might be too much attitude.

Talking was good. Drawing things out. Buying time. And well, this was probably the longest conversation she'd ever had with her stepfather.

Her stepfather sighed. At least that was familiar. "Don't insult either of us by playing stupid. Sarcasm will only shorten what patience I have."

Zuccolin snorted.

Jones slanted an irritated look at the other soldier. "Isn't it about time for you to check in with the rest of your team, Sergeant?"

Zuccolin stiffened but walked away, his footsteps

striking the floor in measured cadence. Only marginally comparable to a toddler sulking and stomping his way out of the room.

"America's finest?" She raised her eyebrow at her stepfather.

No. She hadn't caught the faintest twitch at the corner of his mouth. Had she? Nah. "All this for a choppy video hidden on a dog?"

"The problem with any shred of evidence is that it is still evidence." Her stepfather strode over to a window and gazed out. "However, the canine is not the only reason we are here or even the primary objective. I placed what should have been sufficient resources on surveillance in order to ensure the dog would present no threat to our plans."

"Sufficient might not be the correct term." She bit her lip.

He turned and glared at her. "Over the years, you have made antagonizing me an art form. I assure you, it's not as effective a tactic as you might believe."

"Force of habit." Keeping her responses shorter might be wise but she was running out of conversational cues.

He huffed. Then he continued to talk, surprisingly. "I've had interviews with several local candidates. There's a land-bound military ship just over the bridge in New Jersey used as a training and testing facility. Many IT contractors with appropriate security clearances have gained relevant communications experience there but are dissatisfied with the temporary nature of their contract work. They're looking for more exciting projects with better pay. Not a single one of them displayed the nimble intelligence you exercise just to deliver a witty comeback."

A compliment. Sort of. "I'm guessing social interaction wasn't exactly a part of any of their skill sets either."

Her stepfather tipped his head to one side, considering. "Enough to communicate in a professional capacity, but you make a valid point. Cultural fit isn't a high priority in our search but perhaps it should be. The teams we're assembling will be isolated on occasion."

"And you have to be able to trust the men who are supposed to have your back." David had taught her that.

Jones frowned.

Oh, had she said that last bit out loud? Maybe. Though Captain Jones had always seemed to read her mind as a teenager. She'd like to think her adult mind was less transparent but around him, the temptation to succumb to petty immaturity was about as irresistible as a chocolate cupcake with fudge frosting and salted caramel.

"Building the right teams takes patience and time." Her stepfather clasped his hands behind his back. "Sometimes you need to make do with what's available and cherry pick when opportunity arises."

Whatever he was getting at, they'd gone so far into the abstract she was wondering if maybe she had a concussion because she wasn't tracking anymore.

A shout cut through her sluggish thoughts. A dog's growl followed, loud and deep. It sounded familiar and she was hoping she wasn't going crazy.

Atlas.

Hope shot through her—or adrenaline—she'd take either. She continued to wiggle in her duct tape bindings while her stepfather and the one remaining soldier focused their attention on the approaching chaos.

Sergeant Zuccolin was backpedaling, crossing past the doorway and back out of view in the hallway. A black and tan blur streaked past and a shot rang out.

A dog yelped in pain.

"No!" she screamed, jerking in her chair and tipping over. Her shoulder crashed into the floor. Lifting her head, she craned her neck to see the doorway. "Atlas! Atlas?"

CHAPTER TWENTY-FOUR

Cruz advanced through the doorway, his handgun at the ready, focusing on the armed threat and relying on his peripherals to catch any other threats in the room. Farthest from the ideal situation, but based on conversation he'd identified Lyn and someone she knew. She was smart to keep up the conversation and distract her captors. Her discussion had covered the majority of their approach and the exchange let him get a basic idea of location, at least for the two speakers.

Only the asshole, Zuccolin, had the timing to encounter them when there'd been no cover. Only choice had been to engage without the advantage of surprise or any chance of stealth. Atlas had stayed true to his training and taken point.

But Cruz couldn't think about that now. The primary objective was Lyn. Locate. Extract.

He'd worry about the rest after.

The solider who'd accompanied Zuccolin was drawing his weapon.

"*Stop* moving," Cruz growled. He immediately stepped to one side of the door, away from the hinges, to have his back to the near wall plus a foot or two of extra buffer space. There were a few crates in case he needed to dive for cover. "You're going to want to get the safety back on that and put it on the ground. Now."

A procedure they were both familiar with and in the other soldier's place, Cruz would be fighting a nasty internal battle. But the other soldier valued his life and complied quickly.

Lyn was tied to a chair overturned in the middle of the room, and to the other side of her had to be the person he'd heard her talking with earlier. An older man and an officer, with his hands out to his sides. No immediate threat.

Still, Cruz was only one man and he had two potential hostiles in the room with a completely immobilized Lyn.

"Lyn?" He kept his gaze on the nameless soldier with the officer at the edge of his periphery.

"Hi."

Relief flooded through him and he blinked quickly to keep his sight clear. "Good to hear your voice."

"I'm pretty happy to see you, too." Her words were wobbly but she was talking and making a good attempt at upbeat.

"Can you get up on your own?"

There was a creak as she wiggled on her side. "No."

Her frustration was much better than the possible alternatives. If she'd been hysterical or panicking, or even devoid of hope, he might not be able to get them moving. But his girl had fight in her and he could work with that.

He skirted the room, keeping the wall to his back and getting closer to her. "Hang out for another second."

The nameless soldier's eyes gave away his intent. Cruz charged and crashed into the man shoulder to shoulder as the other man tried to reach down for his gun. The other man stumbled and Cruz followed through with a knee to the head. His opponent fell to the floor unconscious.

Cruz let his momentum carry him forward and gathered his feet under him for a smooth controlled turn, expecting the old man to have taken advantage of his back being turned.

"Son, why didn't you just shoot him?"

Cruz trained his handgun on the officer, the last man standing.

The officer held his hands up, still empty. "Well, don't start shooting now."

"Who are you?"

"Captain Jones..."

"Her father..."

Both the officer and Lyn spoke at the same time.

Well, shit.

"My *step*-father," Lyn clarified. "Which doesn't matter considering the circumstances."

"You are not in a position to fully understand the current situation." The other man's voice definitely sounded patronizing in a familiar way.

"Trust me, I'd be very happy to survey things from a higher viewpoint. All I've got now without craning my neck is a bunch of shoes and an unconscious man. At

least, I think he's unconscious. Hard to tell from here."
For her part, she obviously wasn't letting on whether her
stepfather was a threat or not.

When in doubt, everyone is a threat. Cruz did not
lower his weapon.

Despite his exchange with Lyn, her stepfather was
watching Cruz.

Cruz tipped his head in her direction. "Help her up."

Her stepfather complied with slow, deliberate movements. The man could've yanked her chair up or followed the order in a number of ways that could hurt her.
It was a calculated risk to let the man touch her at all.

But Cruz was going on a hunch.

Her stepfather cradled her head as he helped set her
upright and broke the duct tape binding her to the chair.
Odd gentleness for a kidnapper.

"She wasn't supposed to end up here." Her stepfather
stepped away from her again to a safe distance. "Only
the canine was supposed to have been retrieved."

"Is Atlas hurt badly?" Lyn was yanking off the re-
mainder of the duct tape and rubbing her arms. It'd
probably been tight enough to cut off some circulation.

Cruz ignored her question. "And what were you going
to do once she showed up?"

Captain Jones pressed his lips together. "To be honest, I was weighing my options. However, you arrived.
All the others are...unconscious?"

"Indisposed." Cruz had managed to take out any of
the other guards with Atlas's help, leaving them zip tied
and unconscious.

"How many men?"

Interesting question. Still, Cruz had a feeling Lyn's

stepfather was a man of many layers. Time to give him the chance to peel back a few. "One outside. Two at the top of the stairs. The sergeant outside the door and our friend here."

A sharp bark and a growl had Cruz down on one knee, turning his weapon to the door. A man stumbled through the doorframe with seventy-five pounds of Belgian Malinois on his back.

Cruz charged forward a second time, engaging with the newcomer. The other man had no chance and was shortly on the floor, unconscious.

"Atlas!" Lyn sounded so happy. God, he was glad she could still be happy.

Atlas stood panting, his left shoulder laid open by a bullet graze and trickling blood down his foreleg. But the big dog was looking at Cruz, waiting to be released from his last command given out in the hallway. *Bewaken*. Guard.

Cruz jerked his head in Lyn's direction. "Okay."

Atlas broke his stance immediately and bounded over to Lyn, licking tears off her face. She flinched and Atlas whined softly.

Cruz got a good look at the side of her face and anger burned through him until the edges of his peripheral vision started to darken. There was a horribly spectacular bruise developing across her cheekbone up to her temple. It had to be painful if even Atlas's gentle touch hurt her.

"I'll be making sure the man who hit her will never do it again," Captain Jones said quietly, calm, cold. Very cold.

"You want to tell us what you're doing here, Captain?" Cruz asked. He still hadn't holstered his weapon. The captain hadn't asked him to, either. That made Cruz more certain there was a lot more going on here.

Captain Jones nodded. "I'll be making a phone call shortly to have them taken into custody. The two of you should leave."

"Not the question I asked."

"As I said to Lyn earlier, the less you know, the better," Captain Jones countered.

Cruz shook his head.

The two of them glared at each other.

Captain Jones sighed. "This is a covert investigation. I became aware of this group a short while ago when I was approached with the opportunity to join as a business partner. However, my concern was the recruitment plan. Several soldiers seemed to be a part of the planning process under duress."

"You could say that." Cruz didn't bother keeping the growl out of his voice. He wasn't active duty anymore; insubordination wasn't an issue.

"Your friend, Calhoun, had put in for a transfer. It was denied. When he died and his dog was sent back here, I was asked to intercept. Instead, I made sure the dog got to where Calhoun wanted him to go." Captain Jones shrugged. "It's easier to flush out the true intents of people if you let them act on their plans for a certain amount of time. I sent Lyn so I'd know when you were getting too involved. I've needed time to identify all the people involved, not just those most directly visible. If you forced my partner to move too quickly, it would have been unfortunate."

"For you?" Lyn was on her knees, her arms wrapped

loosely around Atlas's shoulders. Her bravado was good but she needed the comfort of Atlas's strength to hold on to for the moment.

Cruz desperately wanted to go to her, hold her, and check every inch of her for any other hurt.

"Organizations like this are like patches of weeds." Captain Jones's voice took on a patronizing tone. The man really let Lyn get under his skin. "It takes time to determine how far the roots have spread and determine the best way to cut them out. Otherwise, they just pop back up someplace else. When I conduct an investigation of this magnitude, I don't just pull up the visible weeds. I root up every runner and eliminate the issue."

Bastards like these people would always be around. Cruz didn't envy the Captain a job like that.

"I still need to learn more about my...business partner and his potential investors." Captain Jones took out his phone.

"You mean you're still working with this man, whoever he is." Lyn didn't bother to hide her disgust.

"His business plan has serious ethical issues." Captain Jones raised an eyebrow at her. "Currently, there's no proof tying him to all of this besides my word. The best I would be able to manage with any accusation at this time would be a dishonorable discharge. He'd still be free to move forward with his plans, albeit under a certain amount of scrutiny from the US government. That, however, is insufficient."

"There are people being hurt—dying—while you gather your evidence to make sure this guy has no loopholes to slither through." Cruz thought about Calhoun.

A sad look flashed past Captain Jones's eyes and was

gone. "Some are surviving because of my intervention as well. The video your dog had implicates many men who only agreed under duress. It would be unfortunate to catch them in the same net we use to snare my business partner."

Harris had a family. How many others did? How many wives, kids, relatives would be hurt if men like Harris were caught up in legal action?

"I see what you mean." Cruz paused, then tossed a bit of information out. "We have a mutual acquaintance, Evans. He's got a copy of the highlights right now. Probably plans to bring it back to you or your partner in exchange for bailing him out."

Captain Jones nodded. "His ability to identify the entire group here puts this portion of the operation at risk. A good reason to cut losses here and leave."

Cruz had been planning to give Evans enough rope to hang himself. This wasn't exactly what he'd had in mind, but it'd do. The investigation Captain Jones was conducting was serious business, every bit as dangerous as the situations Calhoun and the other men were facing. And then some. If Jones's business partner suspected him, Lyn's stepfather was a dead man.

Captain Jones regarded Cruz with a steady gaze. Cruz gave the man a nod in grudging admiration. This undertaking wasn't easy. And he might never be sure he had every person involved.

"Take her out of here, Mr. Cruz. Do a better job of keeping her safe." Captain Jones's voice cracked. "I will continue my mission. It won't be much longer and then the men who didn't want to be part of this in the first place will be able to breathe. You've done me a favor with the group here. It will be fairly easy to see to it these men face charges while I go back to my business partner and tell him how unfortunate it was that they were incompetent enough to be compromised."

Cruz nodded. What else was there to say? He needed to get Lyn safely out of here and then he could absorb the new information.

"Lyn knows nothing. I'm sure my business partner will keep an eye on her and agree. Especially when he's told the asset was killed here."

"You are not touching Atlas." Lyn shot to her feet.

"Sergeant Zuccolin shot the dog dead. We both saw it." Captain Jones stared at Cruz.

Cruz nodded. "I run a kennel. I could've brought more than one dog."

The other man nodded.

Lyn held her peace.

It would be better for all of them if no one was looking for Atlas anymore. And now that Atlas had chosen his handlers, easier for him, too.

"Take the dog with you." Captain Jones's tone was definitely gentler. "He's seen enough and based on your reports, it's likely his rehabilitation will require further work. It would be best for everyone if he disappeared."

Lyn bit her lip, obviously caught without words.

Well, that was a first.

Captain Jones looked at Cruz. "My condolences for the loss of your friend. This is the best I can offer you in his memory, for now."

It would have to be enough.

CHAPTER TWENTY-FIVE

Minor concussion, if that. Some bad bruising." Forte packed up his med kit. "Pretty sure you'll be all right with some real rest. You sure you two don't want to go to the emergency room?"

Cruz looked at Lyn, who shook her head.

"I just want to stay here." Lyn had curled up on the couch with Atlas, sitting as close as the big dog could manage on the floor.

"Whatever you need." Cruz turned to Forte. "Thanks, man."

"Okay, but if she develops a headache or nausea or starts acting odd at all, she really does need to see a doctor. Call up to the main house if you need anything." Forte left.

Cruz sighed. "Are you sure you don't want to go to the emergency room? Forte is EMT certified but he's not a doctor."

Lyn shook her head slowly. She was in obvious discomfort and the bruise on the side of her face was blooming into an even more impressive sight as the hours went by. Anger burned Cruz every time he looked at her face.

It was a good thing the man who'd hit her would be in prison.

"It feels a hundred percent better just being here." She gave him a smile. "And no headache, just some throbbing when I turn my head too fast."

"Then quit shaking your head." He gave her a kiss to take the sting away from his retort. She was a trooper, no doubt about it. "You hungry at all?"

She wrinkled her nose.

"I'm not saying I'm going to put a full cheesesteak in front of you piled with fried mushrooms and onions." David chuckled. He could go for one of those himself, though. "I was thinking maybe I'd exercise my actual cooking skills and make you a cup of soup."

She stared at him and then blinked slowly. "You mean put powder into a mug and add hot water."

The idea of grilling for her, though—of putting a whole meal he'd made in front of her—that bore some consideration. He'd never thought it'd be worth the effort before, but for her it'd be more than fun. It'd be fantastic.

He grinned. Best to start simple and try not to burn anything on the property to ash. "Boiling water is cooking 101. We all learn to do it."

She huffed out a laugh. "I can't argue with that and some soup does sound pretty good. But do we have any of it here?"

Simple question but there was a tremor beneath her

words. She wasn't quite ready to be left alone yet. Even with Atlas lying on his very own dog bed here in the main living room, she wasn't ready.

Totally reasonable and he didn't plan to let her out of his sight. In addition to her comfort, he'd been looking her over from head to toe every few minutes, reassuring himself she was hale and whole and safely with him. "I'll call and see if Forte can find it in the kitchen. I planned to ask him to include me in the late night order for cheesesteaks anyway."

The look she gave him was skeptical. "You could've told him that before he left."

He shrugged. "I wasn't sure what you were eating yet."

She swatted him on the shoulder. It did his heart good to get her feisty.

It took less than a minute to text Forte with what he wanted.

"I thought you were going to call." Lyn crawled over from her nest in the pillows and blankets on the couch.

He gathered her into his lap while he waited for Forte to respond. "Sometimes I call up to the main house, but generally I don't like to blow up someone's phone with ringing. Heck, when we need to get Rojas late at night we always text anyway because it's past Boom's bedtime. Mostly, it's Forte who calls everyone."

"Hmm." She snuggled against him.

He wrapped his arms around her and finally let himself relax. This. This kind of time spent with her meant so much and he'd almost lost her. And he was possibly going to ruin it by sending her away anyway. But she had to go; she had her life, the one she'd built for herself.

After all that'd happened, she'd be wanting to get back to it and he didn't know if there would be room for him once she took up her old life again.

Chickenshit that he was, he couldn't make himself ask her.

"Penny for your thoughts."

He realized she'd been watching him as he'd run around in circles in his own head.

"You scared me today." First thing he could think to say. And it was the truth, too, because looking at her, all he could do was hold her closer.

She bit her lip. "I hurt you first, then we both ended up scared out of our minds." She paused, swallowed. "I'm sorry."

At some point in the past, it might have bothered him for someone to read him so well, to have seen far enough into him to the vulnerability of fear. But this was Lyn.

He shook his head. "No apologies. You have a good head on your shoulders and you did so many things right today."

"Hello? I got myself kidnapped and dented in the face."

He tightened his jaw and relaxed it deliberately. Good thing Zuccolin had been taken into custody and would be held accountable for what he'd done to her. Her stepfather had assured them both that all of the men involved, including her two initial attackers and Evans, had been arrested by military police and would be awaiting court-martial. Jones's mysterious business partner had withdrawn his considerable influence so there would be no easy breaks for those men.

Leaning close, he pressed his lips gently to her good temple. "You foiled the bad guys and saved Atlas."

"So he could go get you to come save me." A pause, then her tone turned bitter. "As far as my stepfather is concerned, I am still the clumsy idiot blundering around messing up his well-laid plans."

All of the history between her and her stepfather was not going to be healed in one day. "I'm glad he was doing the right thing back there. At first, I was thinking the worst."

She let out a slow breath. "So was I."

Her shoulders slumped with what had to be guilt and she dipped her chin low until it almost rested on her chest.

"Hey." Cruz freed up one of his hands to slip a finger under her chin and tip her face up so he could see her expressions. "You know the truth now and you can act accordingly."

"It's not like I can call him up and say, 'Sorry for almost screwing up your sting operation.' I think that'd expose him in all sorts of bad ways." She rolled her eyes.

Cruz couldn't help a grin at her sarcastic tone. "I'm sure he's glad you are intelligent and perceptive enough to know that's not the way to go."

It was part of the reason why she attracted him. Things made sense to her without effort or arduous explanation or fighting. She got it. All of it. Or at least as much as he'd managed to share with her so far. It could take a lifetime to open up all there was for her to see.

"So what then? I'm not even sure. There'll be future military contracts based on what he said. And we'll have to see how his office manages the press with Atlas disappearing, go along with it. Until then, it's business as usual, I guess?" There were a couple of questions left unspoken as she waited for his response.

He kissed her, because he didn't want to hold off on the things they both enjoyed and because he wasn't sure how she'd feel after he gave her his response. Tasting her, exploring her, enjoying the play of their tongues, he savored every moment. Her hands came up around his face and tangled in his hair.

He wanted this. Working with her, talking, maybe arguing a little, and definitely playing. Filling his days with a mix of these things would be more than he'd ever hoped for in terms of happiness. Fulfillment. All those words he'd taken out of his expectations for himself somewhere in the middle of his time in service.

But if you love something...

* * *

Lyn almost forgot her own question in the midst of their kissing. His hands had wandered too, sliding down her thigh to cup her behind and squeeze. She was wondering if she could coax him into some very gentle intercourse maybe, since she only had a mild concussion.

It'd take her mind off her aches and pains. Medicinal. Really.

But when he drew back, his expression changed from the soft look he only wore for her to a more serious, intense expression.

He hadn't gone neutral, hadn't compartmentalized. This was new.

"Here's the thing." He ran his hand through her hair

and she closed her eyes, enjoying the feel. She relaxed with his touch, listening to the timbre of his voice. As long as it stayed warm like this, didn't go flat or distant, it'd be okay. "Your life has been turned upside down since day one of you getting here. If we think back on it, a whole lot has happened in almost no time."

She opened her eyes, sought his gaze. "It happened, we happened."

Fear pricked at her despite her earlier thoughts. What was he trying to say?

He nodded and kissed her forehead. "We did. I really like us as a thing and I want us to last."

"Good." She settled, relaxing back into his embrace. *Us.* She liked the sound of it.

But he leaned back and tapped her nose with a fingertip. "You might have a different perspective once all the excitement settles down, though. Believe it or not, it gets boring around here. The whole reason Forte chose this location was for the peace and quiet."

Something she had yet to experience. But the location was tucked away and if you didn't drive twenty minutes in either direction on the main road, you wouldn't realize how close it was to the rest of the world.

"With ready access to two major metropolises and several major airports," she countered. "From what I understand, you all took advantage of the city nightlife on a pretty regular basis. This is not exactly a remote small town hidden away in the middle of nowhere and you get a fair amount of business-related traffic coming on site."

Not to mention any number of canine personalities running rampant. When they'd arrived back on site, the three new GSDs had been wandering loose from their kennels. Apparently their intellects combined resulted in Houdini-level escape skills. Alex had been about to rip his hair out getting them back on leads. Their recall was good but not 100 percent, so it'd taken a little effort on Alex's part to get them back into their kennels.

"Point." He gave her a wry grin. "What I'm trying to say is you've been basing all your impressions so far on some high-stress experiences."

She opened her mouth to argue, but he kissed her. And for a minute—okay, maybe several—she was lost. But she pulled herself together as soon as he let her up for air. "Trying to distract me is futile."

He raised an eyebrow. "I like a challenge."

She opened her mouth, closed it, then swatted his shoulder. He only grinned.

"I want you to stay with me, Evelyn Jones," he whispered. "Here, with me. But I want you to leave first. Get some distance and clear your head. Process all the things that happened to you. You might decide you want to leave it all far away. I will understand, no matter what you decide. But I want you to take the time."

Her breath left her and it took a long second for her to pull together her first thought. "You're asking me to go away again."

Her heart twisted in agony at the thought. She struggled to listen as he continued.

"This isn't exactly the same. Before I was trying to protect you, and taking away your work was the wrong thing to do." His arms tightened around her briefly before easing up enough for her to get up out of his lap if she wanted. But he continued, "This, I want for you because what happened to you isn't easy. You were attacked, shot at, kidnapped, and beaten. Not any one of those things is something you'll process overnight. Not tomorrow. Not a week from now. Believe me. And staying here might let you hide from it more than deal with it. A big part of your career has you traveling places by yourself."

Biting her lip, she held her initial retort. He'd been through these things, seen friends go through them. The look in his eyes, the earnest sincerity in his voice, the way he held her against him spoke of how much he cared about her.

"If you give life a chance to get back on track, you'll have perspective. See clearly. And then when you decide what you want, we'll both know it's because it's the right thing for you." He nuzzled her ear. "And you'd be welcome back here if that's what you want. I'll stay by you and work with you through every one of your nightmares. But you'll at least have had a chance to think it all through. Your choice."

Hers. He always made sure to let her know it was her choice. And it meant everything. The biggest difference between him and her stepfather was the way David respected her right to choose. The confidence he had in her ability to make the right decision.

"Don't say anything now." He tucked her head under his chin. "I want you to take your time, go out on a couple of client trips, get back into the rhythm of your career, and then decide. Is that fair?"

Lyn stared at him as her temper simmered. "No."

He blinked, stilled.

Oh, everything he said made sense, especially the consideration of her traveling alone. She'd already had issues glancing out the windows of the cabin into the falling darkness. Reflections on the windowpanes startled her, like strangers staring in for the first few moments before she really looked at what was there. Tonight was not going to be an easy night and she was glad to have the secure warmth of his arms around her with Atlas nearby.

That was her point, though. She didn't need time alone or distance from him to process.

"I don't leave things unfinished." Rising out of his embrace momentarily, she turned and straddled his lap. Resting her hands on his chest, she looked deep into his gaze.

He waited, silent. Listening.

Listening was something her stepfather had never done. At least, it'd never felt like he had. But David always did. He'd taken the time to hear her out every time she'd had something to say while they worked together. And here he was now.

"You're right about there being a lot of things to process. But"—she tipped her head to the side—"I don't need solitude to think straight or see my way clearly and I definitely don't need to go back to my old life to figure out how I want to live my days. If there's one thing I learned from you here, it's that you can't ever go back and being too stuck in the past doesn't work."

A muscle twitched along the side of his jaw. She'd hit a nerve. But that was okay. She leaned forward, her hands flat against his chest, and kissed the spot on his jaw. When she straightened, his lips had softened from the hard line and he settled his hands on her hips.

"I was so caught up in proving to my stepfather that

I could be out on my own, I didn't even realize I'd established myself already. I was just...running, charging forward to prove a point." She gave him a smile and warmth spread through her chest when he smiled in return. "Working with you and Atlas gave me perspective. And maybe I needed some chaos to knock me off my train tracks and really think about what I'm doing, where I'm headed."

She paused and he held his peace, patient. It was never a race to get a word in edgewise with him and for that, she was grateful.

He gave her so many things. Time, consideration, caring.

"What happened is going to give me issues for a good while." She smoothed her hands over his chest, taking comfort from the hard muscles under her palms. "But whatever steps I'm going to take toward recovering from this won't be backward to resuming my old life. I'm moving forward and I want to do that with you."

She held her breath.

His hands tightened on her hips. "You sure?"

"I love you, David Cruz." She kept her gaze steady on his. "And you remember I was first to say it."

He laughed. "I'd have said it first if you needed me to."

"Well, now's a good time." Because she did need to hear it.

He sat up straighter and kissed her first, his mouth sliding over hers in a dizzying, intense kiss. Heat seared through her and she clutched at his shoulders as his arms tightened around her waist, pulling her in snug against him. And still he kissed her, drowning them until they were both breathless. "I love you, Evelyn Jones. Since

I don't even know when. I want you in my life and I'll wait forever if you need me to."

She pressed her forehead to his and closed her eyes. "No more waiting. I'm done waiting for my choices to feel like mine."

His arms tightened around her in a fierce hug, then loosened enough to relax again. "So what's next, Miss Jones?"

His teasing tone made her smile wider. Wow, had she ever been this happy? It bubbled up inside her and she barely knew what to do with it all. "Well, we've got some administrative stuff to work through here with wrapping up the contract paperwork and submitting any reports they'll need."

He nodded, running his hands up and down her thighs. There was a naughty gleam in his eyes and she narrowed hers as she put in the extra effort to remember what she was saying.

"And you were right about my having other clients. I've got people who need me to work with them and their dogs."

Atlas barked.

She glanced over at him, sitting close, his tail sweeping the floor in a happy wag. Reaching over, she gave him an affectionate scratch behind one ear.

"I think he's going to have to accept it's a part of your job." David chuckled. "He's got to learn to share you."

"Mmm." She looked back to David. "I'll still be traveling some and next time I leave, there should be texts. Texts from you, pictures of Atlas, maybe we should create accounts on a couple of social media apps. Whatever it takes to feel connected."

"But you could use this as a home base." He made the offer quietly.

Her words caught in her throat for a moment and she bit her lip as she nodded. It seemed impossible in such a short time, but this cabin and Hope's Crossing Kennels had come to feel like a home in ways her actual apartment way back on the West Coast never did.

He grinned. "I'm on board with that. Maybe we'll travel together, too, go to a few training conferences together and learn some new techniques."

Or he could kiss her some more and remind her of a few of his techniques. She lost time in his kisses, enjoying the taste of him and teasing him back in turn with nips at his lower lip.

Happy. She was so happy with him.

She opened her eyes, met his gaze. He wasn't her stepfather. Hell, her stepfather wasn't even who she'd thought he was. David was everything she hadn't even known she needed and now that she was back in his arms, she didn't intend to give him up.

Lyn took a deep breath. This was it. And if she could let go of everything she believed she knew, quit comparing, she wouldn't mess this up. "No matter where my job takes me, I think I could find my way back here. This is home." She met David's gaze, steady, loving. "*You* are home."

David folded her in close against his chest. "I'll be here for you. Count on it."

Please see the next page
for a preview of

ULTIMATE
COURAGE,

the second book
in the True Heroes series.

CHAPTER ONE

Y ou've got to be insane."

Elisa Hall took a prudent step or two back as the tall man in front of her clenched his fists and glared at the woman in scrubs behind the reception desk.

"I'm sorry, sir, but ambulances take precedence over walk-ins." The nurse held firm. A braver woman than Elisa would've been in the face of rage on a level with the man at the counter.

He was dressed in loose fitness shorts and a close-fitting black tee. His hands were wrapped in some cross between tape and fabric.

Fighter might as well have been printed across his very broad, muscular shoulders.

Actually, now that she was looking, his tee said REVOLUTION MIXED MARTIAL ARTS ACADEMY.

Well then, maybe she could take more ibuprofen and forget about seeing a doctor after all. Getting her own injury examined wasn't worth staying anywhere near this guy.

The nurse glanced quickly at Elisa then returned her attention to the man, her expression softening with sympathy. "As soon as an examination room opens up, we'll get you in to see the doctor. Please, wait right here and fill out these forms while I help this young lady."

Wait, what? The man turned and stared at her. Oh, great.

Usually she envied nurses, their ability to sympathize with so many patients, make such a difference in lives. Now was not one of those times.

Elisa squashed the urge to bolt. Never ended well when she tried it. Better to hold very still, wait till the anger in front of her burned itself out and pull herself together afterward.

But the expected explosion, shouting, other things...never happened. Instead, the man had quieted. All of the frustrated aggression had been stuffed away somewhere.

She swallowed hard. Leaving remained the best idea she had at the moment.

But he stepped away from the counter, motioning with a wrapped hand for her to step forward, and incidentally blocked her escape route toward the doors. He couldn't have done it on purpose, could he? But Elisa took a step up to the reception counter and away from him anyway.

"Yes, dear?" The nurse's gentle prompt made Elisa jump.

Damn it. Elisa's heart beat loudly in her ears.

The nurse gave her an encouraging smile. "Don't

mind him. I've already asked another nurse to bring ice packs as fast as possible. I don't mind if he blows off some hot air in my direction in the meantime. I would be upset too."

Elisa bit her lip. She could still feel the man standing behind her, his presence looming at her back. He couldn't possibly appreciate the nurse sharing some of his private information. And he didn't seem to need ice packs or any other medical attention. He appeared very able-bodied. "It's none of my business."

The nurse placed a clipboard on the counter and wrinkled her nose. "Oh trust me, the entire waiting room knows what his concern is. Tell me what brought you here."

This might be the most relaxed, and personable, emergency room reception Elisa had been to in years, not counting the extremely angry man standing behind her. But the waiting area wasn't packed and no one there seemed to be in dire agony. They were either not very busy—not likely if all the examination rooms were filled up—or extremely efficient.

Efficiency meant she could get in and out and decide what her next steps would be.

"My wrist." Elisa held out her left arm, the wrist obviously swollen. "I thought it was just a bad sprain, but it's been more than a few days and has only gotten worse, not better. I can barely move it now."

And, if she could, she definitely wouldn't have stopped in to get it treated. An emergency room visit, even with the help of her soon to be nonexistent insurance, was still an expense she didn't need.

"Is that your dominant arm, dear?" The nurse held up a pen.

Elisa shook her head.

"Oh, good. Leave your ID and insurance card with me so I can make copies. Take a seat over there to fill out this form and bring it back to me."

Okay then. Elisa took the items and made her way toward the seating area, thankful the nurse hadn't asked her to give her name and pertinent information verbally. It was always a risk to share those things out loud. There was the slightest chance someone would overhear and take note.

She'd learned over and over again. There was always a chance a slip of information in the unlikeliest of places would find its way to exactly the person she didn't want to have it.

It might not be crowded but just about everyone in the room had decided to sit with at least a chair or two buffer between them and the next person. The buffer seats were all that was left and most of the other people waiting to be seen were either men or women sitting with men.

Of course, Elisa wasn't feeling all too sociable either.

Then she caught sight of a little girl sitting with her legs crossed in the seat next to the big planter in the corner. The seat next to her was open, and she was waiting quietly hugging a big blue plush…round thing. Whatever it was.

Elisa walked quickly over and when the girl looked up at her with big blue eyes, Elisa gave her the friendliest smile she could dig up. "Mind if I sit next to you?"

The girl looked around, her gaze lingering on the reception area behind Elisa for a moment before saying, "Sure."

Elisa took a seat.

After a few silent moments, the little girl stirred next to her. "Are you sick?"

Well, paperwork didn't take much of her attention and it'd been a while since Elisa had been outside her own head in a lot of ways. Conversation would be a welcome change as she finished the forms, and a good distraction from the constant worry running in the back of her mind. "Not sick so much as hurt. I won't give you the plague."

A soft, strained laugh. "Same here."

Elisa glanced, then took a harder look. The girl wasn't hugging the big plush toy as she'd first thought. It was supporting the girl's slender left arm, which was bent at an impossible angle.

"Oh my god." Why was she sitting here alone?

"Don't worry." The girl gave her a quick thumbs up with her right hand. "The doctors are really good here and I'm in *all* the time."

Such a brave face. She had to be in an insane amount of pain. And here she was encouraging Elisa.

"Is there someone you should talk to about how often you get hurt?" Elisa struggled for the right tone. It was one she'd heard more than once when people had been concerned for her. Some places had safeguards in place for…

Blue eyes widened. "Oh, it's not what you're thinking. Trust me, people ask my dad. And it's not like that *at all*. I study mixed martial arts. I get bruised and bumped all the time and usually it's nothing, but Dad always makes me come in to get checked."

It was hard not to believe in the earnest tone. But monsters were everywhere.

The girl gave her a rueful smile, still amazing considering how much pain she had to be in. "This time it wasn't just a bump."

"Which is why they're going to see you as soon as they can, Boom."

Elisa hadn't heard the man approach or seen him approach. He was just there, kneeling down in front of the girl, gently tucking an ice pack under her arm while moving it as little as possible. For her part, the girl hissed in pain but otherwise held up with amazing fortitude.

Elisa would've been in tears. The arm had to be broken. It didn't take a doctor to figure that out. No wonder the man had been mad earlier. She dropped her gaze, unable to watch.

"Here." An ice pack appeared in her view. "Your wrist should be iced, too. Take down the swelling while you wait."

Speechless, Elisa looked up.

The man's words had been gruff, awkward. His expression was blank. But his eyes, a softness around his eyes and a... quiet in the way he watched her made her swallow and relax a fraction. Her heartbeat stuttered, but in a fluttery kind of way. A completely different reaction from what she should be experiencing if she were wise.

Learn from your mistakes. You never know who a person really is.

"You should listen to Dad." The little girl had regained her earnest tone. "He's usually right. Even when I think he's crazy, it turns out he's right and I wish I'd listened to him. Besides, he gets hurt even more than I do. He says ice is his best friend."

"So is ibuprofen." Elisa snapped her mouth shut, not even sure why she'd let the comment pop out.

The little girl gave her a brighter smile. "Yeah. He says that, too."

The dad in question stood, his knees creaking a bit as he rose up and took a step back.

Elisa was grateful for the space even though he probably wanted to be near his daughter. His presence was intense even if his movements were all steady and smooth. No sudden or frenetic motion. Nothing to freak her out.

"Have you ever had self-defense?" The girl was continuing. "Dad says every person should take at least one class or seminar. It's what got me started in mixed martial arts. I liked it so much I started taking classes."

"I haven't, no." Elisa wasn't sure if the man minded the conversation, but it did seem to keep her mind off her own wrist, so maybe it was a distraction for the girl, too. If it was, the least she could do was help a girl this nice. "But it sounds like good advice. Will you be worried about mixed martial arts now?"

The girl gave a slight shake of her head, grimacing as she unintentionally shifted her arm. "I want to go back as soon as this is fixed. I've got a belt test at the end of the year, and I want to make black belt before I get to middle school."

"We'll let the doctor take a look and get some X-rays," the man interjected, his voice low and maybe amused. "Then we're going to follow the doctor's orders to let you heal up correctly."

"*Then* I'll go back to class." The little girl was not to be deterred.

Elisa couldn't help but smile. Dauntless. So much conviction in such a young package.

"Rojas?" A new nurse was standing in the double doors leading from the waiting room back into the emergency room area.

Her father straightened. "Here."

The nurse nodded and motioned for a young man in scrubs pushing a wheelchair.

In moments the girl was eased into the wheelchair, big round plushy support and all. She gave Elisa a wave as she was wheeled away to see the doctor.

Elisa waved back.

Wow. Just wow. Elisa took a deep breath. There was one heck of a personality. Someday that little girl was going to grow into a powerful, confident woman.

Someone cleared his throat near her.

She jumped.

For the second time in the space of a few minutes, the man had snuck right up on her. This time he was holding out a cup of coffee and a card. "Revolution Mixed Martial Arts. It's local, if you're staying in the area. There's a women's self-defense workshop coming up in the next couple of weeks. Boom made me promise to come give this to you."

Words stuck in her throat as she stared at the proffered card. It took a minute for her to pull her wits together long enough to take it from him, and the coffee, too. His hand remained steady until she had both in her own. As she gingerly took the offerings, he didn't extend his fingers to touch her the way some men did.

Warm brown eyes, the color of dark chocolate, studied her. "The workshop takes it slow and easy. It's as-